A. Tarrant
Sirens' Island
978-1-895166-52-1
1. Fiction. I. Title.
Printed and bound in North America.
First published in 2024
by Insignificant Diversions
New Brunswick, Canada

SIRENS' ISLAND

A. Tarrant

All men will be sailors then
Until the sea shall free them
– Leonard Cohen, *Suzanne*

Early Summer, 1943

Jimmy Sherman was eighteen years old, of average height, and well-muscled from working on the family farm.

He was at Comer's farm, for the morning, taking care of some chores for Larry who was away for a couple of days in Charlottetown, visiting his ailing mother.

Jimmy stopped work and went to the door of the farmhouse. He asked Larry's new wife, Ellen, if he could use the bathroom.

Ellen, who was only nineteen, went back to the sink where she'd been washing the dishes. She heard Jimmy open the bathroom door and she expected him to go back outside, but instead suddenly felt his presence behind her.

He reached out his hands and took hold of the counter, one arm resting against each side of Ellen's waist, corralling her in.

"Back up Jimmy," Ellen demanded.

"I thought we could be friends," Jimmy replied and pushed up against her. "You should be nice to me, so I don't tell everyone what I saw in Toronto. I'm sure that Larry wouldn't be too pleased if he knew the naked truth about your watery past."

"You're going to get out of my way or I'm going to go crazy and start screaming."

Ellen threw her weight to the left, dislodging Jimmy's grip on the counter. His hand remained extended, sliding over her body as she moved to the side.

Ellen strode to the kitchen door, threw it open, and stood to one side.

Jimmy turned, still standing by the sink, and looked at Ellen. He smirked and said, "You know, I like to go skinny dipping in the pond back of our farm. You oughta come with me. That's something you know all about."

Ellen turned her back to him and snatched an object from the shelf in front of her. She then grabbed the shotgun that stood against the wall beneath the shelf and slid the shell into the rifle. As she turned back to the boy across the kitchen she pumped the slide to move the shell into the chamber and raised the rifle to her chest. She stepped further from the door, out of Jimmy's path, and far enough away to keep the barrel beyond his reach as he passed by.

Nothing further needed to be said to make her point. You can't speak with more cogency than a loaded shotgun.

Jimmy's smirk continued but it was now just the pretense of someone relaxed, with the upper hand. He recalled Larry telling him that he'd taught Ellen how to shoot. She has a steady hand, Larry said, and he had plans to take her hunting.

Jimmy walked slowly and dramatically across the kitchen, feigning self-confidence and bravado.

He exited through the door.

Ellen slammed it behind him and turned the lock.

She swore under her breath. She knew that she couldn't tell Larry about Jimmy. She'd have to explain a lot of other things as well and she couldn't bring herself to do that. They were things that might destroy her life here and maybe her ability to live anonymously and safely.

Ellen recalled having heard that Jimmy would be leaving to study art in Toronto in the fall. Hopefully that would end the harassment. She couldn't change her past, she thought, but she could get a large dog to help control her future.

Late Summer, 1943

With fishing rods in hand, Harry Nelson and Jack Eades, two ten-year-old boys, were walking up the dirt road. They had come from Jack's place and were on their way to the pond trail that began behind Martin's farm. It ran along beside the creek where they fished.

They'd agreed the day before to meet up with Robbie and Eddie Martin, who would already be there.

The boys turned into the driveway of Martin's farm, then walked past the house and the kitchen garden. There was no sign of Ginny or her parents.

They swung to their right to get onto the path that ran along the side of Martin's western field.

They were engaged in a learned conversation about Buster Crabbe, their hero, who they'd seen in films the year before, playing Buck Rogers and Flash Gordon.

"Flash has to stop Ming and Dale's wedding," Harry said, furthering the boys' speculation about what the next instalment of the Flash Gordon serial might involve. Not that Harry cared one way or the other about the love interest in films, but he understood that Flash had to kill Ming and save the girl before they could get home to earth.

They paused briefly at the sound of a siren, looked about and saw a police car drive past the Martin house. The siren stopped as the boys resumed their trek.

They were almost at the creek when they were startled by the sound of a rifle blast nearby. It had come from somewhere in the bush up ahead.

Both boys froze, aware of the danger. Two hearts pounded. Someone was hunting and the boys feared they might be mistaken for game if their movement was spotted.

"What do we do?" Jack whispered. "Should we go back? I don't want to get shot."

"Nah, we keep going," Harry said, affecting Buster Crabbe bravado, "but we go slow and keep our eyes open."

"It's probably Mr. Martin over at the gravel pit," Jack decided. The pit was on the road on the other side of the forested area that began at the back of the field. "I hope he's

there anyway, cus I don't trust that guy not to shoot us. Remember when he threw us out of his house after we went through the ice on the creek? We were soaking wet."

"That was nothing. He didn't know we were wet and we were horsing around."

"It was nothing for you, you live on the very next farm, but I had to walk all the way to my place. The milkman picked me up cus he knew I'd get hypothermia. My old man was really pissed."

Harry shrugged.

"Old man Martin scares me," added Jack.

Harry's brow was furrowed, his thoughts elsewhere. "That shot... That sounded too close to be coming from the gravel pit."

"Maybe the son of a bitch got a bird for dinner off the trail."

"So we go slow."

Warily, Harry and Jack continued along the perimeter of the field, staying close to the edge.

Spotting some movement up ahead they halted, then ducked down into the tall grass growing under and beside the fence. And they watched.

They recognized the person with the rifle who emerged from the pond trail.

Only after the figure had finally made it all the way across Martin's west field, and disappeared into the bush on the other side, did they continue on their way – silently.

They turned onto the pond trail.

"It's okay to talk again," said Harry once he and Jack were in the shelter of the forest.

But Jack wasn't listening. He was absorbed with trying to discern whatever it was that was laying on the path up ahead, back of Martin's eastern field. "What's that?" he said.

The boys sped up, anxious to sate their curiosity.

They abruptly stopped in horror. Laying on the path was the body of a man dressed in a military uniform. Half his head had been blown away. Clothes were scattered on the ground around him.

"Oh my God!" gasped Harry.

"Let's get the hell out of here," said Jack.

Harry didn't move, stunned at the sight of the dead body.

"C'mon," Jack said. "We're gonna head home. And," he added, firmly and decisively, "we're gonna tell nobody what we saw... Right?"

Harry roused himself from his stupor. "Right," he agreed.

1. Saturday, June, 2005

After pulling Heather's Fiat onto the shoulder of the country road, Hugh Martin withdrew a piece of paper from his shirt pocket and unfolded it.

His eyes went back and forth from the hand-drawn map to the vista on his right, imagining the lines on the paper laid over the land.

This was it! He was parked at the foot of what had once been the driveway of his great-grandparents' farm.

The spot where the house and other buildings once stood was now overgrown, as was the old driveway. Stones and chunks of broken concrete, that had been part of the foundations of the house and barn, lay scattered about.

On his drive from Charlottetown, Hugh had passed the ghostly presence of old tractors and other farm equipment, discarded and rusting. And he'd seen a number of abandoned buildings, dilapidated and fallen down, in various stages of being reclaimed by the land. There were sheds, houses, barns, and even a graveyard; all helpless against the power of nature to reassert itself. But this place, the 'ancestral home' as he'd referred to it when talking to Heather that morning, was in a more advanced state of decay than any of them. Anything that nature could swallow up had already been consumed.

Hugh climbed from the car and was immediately greeted by an unseasonably cold and gusting wind expressing its unwelcome.

He made his way up the old driveway towards the crumbling foundation. There was a farm field off to his right – to the east – and another straight ahead, just beyond where the barn had stood. Both fields were in use. To his left, past the site of the old house, was a swath of bush which wasn't quite thick enough to completely block his view of the neighbour's farm. Whoever lived there in 1943 would have known his family.

Hugh walked past the piles of soil, old bricks, and rocks that had been dumped to the right of the driveway. Between two of the piles some purple flowers grew. He couldn't identify the variety but knew that he'd seen them before, in gardens; meaning that these flowers had been planted by human hands – perhaps by his great-grandparents – unlike the wild lupins growing everywhere around him, now in flower.

It may have felt eerie to some people, standing beside the ruins of the house, as if one were in a cemetery, but this wasn't the case for Hugh. The sight of the flowers animated the area, infusing it with melancholy. There had been life here. Laughter. Joy. Sadness. Love. The monotony of the day to day. This had been a home.

He stopped beside what was left of the foundation. There was nothing to see, in one sense, and that had been his expectation, but he'd come here anyway, just to be in this place, to feel its presence, and to breathe the air. This was his home. It was enormously changed from what it had been in the past, but this was still the soil where his roots had grown. It felt like discovering an abandoned piece of himself laying in the Prince Edward Island countryside.

Some movement caught his eye, disturbing his reverie. Looking up, he saw an enormous collie bounding towards him along a path worn through tall grass that began at the end of the former driveway. The path wove its way across what would have been a backyard and, on reaching the back field, connected to an east-west path.

Hugh froze, on alert, but quickly realized that this wasn't an attack but a greeting.

He bent over as the animal came near, slowed, then bumped up against him, pushing its head against his thighs.

Hugh swirled his hand through the fur on the back of the dog's neck. Within seconds, the collie was off, with more interesting things to explore after having said 'hello'.

A middle-aged woman was now visible, tramping up the path, also headed in Hugh's direction. A solid woman with long grey hair tied back. She wore rubber boots and a weather-proof jacket, and she carried a wooden staff.

When she was near enough for her to hear him, Hugh said, "That's a beautiful dog you have there."

"Yes, but he's very stupid." The woman's next word was spoken with a depressed sigh. "Unfortunately."

Hugh smiled uncertainly. "Is this your farm? I'm sorry if

I'm trespassing."

"No, it's not mine. I'm in the trailer beyond those trees." She pointed off to Hugh's left. "This place is owned by a farmer up the road. He uses these fields for potatoes and soybeans. Heidegger and I walk here everyday if the weather cooperates, so I'm pretty certain you being here won't bother Mr. Murphy."

On cue, Heidegger reappeared, ritually circling Hugh's legs again, then heading for the woman. The dog allowed her the privilege of running a hand over his head before, once again, bounding off.

Feeling that he needed to explain his presence, Hugh said, "This used to be my great-grandparents' farm many years ago and I just wanted to have a look."

The woman tilted her head back to get a better look at the young man before her. He appeared to be in his late twenties. He was thin but not willowy, dark haired with fine facial features and the sort of eye colour that defies classification; grey perhaps. "Can I ask you who your great-grandparents are – or were?" she said.

"Thomas and Louise Martin."

The woman smiled, with evident surprise. "My, my, that does go back; much longer than I was expecting! They left here during the war." She looked Hugh up and down as if searching for a trace of Louise or Thomas in him. "So nice to meet you."

"So you know about them."

"Of course. Louise was my friend. She lived in the house here when I first arrived next door as a young bride. She took me under her wing and was very kind to me – like a mother."

It was Hugh's turn to be taken aback. He considered the old lady. She had few wrinkles and moved vigorously. He would have guessed her to be somewhere in her early fifties. It didn't seem possible that she could have been friends with his great-grandmother who, if she were alive today, would be closing in on her 100th birthday.

"I know what you're thinking," the woman said, smiling.

"You look…" Hugh bit off whatever he was about to say.

"I know. I wasn't as old as your great-grandmother but I'm

12

no spring chicken. I recently celebrated my eighty-first birthday." Looking in the direction of her farm, the woman said, "You can't see much of my place anymore – everything's overgrown – but Louise and I used to nip back and forth almost every day."

Hugh could only make out some strips of colour through the trees and bushes.

"The house and farm now belong to my daughter Leona and her husband. I live in the trailer that you can see a bit of. It gives Leona and her family some privacy… May I ask your name?"

"Hugh."

"Martin?"

"Yes."

"It's very nice to meet you Hugh Martin. I'm Ellen Comer. Eleanor actually, but I go by Ellen. So…Martin…the name means, I presume, that one of Louise's boys is your grandfather."

"Robert."

"Ah. I might have guessed. You're tall like him. Is he alive?"

"Yes. He lives in Montreal."

"Still? And you grew up there?"

"No. My parents moved around a lot until ending up in Toronto. I moved to PEI a couple of years ago."

"I see. Well Hugh, Heidegger and I have had our walk. Can I invite you for lunch so we can talk some more?"

"I'd like that very much."

2.

Hugh and Ellen sat at the dining table in her small trailer.

Sneaking glances about the room as they spoke, Hugh noted an apparent fondness for Renaissance religious paintings; heavy and dense imagery picturing the Virgin Mary as a mother; the ideal of Catholic womanhood.

He spotted a large rifle standing beside the door.

"Are you living in Charlottetown?" Ellen asked.

"Yes," said Hugh. "I teach high school history. I'm in my second year."

"Very good. Did you always want to be a teacher?"

"No. A rock guitarist."

Ellen smiled as she slid her chair back. She retrieved a framed, 8X10 photograph from the buffet and set it on the table, just beyond the placemat in front of Hugh. Pointing at the figures in the image she said, "That's me, and that's your great-grandmother. I hate having my picture taken but I wanted to have a souvenir of me and Louise. She was my surrogate mother, as I mentioned. We were very close."

Hugh carefully reached over a mug and sandwich plate to pick up the picture. In it, two women – one of them wasn't much older than a girl – were smiling and standing on a beach. Hugh drew the picture toward his face for closer study. One of his great-grandmother's photo albums contained many pictures of women and their kids by the ocean, likely on this same beach. Hugh was certain that the younger woman in this image wasn't in any of the photos in the album, yet he also felt certain that he'd seen her face somewhere before.

Hugh handed the picture back to Ellen, who'd remained standing, and she returned it to its spot on the buffet. As she was doing so, Hugh scanned the other framed photos.

"My daughter, Leona," Ellen explained, after observing Hugh's interest, "with my granddaughter and my great-grandson."

Sitting back down, Ellen said, "I'm curious. If you don't mind me asking, what prompted your desire to see your great-grandparents' place? Not that you shouldn't want to, but I've never seen anyone else from your family here."

"Well, it wasn't just Louise and Thomas's place. It was in the family for three generations before them."

"So there's a lot of past connected to the area."

"Yes, and the past fascinates me. It's why I became a history teacher. I began researching my own ancestry last fall – I mean, in a detailed way for the first time – and decided that I'd drive up here in the summer to look at the old place. We moved around when I was growing up but I don't think of any of those places as home. This is where my family's roots grew; in this soil. This is my home."

"Hmm," Ellen replied to Hugh's wistful explanation, seemingly lost in thought.

"You look...I don't know...like you maybe think I'm being too sentimental."

"Oh no, sorry." Ellen shook off whatever was distracting her and looked Hugh in the eye, obviously anxious that she might have offended. "No, I don't think that. I understand what you're saying, of course. A lot of families and young people from around here left home for the city and for other provinces. Some of them, and their kids, undoubtedly feel distanced from their past and nostalgic about this place as a result. What I was thinking about was the way you phrased what you said and I was comparing it to my own feelings. In my case, land and soil aren't what I think of when I think of home. I have zero inclination to go back to where I grew up. I think of home as the centre of my current existence. It positions me in the world, but it isn't a fixed geographical positioning because it's moveable and changeable."

"I suppose that researching my ancestry and family tree got me thinking in terms of roots; like I'm connected to those that came before me."

"I understand. Of course you're right that the past exists in the present."

"A part of my interest in the past is because my father's family was uprooted – there's that metaphor again – from this exact place after... My family didn't talk about what happened here and why they left... It was off limits."

"Ah," Ellen nodded in understanding, "but not for you."

"No. Facts are facts."

"You're referring to…"

"The murdered aviator from the RCAF station."

"Yes, of course, but you obviously know something about what happened after that."

"My great-aunt Virginia told me a bit before she died."

"Not your grandfather?"

"No. He told me to mind my own business when I asked him about it. Virginia warned me he'd be like that."

"I'm sorry. What did Ginny tell you about what happened back then – if I might ask?"

"She said that a man who'd deserted from the Mount Pleasant RCAF air base near here, in 1943, was found dead, back in the bush. He'd been shot. I gather that he was laying on a path beyond my family's field; the one behind the house…"

"No. That's where the trail begins. It runs east through the bush, along behind your family's east field, and then back of Nelson's farm. The body was found behind your east field."

"Virginia said that there was a rumour that her father, Thomas, who was out there with a rifle, shot the man, thinking that he'd been visiting Louise."

The old lady studied Hugh's face for a moment. "Yes," she began slowly, apparently reviving long forgotten memories. "It was terrible what a few of the locals said. So unfair. Vile gossip."

"It was unpleasant enough to make Thomas and Louise move to Montreal."

"Yes."

Hugh had never spoken to anyone, except Heather, about the events he'd just described; about the aviator's death and the nasty rumours afterwards. Much about what actually happened was a mystery to him and he was reconciled to the fact that it would always be so. But the old lady now sitting in front of him had, amazingly, been here at that time and been friends with Louise. It sparked some hope that he might learn more about that awful period in 1943.

Hugh said, "I read the autopsy report. It was decided that the man was a deserter from the air base, probably mistakenly shot by a hunter with a shotgun who thought he was shooting at a bird. Apparently the hunters would head up to the bush in the summer – or to an old gravel pit – to shoot targets or skeet and do whatever they do with their rifles to get them ready for autumn hunting. That should have ended the speculation about my great-grandparent's involvement in the man's death but Virginia said that the rumour that Louise was an adulteress and Thomas was a murderer persisted. Do you know why the gossips were saying what they did? Was it just something some locals pulled out of thin air because they didn't like my family?"

"No, I wouldn't say that a lack of popularity was why. The murdered man had apparently been bragging to other men on the base that he was carrying on with a married woman who lived on one of the nearby farms. He'd never said anything about deserting, so on the day that he went missing, his chums who noticed his absence assumed that he'd snuck away to visit the woman. After the guy was found dead, some locals wondered if the married woman in question was involved in the shooting, and they began to speculate about who she was. The gossips could have targeted any of the women in the area as the suspect but it was known that the dead guy had been to Louise's house, and at a time when her husband and kids were away."

"He'd broken in to steal civilian clothes, right before he was shot."

"Exactly, and he had them with him when he was found. And we know that he got them from Louise's house because she told the police that he'd been there. She called from my house to report the break-in. It was Louise and the policeman who discovered that some clothes were missing."

"Calling the police is not the act of someone who wants to hide the fact that a man who they've murdered has just been at their house."

"No. The gossips decided that Louise called the police in case someone had seen the man near her house – or if the police later found blood in the yard – and that she fabricated the story that he was a deserter who'd been at the house to steal clothes. It was even speculated that Tom had placed the clothes near the aviator's dead body."

"Geez."

"I should mention that, so far as I could tell, it was only a few men who spread the rumours about Louise. We women stood by her. I always suspected that the rumour mongers didn't like the idea that a hunter could have shot the man because it would mean that any one of them may have done it. Their rumour took the murder out of the bush altogether and placed it in the vicinity of the Martin house."

"So they were saying that Thomas came home, saw the aviator leaving his house, shot him, and carted the body off to the woods?"

"It was a long time ago, Hugh, but I think that was how it went."

"But you don't think that there was any truth to the rumour do you?"

Ellen smiled and, speaking gently and reassuringly said, "No son. No a chance. There was an inquest as you know, and it was decided from the evidence that the guy was a deserter. Plus, I knew Tom and he would never have killed anyone. He was a good man."

"And Louise… Would she have had an affair?"

"No. These things happened sometimes, of course. There was opportunity. Some of the men around here went off for part of the year to work on logging, and their wives were left alone. And, by 1943, husbands were joining up for the war effort and leaving home. But you know Hugh, if someone wants to, it's easy to make any of the normal things that happened during those times when husbands were away sound suspicious. Like there were men, during the depression, who stopped at houses to chop wood in exchange for a sandwich. Women, on their own, especially with small kids, welcomed that. Natives came by, selling baskets, and people would put them up for the night. Oh, and us Acadians welcomed storytellers and singers into our homes. It can get pretty lonely around here. On top of all that, I suppose there are always some men who are willing to believe stories like the ones the aviator spread about himself, about being a great seducer, you know, because they have contempt for women, thinking them stupid and easy to manipulate, and that men are suave operators. A lot of what men think about women is just male fantasy… Same thing with the stories they make up. The fact of the matter is that there was no reason to believe that the man was actually seeing anyone."

"No wonder Louise and Thomas left here with those type of attitudes around."

"Yes. But they exist everywhere."

"But why, if those spreading rumours were men, would they have blamed Thomas? He was one of them. Why pin the blame on a man?"

"I assume that Tom only got dragged into things because he was Louise's husband. I'm guessing that his pals would have thought that, if Tom did shoot the aviator, that he'd done nothing wrong. It would have been a matter of honour and of saving his home, so he would have gotten off easy in court. Been seen as a hero even. There was a double standard. When a man and a woman got up to something, only the woman was acting immorally. She was a Jezebel. The benefit of that – of defining the woman as immoral – is that, if a man shoots his wife's lover, then she can be seen as the one actually responsible for the lover's death."

"Letting men off the hook."

Ellen didn't respond to Hugh's comment so he continued, "It makes me angry, furious even. My ancestors were robbed of their place in the world in an unfair way."

"I don't blame you. I feel the same."

When it came time to leave, Hugh said, "I have some of Louise's photos. Lots of them taken at the beach, like the one you showed me. Would it be okay it I come back with them some time? Maybe you could look at the pictures and identify the people in them. My grandfather hates the pictures for some reason so I could never ask him about them and now he has dementia. He might remember something or he might not. It depends on the day."

"I'd be delighted to give it a try – anything for Louise's great-grandson – although all of the pictures would have been taken many years ago and my memory isn't what it used to be. Still, a visit would be especially nice since I don't get much company."

3.

Across from the entrance to the first farm that he passed on his return trip to Charlottetown, Hugh pulled Heather's distinctive 2003 red Fiat Panda onto the gravel shoulder.

On his drive up that morning he'd observed the sign on the fruit stand across the road: *Nelson's Fruit, Vegetables, and Maple Syrup.*

The wooden booth sat beside the farm's entrance. It had been empty earlier but Hugh could now see maple syrup bottles lined up along the counter. An old man, staging the last bottle, turned to look at Hugh and nodded.

Hugh climbed from the Panda and walked across the empty road. He said, "Hi," as he approached the man, who stood eyeing the Fiat with curiosity.

"Get good gas mileage with that little car I guess."

"Fantastic; especially on the highway."

The man had undoubtedly been tall in his youth but was now stooped and thin. Dark blue veins stood out on his skinny arms and hands; the skin being diaphanous. He shuffled his way towards a foldable lawn chair and awkwardly sat down, almost tipping the thing over.

Hugh tensed, wanting to grab the chair, but resisted the urge.

The man let out a deep wheeze and then a hoarse cough. Around the legs of the chair were the butts of a dozen or more roll your own cigarettes that testified to the reason why such a simple act as sitting down was a taxing effort.

"I'd like one of these big bottles," Hugh said, pointing.

"Just stick your money in the cash box there," the man replied, neatly economizing his own activity. A bout of smoker's cough followed the simple expenditure of energy.

Hugh took note of the prices listed on the sign, found that he had exact change, and placed two bills in the metal box. There was a clip board beside it and the page attached to it invited people to sign up to the farm's mailing list. Hugh obliged, writing down his name, address, and email address.

By this time the man was rolling a cigarette, shakily, with long bony fingers that were stained nicotine yellow.

"I guess you make the syrup yourself," Hugh said, uncertain of whether he had used the correct verb.

"My daughter's husband does, from the trees at the back of our fields."

"And what do you grow in the fields – if you don't mind me asking?"

"Vegetables and berries, like the sign says. We even have a small apple orchard."

After watching the man light his smoke, then cough with his first drag, Hugh asked, "Have you lived here long?"

"Lived in Summerside when I was a youngster but my old man moved us here to work the farm after my grandfather couldn't do it anymore. Well my father – Freddy was his name – worked it. My mother wasn't a farm person so she soon left and it was just the old man and me who did everything."

"And you're still at it."

"Not really. The wife and I worked it for forty years till Ruth passed. Now it's my daughter and her husband who run things."

Hugh glanced past the man, his gaze taking in the fields and farmhouse, and it occurred to him that it wasn't surprising that so many young people didn't stick around. Living in a place like this – especially for a young person – could undoubtedly be isolating and boring.

"My family's from around here too," Hugh said, "but they left a long time ago. Their name was Martin…" He watched the man's face for a reaction but saw nothing to read there. "Did you know them? It was a long time ago, before and during the war – maybe too long ago to remember."

The man looked appraisingly at Hugh. "Hmm, Martin… Oh yeah, of course." His face brightened. "That goes back. I chummed with a couple of Martin boys when I was young. Jesus, that must have been sixty years ago."

"My grandfather would have been one of the boys you were friends with: Robert."

"Oh yeah, right. Robbie. Tall for his age; and the other one was…"

"Edward."

"Right, yeah, Eddie. He was the older one. Those boys were the best fishermen… So is Robbie still alive?"

"Yes, he lives in Montreal. Edward and Virginia have passed away though."

"Sorry to hear it… So you were up to look at the old place eh?"

"Yes, not much left of it now. I mean, the house and barn."

"No, no, it's been that way for a long time. It's just the fields that get used now."

"I met an old woman when I was at the farm: Ellen Comer. She told me a bit about the times when my family lived here."

"Ellen…right. Haven't seen her in awhile. You'd think I would, living just up the road. I never knew her well cus she's never been too friendly. Well, I shouldn't say she's not friendly, I just mean she's not too sociable. Keeps to herself. My old man used to call her 'the mermaid'."

"Why?"

"She just showed up one day, married to old Larry Comer when he came back from a stint of logging in New Brunswick. Well, he wasn't old, now that I think about it, somewhere in his thirties I guess, but she was only eighteen or nineteen. They said that Larry must have scooped her out of the water cus she had no family that ever came to visit her and, like I said, she keeps to herself." The man leaned forward as if to indulge a secret. "She was a beautiful girl, like those drawings of mermaids you see. My old man said that some of the young guys would drop by Comer's farm to do her."

"Do her?"

"Yeah," the man said with a lascivious smile.

Hugh suppressed a comment that there seemed to have been an inordinate amount of malicious gossip back in the day. He pretended to read the label on the syrup bottle while thinking it was no wonder that Ellen kept herself isolated from people with attitudes like this – he would have done the same. And it possibly explained why she had accused men of making up stories about women because it fed their fantasies.

With nothing else to talk about, Hugh said, "Thanks for

the syrup." He'd begun to turn toward his to his car when he stopped. It had struck him that Nelson was a name he'd come across lately. Pointing to the sign on the fruit stand, he said, "Nelson, that's your name I take it?"

"It is."

"I was doing some research about this area and read about an aviator that was shot and killed the year before my great-grandparents moved away from here. The news article said that a couple of boys – ten-year-olds – found the body, and that one of their names, if I'm remembering correctly, was Nelson. They interviewed him. Harold maybe?"

"It's Harry. Geez! Didn't know I was famous. Horrible thing, that murder. The poor bugger's face was half blown off. I had nightmares about it for a long time after. Even now it comes to mind once in awhile." He took a huge draw from his rollie to calm himself.

"I'm sorry. I didn't… I didn't mean to remind you."

"It's okay… So is that why you came up here? To ask Ellen about the murder?"

"No no. I just ran into her but the subject came up. I've always been curious about what happened. My family never talked about it. I guess the whole thing brought up some bad memories that they wanted to get away from. The police never caught who did it and it seems that some people blamed my great-grandfather Thomas for the shooting – based on no evidence. I was told that he was even shunned. Anyway, it made life miserable enough for him and my great-grandmother that they moved away."

"Did people really say stuff like that? Cruel. I was young so I don't remember much. Plus, I tuned my old man out when he went off on one of his rants about the murder."

"Understandable that you didn't want reminders after what you saw. Anyway, I have to be off."

Harry said, "Listen, if you want my advice, you should leave the past behind. It's done. No sense getting yourself worked up about it. That's the way I am, like with that murdered aviator. I leave the past where it belongs. Oh, and another thing, that old lady you were talking to is more than eighty years old – I don't know if you know that – and they say she's a bit loopy. Her mind has been going for a long time, and her memory too, so you can't be sure that anything she says – about anything – actually happened." Harry coughed up some phlegm and spat it out onto the road.

Hugh nodded but made no reply except to say, "Goodbye."

As he drove home, he thought about Harry's advice: leave the past behind. It went against his own nature; he was an historian after all. Was it possible, he wondered, that the old man was warning him that he might find out that the stories about his great-grandparents were true? The old guy remembered the salacious rumours about Ellen and that his father called her 'the mermaid', so in spite of what he said about having a poor memory, he likely remembered a lot more than he let on. And would it be surprising if Harry not only recalled but believed the stories about Louise and Thomas's involvement with the murdered aviator?

Driving past farm after farm, Hugh once again thought about how lonely it might feel to live on one of these farms. Was it any wonder that a murder would stir up local gossip and theories? It would have been a bit of excitement to break the monotony. On top of that, a person might feel less vulnerable living in such isolation if they didn't think there was an unknown murderer roaming around. Blaming someone was maybe essential.

Panel from Heather Bruce's Siren video

In the beginning, before the appearance of Mermaids, lived the divinities known as Sirens: half woman and half bird creatures with fierce talons that could tear men apart.

The Sirens famously appear in *The Odyssey* by Homer, the story of Odysseus and his men's return from war, back to their homes and their land, back to the place where their journey began.

The Sirens' beautiful voices lured sailors to the cliffs of the Sirens' island where their boats were smashed on the rocks. The men would be drowned or torn apart by the Sirens.

Siren myth reflects the fear of men who set sail: the fear of not being able to return home.

The mythical significance of the story of Odysseus usually focuses on 'the journey theme', about an adventure which goes full-circle, bringing us back home, changed by the experience. But perhaps its significance is in the obstacles encountered along the way, especially those which are categorized as dangerous to a man's quest for home: such as women who lure sailors to their destruction.

4.

The Prince Edward Island women's art collective that Heather Bruce belonged to had recently had an arts grant application accepted. The proposal was to stage a multi-genre art exhibition at the university, entitled, *Sirens' Island: Myth, Power, and Silencing Women's Voices in PEI.* The application had stated that the works would be wide-ranging but thematically connected.

It would be the group's third show. The first two had gained them a reputation for being provocative and issue oriented.

The idea for this latest project began after someone spray-painted graffiti on the window of the downtown storefront where the collective rented studio space. The message read 'hell is this sirens island' – the reference being to the murderous female creatures of Greek myth.

The members of the collective discussed the meaning of the graffiti. To them, it indicated that the graffiti writer felt that Prince Edward Island was now an enclave where men were under attack from women who were using their voices to gain control. By referring to the artists as sirens, it implied that they were anti-men, and that their voices were destructive to men. The ultimate, irony-free meaning of the graffiti was that PEI women should shut up.

The collective decided to respond by co-opting the phrase 'sirens island' and owning it.

In addition to being spokeswoman for the exhibition, Heather was doing research for a video installation, a feminist polemic on siren myths.

Hugh and Heather were standing side by side, facing the kitchen sink in their main floor apartment. Heather was washing and Hugh was drying. They were of similar height but Heather was more athletic and vigorous in her movement. Her long ginger-coloured hair attested to her Shetland Islands parentage.

As always, the after dinner ritual began with the two of them noting the state of the backyard since the window above the sink looked out on the yard they shared with their upstairs neighbours.

"Still no ducks," Heather joked. Charlottetown had just gone through a period of two weeks of almost constant rain. She prompted Hugh to continue his story, "So you were talking about the old guy with the maple syrup stand that you met on your way home."

Hugh replied, "Yes, Harry Nelson. He said that the old lady I mentioned – Ellen – was nicknamed 'the mermaid'. How's that for a coincidence? While you're beavering away, researching mermaids, I actually ran into one."

"Ironic since, in my experience, running into mermaids isn't something that happens every day. Did you get an explanation of why Ellen was called 'the mermaid' – behind her back I presume?"

"I suspect she knew about it because she told me that some of the stuff that men say about women is a reflection of their fantasies. Anyway, Harry said that she was called 'the mermaid' because she just showed up one day accompanying her much older husband – meaning that he must have fished her out of the water. Oh, and no one ever met any family of hers – like she didn't have any. And she kept to herself. So presumably no one asked her about herself."

"Or maybe someone did ask and she didn't tell them because she wanted her privacy."

"Harry also said that she was beautiful and that young men would go by her house and sleep with her."

"Oh really. Assuming that she wasn't sexually free, I agree with your Ellen… That sounds like a characterization taken from stuff these guys heard about mermaids. Like they laze around naked, perched on a rock, brushing their hair and desperately longing for a man. A man's perfect fantasy."

"So maybe the young guys around there fantasized that she really is a mermaid."

"Yes. And maybe she is," Heather said, smiling, then added with mock seriousness, "One could make the case…"

"That Ellen really is a mermaid?"

"Absolutely – in hiding."

"Okay," Hugh said, nodding and donning the expression of

one engaged in a serious debate. "What's your case?"

"Well her age is the big one. You said that she was over eighty but looked and moved like she was fifty years old or so… Here, wait a second." Heather shook the soap suds off her hands.

She left the room and returned in less than thirty seconds, a dog-eared copy of Hans Christian Andersen's fairy tales in hand. She began flipping through the pages.

"Right, here it is," she said. "The little mermaid is asking whether humans die."

Heather read the words of an ancient mermaid:

> *"Yes," the old lady said, "they too must die, and their lifetimes are even shorter than ours. We can live to be three hundred years old, but when we perish we turn into mere foam on the ocean, and haven't even a grave down here among our dear ones."*

Hugh countered, in a theatrical, pseudo-intellectual voice, "So you're arguing that Ellen's on a different biological schedule than the rest of us. Well, I can easily refute that argument by pointing out that *The Little Mermaid* is a fairy tale."

"So you say, but Andersen would have done his research. Plus it's not just him who's made these kind of claims. Ancient Greeks said that mermaids can live to be thousands of years old."

"And what about the fact that Ellen has a kid; a human child, yet she's half fish?"

"Oh bosh! That ancient gospel of old truths, *The Arabian Nights*, tells the story of an ocean girl. And according to that work, these creatures are anatomically the same as humans."

"And how exactly – physically I mean – do they breed?"

"Is it a pornographic image you want me to conjure for you?"

"Merely a medical one."

Heather set down the Andersen book on the kitchen table and returned to her spot at the sink.

"Well, here again," she said learnedly, "there's anecdotal but solid evidence of human and mermaid inter-breeding. It's believable because it comes from my homeland, so be careful what you say next." She looked sternly at Hugh. "According to my nana, a mermaid's tail is just the skin of a fish that can be removed and put back on."

"Well, I'm lost if you're allowed to cherry pick stuff from mythology to prove whatever you want."

"But I am. Why do you seem so surprised? You're a pretty slow learner." And she leaned affectionately against Hugh.

Their relationship was still quite new and its original magnetic properties were strong. It frequently brought their bodies against each other throughout the day, providing a sense of completeness and assurance.

Hugh said, "Actually, there's something else about Ellen that might support your contention that she could be a mermaid."

"So you're seeing sense, but what, pray tell, is that?"

"I was telling her about my quest to be on the land where my relatives came from, where my roots began, and she had a strange look on her face. I asked her about it and she said that she misses home, but not any land; that land and soil aren't home."

"Meaning she sounds like someone who came from the ocean?"

"Yes."

"Except there are other reasons why people could object to associating land and soil with home."

"Such as?"

"Well, given her age, Ellen lived through World War II. She might remember the Nazi slogan, 'blood and soil', where fascists sought racial homogeneity in their homeland, and also used the idea to justify the conquest of other people's land and the genocide of the inhabitants."

"Okay… I hadn't thought of it that way."

And with that the conversation fell off, from the end of the humour.

Heather knew that Hugh felt a connection to this place because it was where his paternal ancestors had lived for generations. In one way, this was the home he'd always sought. She felt that there was a bit of romanticizing behind his attitude about the place – which she couldn't criticize – but it wasn't anything that she could relate to. She'd been born on the Shetland Islands in Scotland, lived there until the age of three when her parents moved to PEI, and she planned to stay here. Her parents had returned to Shetland three years ago, to the island called Mainland. In Heather's mind it was a beautiful place, but it wasn't 'home' because it was where her life began.

"Speaking of mermaids," Hugh piped up, a few moments later, "how's your show shaping up? Any progress today?"

"There was." Heather brightened at the subject. "The show's not about mermaids specifically," she corrected, "it's theme is sirens and a mermaid is a hybrid siren."

Hugh said nothing in reply, looking expectantly in Heather's direction.

She continued. "We've all begun work on our projects."

Heather went on to bring Hugh up to date. Penny, a sound artist, was out recording the ocean and the voices of PEI women. Darla had completed some sketches of her proposed performance art piece. Katarina was busy taking photographs of the ocean while Gillian, a filmmaker, was making progress on her storyboard, a re-imagining of a lost silent film from 1919 called *The Siren's Song*. Gina was researching the historical sightings of sirens and mermaids in the Maritime provinces, while Francis and Myrna were making progress on their artworks. Francis was working on a large collage and Myrna was doing an oil painting; both focused on kitsch and the depictions of mermaids and sirens.

"And how's your video going?" Hugh asked. "You're obviously doing your research."

"Only to a certain extent because it's not an essay. It's an idiosyncratic dissection of the views about women that the myth expresses."

Heather's proposed video would mix text and images, old and new, to show the continuity between the misogyny of the myth when it arose, and the misogyny of today.

"I'm thinking of setting up a monitor inside an aquarium type structure. People can put on headphones and view the video through glass. It will help shut out the sound and imagery all around, and the aquarium shape will make the experience similar to the way we observe fish, although the fish, in this case, will be sirens and women on a screen…so inside a glass box as it were. I'm hoping it will make the point that there is continuity between male attitudes about women, from ancient myths to how television presents women for the male gaze. Women trapped in boxes, like home and television. My pseudo aquarium is meant to be an inversion of what I read is happening in that new bar downtown, where there's an aquarium behind the bar, and a scantily clad miss in a mermaid tail swims inside it for the entertainment and gaze of the customers. Like a strip joint but more upscale and supposedly artistic. In my installation it will be clear that women, as part of nature, are imprisoned like mermaids inside aquariums. They are silenced, and their world is limited and controlled. They are there to be looked at; not to speak."

"And what will the soundtrack be? A siren song?"

"Well… What would a siren's song be these days? A seductive voice cooing about how handsome you are maybe? Ohhh, let me touch your muscles. Irresistible stuff for some men. I'll have to think about it and get back to you… Oh, you know what just occurred to me?"

"What?"

"That old woman you met – the mermaid – that she'll have a story to tell and it would be fascinating to hear it; to hear how people treated her because of the way she was seen. She sounds perceptive."

"I think you'd like her. I'm guessing she's a feminist since way back, judging by her opinions. She told me that the rumour mungers who were whispering stories about my great-grandfather being a murderer did so because they didn't like the theory that the killer was a hunter; meaning it could have been one of them. But when I asked her why they would have thrown my great-grandfather under the bus, even though they would have been his buddies, her view was that, in saying that a husband shot a guy who was sleeping with his wife, the men were really blaming the wife for the killing because they would have seen the husband's actions as justified and caused by the wife's betrayal of her marriage vows."

"Ah, and peace loving men go to war because of women like Helen of Troy. Yes, that's consistent with my views about siren myths. Women are supposedly responsible for men's violence."

"They're seen as 'Jezebels' was Ellen's word, who lead men astray. So do you want me to ask if you can interview her?"

"No, absolutely not. For all we know she didn't even know that people called her 'the mermaid'. No, I don't want you to even mention that to her. But if and when you visit her, if she brings up the subject, then it would be alright to ask if I could speak to her about it. But, as I say, only if she brings up the subject. She obviously wants privacy. You've gotten me very curious about her."

"Maybe she'll mention something when I take my great-grandmother's pictures to show her. She said she'd look at them. I thought she could tell me who the people in them are. I plan to focus on the ones taken near the water, like the picture she showed me. I'm guessing that she was there when they were taken and will know everyone in them."

"Nice…"

"But you know what's odd?"

"What?"

"Ellen isn't in any of my great-grandmother's pictures, although she says that they were very close."

"Well, she might have been the one holding the camera, or maybe she's just camera shy."

"Oh yeah, that's right. She said that she was."

"But yeah, please let me know what she says…about anything really."

5. Sunday

Heather was the same age as Hugh and, like him, had originally sought a career in an artistic field.

In Heather's case it involved studying graphic art at college. But the closest she had come to working as an artist after graduation was a job that involved painting and building sets at a local theatre.

Also, like Hugh, she eventually returned to school for a teaching degree to give herself a steady income. It hadn't been the end of her artistic aspirations but rather a means to accomplish them.

Her involvement in the founding of the women's art collective had come from a desire to share studio costs, and to find camaraderie, feedback, and encouragement. The group had created a sense of community where members received support without regard for whether they were professionals or amateurs and regardless of the sort of work they did.

As she was becoming more involved in her video project for the siren show, Heather found herself increasingly absorbed in the work and enjoying it.

She sat down at her desk on Sunday morning and continued on with the first draft of the script.

She'd been thinking about the dualities found in siren myth. For example, sirens were half human and half bird. Birds could make beautiful music or they could be birds of prey. These things needed to be incorporated into her video.

Heather also had a thought about the video's soundtrack. Since dualities are a characteristic of all nature, including the sounds one hears in nature, the soundtrack could reflect this. And not just by using opposite types of birdsong.

'Birds', she thought, was old British slang used by young men to refer to girls or women. Her mother had been called 'hen' when she was young, in Glasgow, Scotland. And women only gatherings are called 'hen parties'. But why the association of birds and women? Was it because it suggested a dual nature: beautiful and delicate but also potentially deadly?

Her thoughts were soon hijacked by remembrances of her

talk with Hugh the evening before, especially about the story that some local men in 1943 had spun about his great-grandparents. It was myth making. In the view of Ellen, the old woman that Hugh had met, some men invented the tale to exonerate themselves and to blame a woman for the murder of a dead aviator. The idea reinforced Heather's view that myths were self-serving; bolstering the views of the groups the authors belonged to.

Perhaps this idea could be extended, she thought. Myths, with their patina of truth, shield a group from criticism and provide safety for its members, but they also create a shared set of views which give birth to a new reality and determination of what is the truth. This leads to a set of shared values among the group and to common cause – the way it happens in the military for instance: identify the enemy and their nature by inventing stereotypes. Myths solidify power.

Her thoughts spawned the idea that, perhaps, for the final segment of her video, that she could rewrite siren myth in a way that reflected a woman's perspective. It would be based on the premise that men have wielded the power to describe women, and to see their actions from a man's perspective. A revised myth would be a refusal to accept men's myth-making about women. It would be a refusal to be silenced and an insistence that women's voices be heard.

Panel from Heather Bruce's Siren video

The Sirens were thwarted in the *The Odyssey*. The crew had their ears stuffed with wax to deafen them to the voices of the Sirens, allowing them to continue their journey past the Sirens' island, while Odysseus had himself tied to the ship's mast so that he could listen to the Sirens, and, although he would be driven mad by desire, he would not respond. He could indulge in beauty and pleasure without succumbing to women: a dominant hero in a gendered competition for power.

Only if the Siren's voice is silenced, or not responded to, says the myth, can men survive and make it home.

By extension, this lesson, when applied to life, indicates that men's attempt to silence women is an admission of a fear of the power of women's voices; seeing them as deadly.

6. Monday

As they set off on the drive to school on Monday morning, the final week of school before the summer holiday, Heather told Hugh about the first segments of her video essay.

Hugh made some positive comments but then became distracted.

A block before their arrival at the school, he came alive and said, "I was just thinking about what you said last night about being interested in the old lady I met in Mount Pleasant."

"Yes?"

"Harry said she was called 'the mermaid'…"

"Yes. So what are you thinking?"

Hugh could hear the hint of amusement in Heather's voice but he wasn't about to pick up on their mock debate of last evening.

"I was wondering if she was called 'the mermaid' because some thought that she was involved in the death of the aviator."

"What? My interest in her was not about… Okay, go on."

"Well Harry said that she was called 'the mermaid' because she'd arrived suddenly in town and the rest of it…but what if that was the kid friendly version? In *The Odyssey*, sirens killed men returning home from war. Is it possible that Ellen was called 'the mermaid' because some people thought that she was the one who had killed the deserting aviator?"

Heather pulled her car into her usual parking spot at the school but instead of shutting off the motor she twisted in her seat to look at Hugh. "Well…" She slowly exhaled, lost in thought for a moment before continuing. "There's a few problems with your theory that occur to me. First, I gather from what you've said, from your family lore, that the rumours around Mount Pleasant were that Louise was sleeping with the aviator. We can assume that was how they went because the rumours were the reason that Louise and Thomas packed up and left. If the gossips had pointed their venom at Ellen, your great-grandparents might have stayed on in PEI. The second issue I see is that the gang who

supposed that the aviator was carrying on with a woman –
and that's why he was killed – didn't think that he was a
deserter, so they wouldn't have seen him as a man on his way
home, like Odysseus was when he met the sirens. Your theory
only makes sense – I mean, that the men were borrowing
from *The Odyssey* – if they thought that the aviator actually
had been a deserter, was heading home, and was seduced by a
siren along the way, which led to his death. Plus, I'd have to
question whether a handful of small-minded gossips would
know enough about *The Odyssey* to know the story of
Odysseus."

"Not for the most part, I wouldn't think. I can't speak to
that, but could there not have been a counter-theory that
imagined a scenario where the aviator was indeed a deserter
who had been seduced by Ellen and was killed by her?"

"Like one of those bugs who kills after mating?" Heather
laughed. "If there was such a theory it doesn't make sense
either. Odysseus met sirens, not mermaids. Mermaids didn't
kill men by tempting them onto rocks; real or imagined. Only
sirens did. Mermaids supposedly love men. So there seems to
be no other reason for postulating that Ellen is a mermaid,
other than the ones you mentioned: her beauty, her
mysterious background, and men's sexual fantasies."

"I wonder though, if most people could explain the
difference between sirens and mermaid."

"I'll give you that. Oh, but since you're looking for other
reasons why a few men called Ellen 'the mermaid', let's not
forget, as I so brilliantly argued last night, that she might
really be a mermaid and that's why they called her that.
Actually, that's my theory until proven otherwise."

7.

Both Hugh and Heather were busy with year-end work during the evenings that week, but Heather found some time for writing and research while Hugh made inquiries into the 1943 murder behind his family's farm.

He re-read the transcript of the inquest into the murder of Samuel Marsh. Marsh, it had been decided, was a deserter from the local RCAF air station.

On his person, when his body was found, was a letter from his mother, Deborah, begging him to return home to Nova Scotia if he could honourably get out of the air force. Samuel's father had been working on the construction of a log home and a log had rolled backwards off of the loader of the tractor he'd been driving and crushed him. His back had been broken, leaving him laid up in bed with no one to provide for Samuel's three siblings, all of whom were under ten.

As to the rumours about Samuel sneaking off the base to meet a woman – the judge at the inquest made it clear to the jury that they were to give zero credence to any and all speculations about the murder that had no factual basis. It was a fact that the aviator had been in the bush near the base because he was a deserter. The letter on his person attested to this, as did the fact that he had stolen some men's clothing which was found laying near his dead body. There was no evidence that the man had been having an affair with anyone or was off the base to visit a woman. In his instructions to the jury the judge even chastised those who spread 'fanciful rumours'.

While the judge's injunction appeared to have been taken to heart by the jury, Hugh knew, from the fact that his great-grandparents had later fled the area, that the man's words had little impact on a small group of people around Mount Pleasant.

It was the conclusion of the inquest jury that the aviator had been murdered by a person or persons unknown; possibly by a hunter and likely by accident.

Hugh knew from his previous research that no one was

ever charged with the murder. And obviously, no possible motive was put forth during the inquest to suggest that the murder was planned.

The lack of certainly about who killed Samuel Marsh had set the local gossips off speculating. But, Hugh wondered, were their theories 'fanciful'?

If one genuinely rejected the possibility that a local hunter with a rifle would have acted so rashly as to just shoot at any movement or noise near him, especially in an area where there was a creek where local boys went to fish, then didn't it follow that the aviator's murder had been intentional? And in that case, the most likely murderer might be a cuckolded husband since no other motive had been brought up and the aviator had been telling everyone that he was carrying on a romantic affair with a local woman.

But nothing pointed to Thomas and Louise as the couple in question. Hugh agreed with Ellen's view that the rumour about Thomas and Louise being behind the murder spread because the aviator's body was found behind one of their fields.

But proximity wasn't a sufficient basis in itself to conclude anything from. Louise was not a suspect mistress because the man was murdered near her farm. There wasn't even any evidence that the guy had been seeing anyone, little own Louise.

To blame Louise and Thomas for the murder had demanded blindness to facts and evidence. It even suggested willful misrepresentation.

It was evident that Marsh was a deserter. He had left the Martin property with civilian clothes and was headed for the highway to hitchhike. That's why he was where he was. There was nothing that connected him to the farms near where he was killed.

Nor did it connect the murderer to the area. He may have stumbled upon Marsh while walking somewhere.

Another possibility… If the murderer had followed Marsh from the base – assuming the killing was deliberate – then the person could have lived in any direction from the air base.

Hugh's thoughts strayed to the rifle he saw in Ellen's

trailer. He didn't see Ellen as a murder suspect just because she lived near the murder scene, but the image of that gun brought to mind the possibility that it could have been a woman who shot the aviator. Marsh might have been harassing a woman, as one possible motive. Or deserting her.

Hugh's curiosity about Ellen's mysterious background came to the fore and he went to the ancestry website he used. A quick search led to Eleanor Comer's marriage certificate to Lawrence (aka Larry) Comer. They'd married in Summerside in 1942 when Ellen – sometimes referred to as Helen in documents – was eighteen and Larry was thirty-six.

Searching further, Hugh discovered that Ellen had been born in Moncton, the third child of Pat and Frank Lange, both of whom had died in the 1970s.

Neither theirs, nor the brief obituaries for Ellen's older sisters, made any mention of Eleanor.

That fact struck Hugh as odd. Ellen hadn't been adopted out as a baby because her name appeared on the census information he'd seen. The listing of residents included the names of both her parents and those of all three of their children; including Ellen. So why hadn't Eleanor been mentioned in any family obituaries. Had there been a falling out between them? Had Ellen been disowned? Or had she disowned her family?

Ellen remained a mystery.

And there was more. Why, for example, had she been in Summerside at age eighteen?

Hugh suddenly wondered if he should be looking into Ellen's background. It seemed quite natural to him to do so; a benign activity. He was an historian after all. He had delved into Heather's background and that of his friends, and then passed along information to them. All had shown an interest in his findings and no one had objected to his researching their families. But he recalled his conversation with Heather when he'd told her about Ellen. She was curious about the old lady but insisted that there should be no prying into Ellen's background without her permission. Ellen was entitled to privacy and one could presume, based on her actions, that she wanted it.

Hugh closed the ancestry website and decided to say nothing to Ellen about his findings.

Hugh also spent an evening that week going through his great-grandmother Louise's photo albums.

The albums had passed from Louise to his great-aunt Virginia, her daughter. After Virginia's death the albums had (for some inexplicable reason) gone to her brother Robert. Hugh's suspicion was that they'd actually been given to Robert's late wife, Marianne, Hugh's grandmother.

Robert had gruffly told Hugh one Saturday, when his visiting grandson was looking through the albums for the umpteenth time, that if he liked them so much that he should take them. "I have no interest in the damn things and if you don't take them they'll only end up in the garbage."

Hugh had seized the moment – and the albums – but he was immediately faced with a problem: he didn't know who most of the people in the photos were, and given his grandfather's attitude and the recent death of his uncle Edward, there was no one to ask for information.

There were many pictures of the family: of Robert, Edward, and Virginia growing up, taken mostly on special occasions like birthdays and Christmas. For those pictures, Hugh had been able to attach names to faces.

But there was one photo album that was still a mystery. It contained the beach pictures, like the one he'd seen at Ellen's. Mothers and kids. Edward and Robert cavorting in the water with their pals.

Hugh had unhappily decided that the people in the photos were destined to remain nameless. A lost community of families. But now, here was Ellen, and the thought of it once again buoyed his hopes that he might get some answers after all.

Panel from Heather Bruce's Siren video

Sirens reflect some men's fear of womanly seduction, believing it to be an act that overcomes their ability to go home.

But the nature of the Sirens who destroyed men is also a significant cause of fear. In some versions of the myth, Sirens were described as independent women with their own community; and they refused sexual congress with men.

If Siren myth provides a life lesson, it says that women's sexuality, freedom, voice, and community are enemies of home.

When men are away, home must always be maintained as if the man is there – its head – no matter where he is off to.

Men must even fight sometimes when they return from war, to regain their home. Odysseus (aka Ulysses), with help, killed Penelope's suitors. His form of masculinity demands domination of home.

8. Friday

The upscale bar, The Sailor's Roost, had cleared out. The Friday night staff were gone. The front doors locked.

As was always the case on Friday and Saturday nights, a handful of friends of Jason Hopkins, the owner, stayed on upstairs in The Mermaid Lounge.

Alex Callas was new to that scene. He'd been coming to the bar for over a year, hanging out in the lounge, but he wasn't part of the group that inhabited it after hours. Tonight was a first.

The bar was still relatively new to Charlottetown, as was Hopkins. Speculation about him and The Sailor's Roost went in several directions. He was a shady character involved in the drug trade. He was an investor and model citizen. The after hours activities in his bar included orgies. Or they didn't.

All rumours were unsubstantiated.

Alex was in the lounge, sitting in a large velvet chair where he was making out with Bethany Yeats who was curled up in his lap, her arms wrapped around his neck.

"It's about time we ended up together," Bethany whispered in Alex's ear, then began darting her tongue around inside it.

"We should find somewhere private," Alex said, closing his eyes to fully enjoy the luxurious experience.

Bethany slid her hand up one of his arms, and pulled her head back momentarily to admire the limb. She muttered "Beautiful physique," then went back at Alex's ear with ferocity.

Alex was a handsome man, and he'd made a concerted effort to be a tough one too, perfecting a quiet swagger. He'd had his eye on Bethany since their paths first crossed a year earlier. She was married but her husband Butler was vacationing in the Correctional Centre where he'd been resident for awhile. He was expected to be living there for a further year.

Alex had the impression that Bethany was seeing her boss, Jason Hopkins, but even so, he'd been certain that they'd hook up one day at a time of his choosing. "She makes my balls ache," he'd told his buddies.

It was Bethany who'd made the first move that night, shortly after the incident between Alex and his best friend Dave Seaver, around midnight.

Alex and several other young men had been sitting in the chairs loosely spread around a low circular table in one corner of The Mermaid Lounge. It was in front of the hallway that led to Jason Hopkins' office. On the wall above the table were two large, titillating, Herbert James Draper paintings, circa the turn of the nineteenth century to the twentieth. *Ulysses And the Sirens* was a curious depiction of Ulysses' ship being swarmed by a fetching young group of 'sirens' – which appeared to be a mermaid and two naked women. *The Sea Maiden* depicted a number of men trying to haul a terrified, and naked young woman from a net, as if she was a giant tuna.

Hopkins was absent from the informal get-together; 'away on business' as they say.

The atmosphere among the men was convivial, with lots of laughing, until, quite abruptly, Dave strode up to the table. Nobody had noticed him enter the lounge.

Alex smiled at the sight of his friend, but his expression soon changed after noting the furious look on Dave's face.

Dave went straight for Alex who was sitting in a relaxed manner with his left foot resting on the glass-topped table.

Dave straddled Alex's leg then bent over him, grabbing the front of his shirt and tightening it in his grip. "What the fuck were you doing with my wife last night?" he shouted.

Alex's free foot flashed upwards, squarely catching his assailant in the testicles, and lifting him slightly into the air.

Dave ended up on the floor, holding his groin and contracted into a fetal position.

Alex knew enough not to sit and savour his victory. He stood up and withdrew a knife from his pants' pocket, which he immediately popped open. He yelled, "Keep the fuck away from me. Don't ever come up on me again. Next time I'll cut your balls off."

Alex's eyes flashed with anger as he stepped away from the man on the floor; all the while watching him intently. For all he knew, Dave had a handgun on his person.

The other men in the room had initially been stunned by the attack, but two of them now stood and moved towards Alex with the intention of managing the situation. Each of them lightly took one of his arms. They spoke firmly, telling him to relax and to put the knife away.

"Let's take a walk," one of the guys said. And with that the three began to slowly exit the lounge with Alex looking over his shoulder to keep Dave – still curled up on the floor – in his sights.

Alex was escorted down the stairs to an empty table in the bar where the men he was with proceeded to calm him down.

Bethany Yeats soon joined them, with two drinks in hand, and told Alex's minders to go back upstairs.

She took hold of one of Alex's hands and spoke soothingly while sliding him a glass. It was time to chill, she said.

Closing time soon arrived and Bethany reminded Alex that she worked at 'The Roost' and had clearance to be in The Mermaid Lounge after hours. She asked if he'd accompany her there.

Anticipating the evening to come, Alex quickly agreed.

Soon after, Bethany got out of her chair, plopped herself onto Alex's lap, and the pair began making out.

The lights were dim, as was the music; as they had been since closing time.

A couple near Alex and Bethany were likewise grappling with each other.

A high-stakes poker game was underway at a table in front of the bar. Four men seated at a round table, looking somewhat like an enactment of dogs playing poker art. The participants punctuated the night with occasional bursts of surprise, triumph, or frustration, when final hands were slammed down on the table.

There was no set agenda for this night – certainly no plan for an orgy. It wasn't a Saturday night after all.

No one noticed when an individual in a black hoodie slipped silently into the upstairs lounge.

The intruder had crept up the stairs and entered near Alex and Bethany.

The figure stepped to the right, slipping into shadow, then surveyed the lounge for a full fifteen seconds. Making sure.

Alex and Bethany were two metres away.

The only part of Bethany that the intruder could make out was her back, mostly covered by a mass of long blonde curls. Alex was almost hidden from view, behind her, but his head was partially visible in profile.

The shadowy figure's black-gloved hand slid the handgun from the spot where it was secured between stomach and belt.

Bethany leaned forward and pulled off one of her shoes.

The intruder strode forward, put the gun to Alex's temple, and fired.

Bethany screamed. She fell to the floor.

People around the room dove for cover.

The figure in black ran to the head of the stairs and hurtled downward.

No one followed.

No one was prepared to move until they had a grasp on what was happening.

Panel from Heather Bruce's Siren video

Over time, Sirens were re-imagined by artists as beautiful human women. Siren porn. Presumably, since visuals couldn't reflect the beauty of Sirens' voices, it was now their physicality and sexual allure that drew men in. If men were in danger it might now be from being fucked to death.
Beauty as power. Beauty can kill. Like nature. Like the ocean.
Seeing Sirens as human women laid bare the fact that the myth had always been an allegory about power relations between men and women.
It is a fear that is always heightened when men go off to war. Inevitably, it is a fear of the latent Siren in all women, including wives who can destroy what many men feel is the multi-faceted natural order of home: a site of refuge, control, happiness, peace, and men's dominance.
There is also a homoerotic element in this, among the sailors. Succumbing to women destroys the group of men.

47

9. Saturday

It was the first full day of summer holidays.

Hugh and Heather had been looking forward to it. It was the conclusion of their second year of teaching. Their work load had been lighter than year one when every unit and lesson plan had to be created from scratch, but in spite of the fact that a portion of their lesson plans had been adopted from the previous year, Hugh and Heather still worked late on most evenings.

It was a wearing schedule and summer break had been eagerly looked forward to as a chance to work on personal projects. And to sleep in, followed by lingering in bed with each other.

It was around 10:00 in the morning when Hugh dropped Heather off at their co-worker and friend Penny Callas's apartment.

He then left in Heather's car, heading for Mount Pleasant.

As near as two months earlier, Heather would have accompanied him to Ellen's place, but they were making a concerted effort to return to a life where they weren't always in each other's shadow.

The pair had met a couple of years earlier, when they were both beginning their teaching careers at the same high school. It took awhile for them to become friends but there was no question of being more than that since Heather had a longtime boyfriend.

In spite of that, Heather and Hugh both began to harbour feelings that they either couldn't allow or expect to be reciprocated if they gave in to them. At least until the afternoon of the last day of school for the year when they both went solo to a barbecue at the home of another teacher.

The pair left the barbecue together, planning to walk to their apartments downtown, but a half hour later they stopped and sat on the grass of a park – for a break.

Soon they both lay back, wrapped up in their discussion, but almost immediately, with all the intensity of pent up feeling, the two were passionately kissing and embracing.

There was often still an echo of that during the day: the

intense desire to feel that surprising intimacy, that satisfying sense of completeness from contact when the two would become magnetized and end up pressed up against each other while they were engaged in some otherwise mundane activity.

As Hugh drove through Mount Pleasant he found himself – for the fifth time that morning – worrying that he wouldn't find Ellen at home and that his drive would end up being a waste of gas and energy. He'd been kicking himself for not getting a number for the cell phone he'd spotted on her kitchen counter the previous Sunday. He'd found nothing online.

Passing the fruit stand belonging to Harry Nelson, Hugh raised his hand to wave but, at the moment he went by, Harry was fussing over his bottles of maple syrup, leaning against the stand with one hand, his other doing the work, with his back to the road.

Hugh turned into the drive at the farm, past a sign that read: *Vezina/Comer*. A pickup truck and a white compact were parked beside the main farmhouse, on his left.

To his relief, a Toyota Corolla was sitting in front of Ellen's trailer, as it had been on his first visit.

When he approached the trailer on foot, Heidegger's barking fired up.

Hugh wondered if the dog was excitedly thinking that the person approaching his door was one of the family or if he could tell by the sound of Hugh's steps that he was a stranger who Ellen needed to be guarded from. He recalled a history book he'd once read. In it, an old man told a WWII historian that when anyone could be heard opening his garden gate and approaching the side door of his house, that his dog would bark vociferously. The window in the living room, where the man and the dog would sit in the evening, was too high for the dog to see out of but he recognized the sound of the children's steps so when one of them approached the house, instead of barking, the animal would run to the kitchen door, his tail wagging. The old man told the historian that his oldest son was away from home for five years during the war. On the evening the son was expected home, the man and the dog were in the living room when they heard the creak of the side gate, and then steps approaching the house. The dog jumped to his feet, cocked his head and listened intently, but instead of barking he ran to the door to welcome home the young soldier. Even after five years the dog still recognized the sound of the eldest son's walk.

Ellen responded to Hugh's knock by opening the door a crack and peeking through the narrow opening. Heidegger's nose poked vigorously in and out of the space.

For a moment, Ellen appeared to be at a loss, but then quickly brightened.

Heidegger's enthusiastic barking had been replaced by an intense effort to free himself from Ellen's grip on his collar and give Hugh a proper welcome.

"I thought it was my great-grandson," Ellen said, smiling, "and was wondering why he was knocking and not walking right in, and why Heidegger was barking. Come in."

She stepped back, and finally let go of the dog's leash once Hugh was inside. Heidegger immediately mashed his head against Hugh's legs in welcome.

"I'm sorry I didn't call first," Hugh said as he entered the trailer. He stooped, tussling the fur on the top of the dog's head, and added, "I couldn't find a phone number for you to ask if you were home. I wanted to show you some of my great-grandmother's pictures, like I mentioned last weekend. I hope this isn't a bad time, I could come back if it is."

"No, no, it's fine. I have a cell phone but I almost never use it... I mean, who would I call, or vice versa? I'll give you my number before you leave."

Panel from Heather Bruce's Siren video

Sirens, in their manifold versions, can be infinite sources of metaphor, but their stories have been told by men.

The myth of Sirens, half animal, somewhere between nature and constrained civilization, singing like all birds, can be re-imagined. And a few women artists have done this.

Consider Henrietta Rae's *The Sirens*, from 1903.

There are no men in the piece. There is a ship of men in the distance, out there: an ominous threat that must be guarded against. This painting reflects the Sirens' perspective. It is an image of a women's community. Sirens are part of nature, nakedly embodying it in their own lovely Pagan world, filled with music. Their nakedness is not for the male gaze, or to seduce men, or gratuitous. Nakedness does not always imply sexual availability for men, or is it even about sex.

In this world, if there are sexual relations, they will be between women. The painting, though, is not a depiction of sex, but of Sirens' communal life.

This reimagined myth depicts Sirens with empathy, as creatures who desire privacy and security for themselves, and for their own unique community. It differs from men dominated society and is threatened by men.

If a myth presents 'the truth' from the perspective of its author, than this is a radical revision of the 'truths' in Homer's *Odyssey* about sirens.

10.

Penny Callas's apartment – like Heather and Hugh's – was one half of a converted old house.

Penny, a sound artist, was working on the siren project and Heather was on her way to visit in order to listen to some of Penny's recordings of the ocean and to provide some critical comment.

The two women had met the previous fall when Penny joined the staff of the school where Heather and Hugh worked. The women were fast becoming close friends, with a shared interest in the arts.

Penny taught business and mathematics but, like Hugh, had grown up wanting to be a musician.

Her wealthy and controlling father, Hector, disapproved however, having tabbed Penny as heir apparent to run the family business, even though she'd made it clear that this was not what she wanted. But Hector, who had always preached 'family first' to his daughter, didn't care, and went to work trying to convince her that she had to succeed him.

Penny understood her father's position. Her younger brother Alex was filled with grandiose dreams of wealth and power, but he was all talk, having never demonstrated a commitment to anything. Nor did he have a love of work. And their much younger sister Selene had no interests other than being with her friends.

If the family business was to survive her father's retirement, then Penny would have to take over the running of it well before that time.

So Penny put 'family first' and agreed to study economics and business. And after graduation, she took a job in the family business. It was soon apparent to her that this was not something that she wanted to do in the long-term. Nor could she live her life solely for her family.

Penny made other plans and, during her three years working for Hector, she saved as much money as she could.

Her announcement that she was leaving the company came as a shock to her father, and he voiced his disapproval, but his further appeals to family obligation came to nothing.

Penny moved out of the house, got a part-time job, and returned to university to become a teacher.

Teaching gave Penny an income and some freedom from the obligations of family and home, and allowed her the time to create art and music; her hobbies and passions.

Penny's piece of sound art for the siren exhibition involved recording the environmental noise of the ocean surrounding PEI.

She especially loved working on the water and spending time there, which she attributed to being a descendant of fishers and sailors.

Her ocean recordings captured sounds in a way similar to how photographs capture the visual environment but listening to them provided a more immersive and enveloping experience than looking at pictures.

Her piece was based on the premise that environmental noise is fundamental to our understanding of the unique soul of every space. The sounds of the ocean remind us that it is primordial, before music and the organization of sound – before the sirens even.

To capture this, Penny had begun to make recordings of the ocean around PEI in different locations, at different depths, and in different weather. The recordings would demonstrate that the sound of crashing waves, for example, was substantially different than the sounds five metres below the surface in an area where motorized boats passed above. The soul of the ocean changes because it can be myth or it can be commerce.

Penny's intention was to surround the exhibition space with small speakers; each of them playing a recording of the ocean in one specific geographical area. There would be photographs of those areas, posted by the speakers, and the exact locations marked on an accompanying sonic map. The exhibition visitor's experience would be affected by the time they spent listening to each.

She also planned to record human sounds: the voices of women who work or play on the water, speaking about their experiences and lives. Telling their stories. The overlapping women's voices would be organized like a piece of music.

As a whole, the piece would demand of its audience that they listen closely to sounds that they often don't pay attention to or appreciate for their musicality. Only if we listen closely do we take note that these sounds are never repetitious, as we assume, but are always unique. And when that happens we are drawn in by them.

Heather knocked on Penny's apartment door.

When it opened she could see that Penny had been crying – in an intense way.

Penny stepped back to allow Heather to make her way inside.

"Are you okay?" Heather asked with deep concern as Penny closed the door behind her.

"My brother Alex is dead," Penny blurted and she lunged across the distance between her and her friend. She threw her arms around Heather and began to sob.

Heather chauffeured Penny across town.

When they arrived at the Callas family home, Heather had to make due with parking a block away. It was a large house, with a double driveway, but it was filled with cars.

Several more vehicles were parked at the side of the road, in front of the house, and one of them was a police cruiser.

Immediately after Penny opened the side door of the house a group of distraught people arrived in the hall doorway, four stairs up. Penny bolted up the steps and began hugging each of her family members, inducing new tears from all of them.

Heather stood anonymously on the landing below, largely invisible to the group above.

The family soon slid off together down the hallway toward the living room.

Only Penny's sixteen-year-old sister, Selene, remained. Heather had never met the girl before but it was obvious who she was. She had the same dark curls and round face as her older sister.

Framed by the doorway, looking down at Heather, Selene said, "Come up," before she too disappeared, heading in the direction of the living room.

Heather looked about and saw no shoes anywhere so she didn't remove her own.

At the top of the stairs, she looked to the right, saw that it led to the kitchen, and turned in that direction – away from the living room and the family.

The kitchen was empty except for a willowy teenage girl leaning against the counter. It appeared as if the cupboard was holding her upright. She was dressed in black – which made her waxen complexion even paler – and she sported large round glasses. Her hair was dyed pink. The girl gave the impression of being depleted and bored with the conventions of life. She looked up at the arrival of a stranger and nodded to Heather who responded by saying, "Hello, I'm Heather," and explaining that she was Penny's friend.

"Yes, I know," said the girl. And that was it. As if she either saw no obvious need to introduce herself, or feared the effort might be too taxing or too suburban. She immediately looked back down at the floor.

Heather watched the girl for a moment, waiting for a name, before glancing about the kitchen. She noted the unwashed breakfast dishes which suggested that the news of Alex Callas's death had come very recently. The household would obviously still be in the initial stages of shock and disbelief since it was only mid-morning.

Heather began to slide a kitchen chair out from the table but stopped after moving it a few inches. She returned it to its place since sitting down would be too much like treating the circumstances as a social visit.

She then copied the nameless girl and leaned against the cupboards where she stood as if the two of them were waiting for a bus.

"Please sit down Sally, and you too…" a woman, who'd noiselessly appeared in the kitchen doorway, said softly.

"I'm Heather, Penny's friend," Heather explained.

"I'm Doris, Penelope's mother." It sounded more like a question than a statement. "Are you both okay?" Doris added.

"I'm so sorry for your loss," Heather said, but received no acknowledgement. Her impression was that Doris had floated down the hall. The woman appeared to be lost, maybe disconnected from the events around her.

"Can I get you something?" Doris asked. At the sight of strangers she'd taken on a familiar role.

"They're fine Mom," Penny said, having suddenly appeared behind her mother. She placed her hands on Doris's shoulders and gently turned her. "They can take care of themselves. Come with me, we need to be interviewed by the cops."

Doris allowed Penny to lead her out of the room.

11.

Constable Ted Johnson, from the police Major Crimes Unit, told the family that he was leading the investigation into Alex's murder.

Penny thought it odd that a Constable would have been given this role and wondered if he was a Detective Constable.

Johnson had begun the meeting – held in Hector Callas's study – with a summation of the events surrounding the murder.

Thus far, Johnson had paid particular attention to Alex's grieving father Hector, and his heart went out to him, but the man's demeanour wasn't something he could relate to. If it was his own son who'd been shot, Johnson was certain that he'd be angry, and determined to tear apart whoever had done it, but the man in front of him was deflated and crushed.

Teen-age Selene stood off to one side. The import of her brother's murder didn't seem to have yet registered.

Her mother Doris sat on a love seat, with Penny sitting beside her, holding her hand.

Johnson and Hector were sitting, face to face, on the chairs in front of the desk.

"I worried that something like this might happen," Hector said, shaking his head. "Alex was a roughneck and he'd lately taken to hanging around with a bunch of punks, according to his wife, Hazel. She told me that she found a knife on him. After that I tried a few times to get ahold of Alex to warn him that he was playing with fire but he never answered his phone or returned my call." Hector paused before saying, "Do you know who did this?"

"No," said Johnson. "We spoke to everyone who was in the room with Alex. No one saw anything apparently. It was dark in the lounge. So far as anyone knew they were the only ones in the building, and all of its exterior doors were locked for the night. Still, someone slipped into the lounge, fired some shots, then ran away... Do you know Dave Seaver? I understand that he's your son's best friend."

"Of course we know him," said Hector. "They've been best pals since they were small kids." His voice rising with concern, Hector added, "Was Dave at the bar with him? Is he okay?"

"I assume so. Dave had been at the bar earlier, but he'd left. We haven't managed to get hold of him yet…" Johnson's voice trailed off as he remembered his interviews with the people at the bar. He'd been told about an incident before the murder when Dave accused Alex of having slept with his wife. The men had been separated and Dave left the bar. The patrons all seemed to be of a mind that Dave must have returned later with a handgun.

Johnson continued. "As I mentioned, Alex was with a young lady – um, let's say they were romantically entangled – when he was killed."

"Does it matter?" Hector asked dismissively.

"It depends. Did he routinely get together with women besides his wife do you know?"

Hector replied, "Ah…he might have had a dalliance or two. He was one of those men I guess. All man. And the bloody women wouldn't leave him alone. He loved his wife and baby though."

The policeman looked about the room and none of the women returned his gaze. Hector's comment that Dave and Alex were best friends had suggested to Johnson that this case may not be as slam dunk as it seemed. Just as well. The theory that Dave Seaver was the killer seemed too pat. A police check revealed that the bar's back door was unlocked. That was fishy. It was simply too coincidental that the door had been accidentally left open on the very night that someone wanted to slip into the place after hours. It said that the killing wasn't an act of impulse by an outraged husband but had been planned in advance.

Johnson changed direction. "I was told that Alex owned a store for weightlifters and athletes. Do you, or any of you, know anything about that?"

"I don't know what there is to know," said Hector.

"Well, when did he buy it?"

"Last summer."

"Buying a store would take a fair bit of money. Did your son receive an inheritance, or a get loan from somewhere?"

"No, no inheritance…"

"Did you loan him the money to buy the store?" Johnson asked, directing his question to Hector.

"No. He never asked me for it. I suppose he got a business loan from the bank."

"So you think he had a good enough credit record to get a bank loan?"

Hector hesitated. "Must have."

"Did he have a job before buying the store?"

"Yeah, he worked for me."

"Good job?"

"Low-level stuff."

"Pay much?"

"Not a lot, but he could have saved some. His wife worked for me too. I don't know about her finances. Maybe she got a loan or co-signed for one… Why are you asking about this? Do you think the money figured in Alex's murder? Do you think he got money from a loan shark or the Mafia? Is that what you're on about?"

Johnson said nothing for a full five seconds. Just when it appeared that his motives would remain a professional secret, he replied, "I'm just trying to get a background picture."

Hector said, "What about that guy who owns the bar…? You said Alex was there after hours so they must have been friends. They say that guy's wealthy; has his hand in a lot of pies. Maybe he's Alex's business partner."

"That's possible. The man's away on business but we'll talk to him when he returns… Do you know if your son had any enemies who might have wanted to hurt him?"

"Not that I know of."

This time, when the policeman looked around the room at the other family members, his eyes settled on Penny, the person he deemed most likely to know things about Alex that the others didn't. "Do you know of anyone Penny?"

"No," she said flatly. She knew there was a small army of pissed off husbands and boyfriends who hated Alex but none of their names.

Looking back at Hector, Johnson said, "You said Alex was a…a 'roughneck' in your words. Was he a scrapper?"

"When he was young I had a few calls from school but that was all. Kid's stuff. He was just a boy's boy…"

"And these punks you said he was hanging around with, can you tell me anything about them?"

"No, I don't know them. Just what Hazel told me… You know, you should talk to her. She could tell you about the store and Alex's finances much better than me, and who he was hanging out with."

"Did Alex ever mention the name Butler Yeats?"

Hector considered the matter. "Not that I know of. Who's he? A local criminal?"

"You could put it like that… He's a biker, and part of a gang that's moved into the area. They're bringing in illegal drugs. Butler is currently in prison. I'm not saying Alex was involved with drugs but I have to consider the possibility that he'd gotten himself mixed up in something he couldn't handle…"

"Cus he had the money to buy the store?" Hector replied angrily, while shaking his head. "Alex wouldn't have gotten himself involved in anything like that. Or do you know something you're not telling us?"

"I can tell you that Alex's name hasn't come up in connection to Yeats, except for… What about Bethany Yeats, the woman he was with? Have you ever heard that name?"

"No again," said Hector with annoyance. But then a light went on. "Oh Jesus! Same last name. Are you telling me Alex was screwing the wife of this druggie criminal?"

"I'm not telling you anything of the kind, but the fact of the matter is that he was with Mrs. Yeats last night when he was killed. I understand it was the first time anyone who stayed late at the lounge last night had seen them together. The first time that Alex had been there after hours too."

"So this floozy seduced him? Lured him to his death? Do you think her husband killed Alex?"

"We're considering all options at this point."

"Isn't there security footage?"

"It's inconclusive. As I said, it was very dark in the room."

Hector began to shake. The helplessness and frustration were too much. He buried his face in his hands and sobbed.

Panel from Heather Bruce's Siren video

For some men, the naked woman's body is only ever about sex, and meant for their gratification. And these men feel that only they are entitled to sexual gratification in a civilized world.
Siren-like women supposedly wield sexual power, and they are cruel with it. They are primal and animalistic. They are seductresses who hunt and bring men down when they are allowed to slip free of the boxes and cages that confine them. They, their voices, and their sexuality must therefore be controlled.

12.

While the immediate family were being interviewed, several members of the extended Callas clan wandered into the kitchen. They smiled broadly and said 'Hello' in the direction of Heather and Sally as if the kitchen was an oasis of normalcy in an otherwise strange world. Some of the nomads even made a comment or two before they once again donned a painful expression and exited, returning to the intensity of the living room.

Shortly after 11:00 a.m., Heather answered a knock at the side door and went down the stairs to answer it.

Opening the door she saw a middle-aged woman dressed in black, looking clearly uncomfortable and distressed, who introduced herself as Vera James, the next door neighbour. She expressed her condolences and handed over a huge platter of sandwiches.

Heather felt for the poor soul. It was possible, she thought, that the woman had known Alex all his life. Maybe her kids had played with him when they were younger, and maybe they were still friends.

Heather assured the woman that she would pass on her condolences and thanked her for the platter, saying that it would be greatly appreciated.

Closing the door, it occurred to her that word of Alex's murder must be all over the local news and social media. Of course it would be. This was Charlottetown. Murders don't happen here.

Heather took the platter into the kitchen and put it on the table without removing the stretch wrap over the sandwiches.

She cleared the table then went to work washing the dishes. Sally silently grabbed a dish towel and assisted.

When they were finished, Heather took the stack of bread and butter plates from the cupboard and placed them on the table beside the sandwiches. She spotted a napkin holder, already on the table, and placed it beside the plates.

Looking up, she saw Selene enter the kitchen and then stop, her eyes going to the table.

"Sandwiches, from Mrs. James," Heather explained.

"Thanks," Selene replied absently, then, looking at her friend, she said, "Let's get out of here. I can't stand it."

Sally bolted across the room, obviously thrilled at the prospect of leaving.

The pair immediately departed.

Now alone, Heather glanced at the clock on the wall. She'd been in the house for only forty-five minutes but it felt like it had been hours. She removed the stretch wrap from the platter, folded it, and put it on the counter, then resumed her old post, leaning against the kitchen counter while watching the clock tick off the seconds.

Eventually, Penny walked into the kitchen, looked at her friend, and shook her head in a signal of exasperation.

"Mrs. James brought sandwiches," Heather said, and pointed. "And asked me to pass on her condolences."

"Oh?" Penny replied blankly. "Thanks. I'm sorry I deserted you."

"Not a problem."

"Can we go out to the backyard? I need to take a break."

Heather and Penny were soon sitting face to face, on deck chairs, beside an inground swimming pool.

Penny took a deep, audible breath, and said, "We – the family I mean – were just interviewed by a cop. It was emotionally draining to say the least…" She sharply exhaled to retain her composure and said, "Alex was shot…" followed by another long exhale. "He was with a woman, who he'd never been with before, at a bar called The Sailor's Roost, and I gather they were making out when someone snuck into the room and attacked him."

Heather spotted a man approaching.

As he drew near, he latched on to an empty deck chair and set it down beside Heather. He seated himself then turned his head towards her. "I'm Penny's father, Hector," he said.

"I'm Heather. I'm sorry for your loss."

Hector nodded. He had evidently picked up on the last bit of what his daughter had been saying because, when he looked back in her direction, he said, "I've never heard of the place until now. Makes me realize how little I knew about my son's life."

He explained to Heather, with a look of disgust on his face, "The policeman told us that Alex was there with some floozy." Hector shook his head in disgust.

Penny's demeanour suddenly changed. Aggressively she said to her father, "Why did you lie to him – to the cop I mean – about Alex? You made him sound like a choir boy. You know that he was always in some sort of trouble growing up. Surely they're going to find out about stuff, and that Alex had a record, which will just make you look like a liar."

"It was kid's stuff. Irrelevant."

"That's debatable. Plus, you made it sound like he was an innocent who was seduced by some harpy when you know very well he was always on the make. And then there's the drugs…"

"Alex was not into drugs," Hector boomed, as if he could control reality by using a louder volume. "And what does it matter now how many women he slept with? He was just doing what lots of other men do."

"Well that's certainly debatable too. It sounds like you condone his affairs."

"No. Hazel told me about this waitress he was shacked up with and I left a message for him to knock it off and avoid the woman, she was bad news and was destroying his marriage. I told Hazel to wait it out, that Alex would be back; that he just made a mistake and was sowing some wild oats… But it went both ways, you know. Hazel told me that there was some older man interested in her. How'd she know that unless she was out looking around?"

"Oh please. Gimme a break. It's Hazel we're talking about. Poor bloody besotted Hazel. And even if she had been looking around I can't blame her. Maybe she was looking for a man who would treat her right."

"Could be," Hector conceded.

"I would have told her to get a divorce and marry the guy because Alex would never change. Did you know Alex was coming over and sleeping with Hazel whenever he wanted, even though he'd left her to live with this other woman? He's my brother and I love him but he was a prick sometimes."

Hector looked to the sky and scowled.

Penny continued. "Don't you think the cops should know that Alex wasn't the devoted family man that you told them about and that he was living with another woman? Maybe she had something to do with his death. Maybe she has a jealous husband."

Hector dodged the question. "What does it matter, the constable thinks the husband of the floozy Alex was with when he was shot is responsible for it?"

"He didn't say that. He said the guy in jail was part of a drug gang and wondered if Alex was involved in the business…"

Hector swore under his breath at the mention of drugs. "The floozy's husband probably found out about them and shot Alex. That's the most obvious explanation."

Heather, who'd been silently watching and listening to the father-daughter exchange, wanted to voice an obvious objection to Hector's suggestion but decided to keep out of family business.

"I wish you would quit calling the woman Alex was with 'the floozy'," Penny said. "You don't know anything about her. She maybe wanted to hook up for one night. Maybe she's lonely. Her husband's in jail after all. Besides, how could the husband shoot anyone when he's in jail?"

"Just put out a hit."

Before she could stop herself from speaking, Heather blurted out, "I thought it was the first time Alex and the woman were together."

Neither Penny nor Hector seemed disturbed by Heather commenting. They looked at her blankly for a moment before Penny said to her father, "That's right, so how could the husband know about his wife and Alex?"

"Maybe he just knew she'd be with someone," Hector fired back. "She probably likes to seduce men regularly."

"Jesus. Alex didn't need to be seduced? He was acting the way he thought men were entitled to act."

That was going too far. Hector didn't answer. He frowned and shook his head. His daughter's comments had deeply annoyed him. "I don't need to listen to this," he said loudly.

All eyes turned toward a figure walking in their direction.

Heather guessed that the woman was Hector's sister, given her marked resemblance to the man sitting beside her.

"Sorry to disturb," the woman said in a hushed tone, "but Hector, you're needed inside."

Hector replied by way of getting to his feet and following the woman back into the house, his shoulders slumping at the prospect of re-entering the fray.

Penny watched her father go before looking back at Heather. It brought it to her attention that her friend didn't know any of the background that she and Hector had been alluding to.

Penny said, "Alex was always getting involved with married women, and with single women who were in relationships. He was very handsome." This was not said as an expression of pride, but as simple fact. "He got beaten up more than a few times for sleeping with women – by their boyfriends or husbands – even when he was in high school. Chasing women was an obsession with him. He even told me once he couldn't help himself. He's like our father…"

"Your father?"

"Oh, yeah. It's an open secret that he had more than one affair over the years…"

"And your mother…"

"Oh, she tolerated it, at least in public, and around her kids. Stiff upper lip. Turn a blind eye. Maybe she figures that all men are like that. I think that Alex admired Dad for it, in a way. He told me that he thought it was normal for men to sleep around, and that one woman wasn't enough… At any rate, he was never critical of my father. Did you see how pissed off my dad got when I said that Alex's fooling around wasn't surprising? It's because I was implying that Alex was the way he was because he'd learned it from his father."

"Well, since your dad thinks that Alex's murder happened after he willfully went with a woman who wasn't his wife, he maybe thinks that you're blaming him."

"Oh. Maybe. But anyway, the jealous husband scenario is just one theory at this point about who killed Alex."

"I hope I'm not being too nosy, but I was trying to follow your conversation. So Alex was living with a new girlfriend?"

"Yeah. Alex was always chasing women when he was with Hazel. The store he owned was open late. He liked to go to parties after he closed it for the night; parties where I'm sure he would hook up with women. Some nights he didn't even come home, according to Hazel. When she figured out that he was staying at one woman's place in particular she told him to leave if he didn't stop the affair. She gave him an ultimatum. Put her foot down. Her or me. But it backfired. Alex left and moved in with the other woman – a young one who works in a bar, according to Hazel."

"But he would…visit Hazel after he left, you said."

"Yeah. Kept coming around to sleep with her."

"Why would she have put up with being used that? Like the self-help people say, 'Don't make someone your one and only if it's not reciprocal'."

"I don't know why anyone would consent to being a dishrag. Low self-esteem maybe. Or maybe she felt she was doing her duty, like my mother, protecting home and family, and thinking she could win the guy back with sex."

"It's just one scenario, you said, but do you suspect that Alex's murder was connected to his philandering?"

"I don't know. Maybe. The cop also asked if Alex was involved in the illegal drug trade. And he might have been."

"Your dad sounds pretty adamant that he'd have nothing to do with drugs."

"When Alex was a teenager my mother found various drugs in his room, so my father knows the truth. My assumption is that he's trying to protect his son's reputation. Or maybe protect his own; like anything Alex did reflects back on him and his influence over the family. I don't know. He's one of those people who wants to keep everything inside the family. Anyway, the cop actually seemed more focused on the financing around the store that Alex bought than anything else. I think he wonders if Alex got into hock to a loan shark and couldn't pay him back so the guy had him killed. At least that's what it sounded like to me. He could be thinking something else altogether."

"So Alex borrowed the money from someone to buy his store but nobody knows from who?"

"When I asked Alex where he got the money he laughed and said something like, 'I have my ways'. He obviously didn't want to talk about it so I left it at that. Maybe Hazel knows where the money came from. There's no way that Alex scrimped and saved, and unlikely that he got a bank loan given his age and lack of credit history. He probably got a personal loan from some someone dodgy; and with a usurious interest rate."

"Which could be playing with fire; associating with characters like that."

"Yes indeed. But, knowing Alex, he could have been working some woman for it."

"So what kind of store was it that Alex bought?"

"It's a store for weightlifters. It sells mostly supplements and equipment."

"Steroids?"

"Possible I guess. I don't know anything about stuff like that. Anyway, I think what adds to the mystery of how Alex bought the store is that it's an established business. It would have taken a few bucks. But yeah, maybe he got a loan and was paying it back by selling steroids. But, then again, the subject of drugs came up because the cop asked if Alex was involved in the drug trade. He didn't say steroids so I assume he meant something more serious than that."

"So Alex could have been involved with both a loan shark and with drug dealers – two scenarios that might end badly."

"Exactly. And that's why I don't like my father lying to the cops, saying that Alex was not involved with drugs because, if they believe him, it might turn them away from the real culprits. Between you and me, as much as I wish I could disbelieve it, it's possible that Alex had gotten himself tied up with bikers. Last spring – so over a year ago, before he bought the store – I was talking to him about this and that, and the conversation turned to news stories about biker gangs popping up in PEI and bringing the drug trade with them. Alex said he wondered if we were going to get flooded with illegal drugs from the rest of Canada and from other countries. He was really interested in talking about drug smuggling and was wondering how smugglers operated."

"Could it have been a casual conversation?"

"Yeah, it could have been. I assumed it was so I thought nothing of it…until this morning. Anyway, that day we talked about it I told him that – in my opinion – someone would have to be an idiot to think that they could smuggle drugs into the province and he just smirked in that smart-alecky way of his. He said that no way would he get busted if he did it because he was too intelligent."

"And you thought it was just bluster?"

"Yeah, some adolescent-type bullshit about being a wheeler-dealer and gangster. He had an adolescent admiration of outlaws. He was often in trouble for stuff, but now I wonder if he got into something illegal on a much bigger scale; maybe just to prove to the world that he was too clever to get caught."

13.

Pointing, to a photograph of a woman in a bathing suit, Ellen said, "That's Cecile Landry and this one…" pointing to another picture, "is Betty Simpson. They were Louise's friends. They seemed like old women to me at the time." She laughed in response to her remark. "They would have been somewhere in their thirties."

The photo album that Hugh had brought with him held pictures taken during summer visits to the ocean. They depicted women standing with each other or children playing – all in bathing suits.

Ellen told Hugh that they always went to the same beach and explained where it was located.

The picture that she next focused on was of Louise, smiling, as were the two women beside her.

"The woman on Louise's right is Lorelei Nelson. She was younger than the other women; probably in her late twenties when this was taken."

"Is that Harry Nelson's mother?" Hugh asked, craning his neck to get a closer look. "I met Harry last week when I was driving back home from here. I stopped at the stand he has on the side of the road, where he sells maple syrup."

"Yes, Lorelei's his mother. Did you know that Harry found the body of the murdered aviator?"

"I did."

Ellen looked closely at at the picture of Lorelei, moving her face nearer to study it. Wistfully she said, "She was a beautiful woman, but almost childlike in her manner; always smiling and singing. You worried about her because she seemed ripe to be taken advantage of. I didn't remember that she came to the beach with us, but here she is, so she did, at least this one time. Her husband probably forbade her to come again. What a shame he was the way he was."

"How was that?"

"He was the sort who likes to be in control. Loud. Aggressive. I remember often feeling sorry for poor Lorelei. She was always looking over her shoulder when she stopped to talk, like she was afraid her husband, Freddy, would come along. I wondered if he'd told her not to talk to me."

"Why would he have done that?" Hugh felt a flash of hope that Ellen might begin talking about being called 'mermaid' by some of the local men, which would provide an opening for him to ask questions that might elicit some information about her experiences – something he could report back to Heather – but it was not to be.

"I think he just wanted to keep her under his thumb, waiting hand and foot on him. Some men are like that. Jealous beyond belief. They're always suspicious and accusing, and women find it easier to indulge them than to insist on their own independence. These women are perpetually afraid. It's a little different now…I hope. Lorelei eventually up and left one day – leaving Harry with Freddy – and headed out west."

"She had no one here to turn to? No family?"

"Whoever there was, was out west."

"It looks like the women here were a close knit group."

"We were, like any island colony… Maybe that's not the right word. I suppose I'm thinking of gulls and some other birds…but mutually supportive and protective. Maybe husbands leaving for military service led to a strengthening of the bonds between us."

Ellen went through the pages of pictures. Smiling at some. Laughing now and then. Sinking into her memories. "I don't remember who most of these children were or who they belonged to. Leona, my daughter, was very young so she didn't interact with many of them."

Hugh brought things back to the moment by pulling out a fistful of old Christmas cards: faded and musty smelling artifacts. Some had zig zag edges, as if cut by pinking shears, suggesting bespoke customization by the sender, while others sported ribbons, now flattened. One card folded in from each side like a book. "I wonder if you would look at these," he said, holding out the cards. "Maybe you'll recognize some names."

Ellen dutifully went from one to another of the cards. Some of the notations only included first names. "From Bill, Noreen, and family," read one. Others were inscribed with notations like, "From the Smythes." As she got down to the last couple Ellen finally said, "Sorry. None of these names rings a bell. My guess is that the cards were from women Louise knew when she was a schoolgirl, and kept in touch with; so before my time here. And the cards are all from couples too, meaning the girls had married, changed their surnames, and possibly spread out all over the country. They're a testament to how much Louise was loved." After opening the last of the cards, Ellen amended her comment. "Oh, I spoke too soon. This one's from Leslie Eades. Do you know when this was sent?"

"No. There were no envelopes with postmarks…"

"Her son Jack was, I think, best friends with your grandfather Robbie…for a time anyway. Jack began to chum more with Eddie, if I remember correctly."

"I've never heard my grandfather mention either Jack or Harry."

"Did you know that Jack also found the aviator's body?"

"I did. I remember seeing his name on the inquest report."

"Poor boys. The scene they came upon was unbelievably grizzly. Harry kept to himself after that. When he'd pass by the house I'd call his name and wave, but he'd start running rather than wave back. No surprise that a young boy would be severely traumatized."

"I can only imagine how horrific their experience must have been."

"Jack fared much better… His mother was housebound, due to illness, so he used to come around here a lot, and we got to be good pals. He liked to talk about the things going on in his life – which often weren't easy – and I think it helped him to escape them, especially after that aviator business."

"How's he doing now?"

"Oh…ah, fine. He's lived in Charlottetown for ages so I don't see much of him anymore, but he phones me once in awhile."

"Something I've been wondering about… I know that my great-grandparents struggled after the aviator was killed because of the rumours about their involvement. But I was wondering about the kids. Did they get teased do you know?"

"Oh yes. They had a hard time in general. Other kids calling them names, saying their father was a murderer and the like. It takes one person to start a stupid rumour, but they spread, and that's the problem. It didn't surprise me when you said that Robbie didn't want to talk about the past. I think that he and Eddie being bullied at school was the big reason why Louise wanted to move. Not because she felt the boys were vulnerable – they had friends who wouldn't take any nonsense from a handful of ignoramuses – but because she didn't want her kids to hear what the rumour group was saying about their father being a murderer and her being… well, you know."

Panel from Heather Bruce's Siren video

Seduction is seen as evil when practised by women; they are being guided by their animal lust and instinct. Seduction is seen here as a means to achieve power over men.

We see in the Siren the mythical basis of the archetypal image of the female human as a bird of prey, but one who hunts by seduction. And men are her target. Men cast themselves as victims while assuaging their egos with narcissism about their desirability.

The seduction and ill-treatment of women is justified as a response when men see themselves as being at war with women. They can convince themselves that they are soldiers, slaying the bird of prey, using seduction against the seducers. This seduction is the opposite of love. It is self-absorption. It dehumanizes women. With proper training, all men are potentially soldiers and sailors in the fight. They learn entitlement, and to lack empathy. If they seduce women they become like Odysseus and other warriors: heroes who bested their enemy. Seduction is an intended attack on women's autonomy, sexuality, strength, and their lack of attention to men. It is an attempt to humiliate women.

14.

Hugh arrived home from Mount Pleasant, late in the afternoon.

He sat down in the living room and turned on the TV, hoping to occupy himself until Heather returned. They'd made plans to go out for dinner.

Time passed, and no Heather, and no phone messages.

At 6:00 p.m. Hugh called her cell but she didn't pick up.

He was becoming worried by the time he heard the apartment door open around 7:00 and was immediately up on his feet and at the door.

Heather looked drained.

"Sorry I'm late," she said, "and sorry I didn't answer your message. Penny had an emergency and I got caught up trying to help her."

"Is she okay?" Hugh asked, taken aback.

"Not really, no. I shouldn't phrase it like that. She's physically okay but when I got to her place she'd just gotten word that her brother died last night."

Heather slouched off towards the living room.

Hugh, trailing, said, "Geez, poor Penny. What did he die from?"

"He was murdered." Heather sprawled onto the couch.

"What! When?"

"Late last night at a bar, after closing time. That newish one with the mermaid tank… I think its called The Sailor's Roost."

"I know the place. A bar and lounge, I think."

"Sounds right. Alex was in the lounge with a woman, after hours. Someone walked in and shot him."

"So he was targeted sounds like… Did they arrest anyone or know who they're looking for?"

"Not so far as I know – to both questions. Let me close my eyes for a few minutes then I'll bring you up to date. Oh, and I don't want to go out for dinner if you don't mind."

"No, no, of course not."

Hugh waited until Heather was back on her feet, then he

cooked something for the two of them.

He watched Heather push dinner around her plate in a lacklustre way.

She was eventually revived enough to talk about the events of the day, beginning with her arrival at Penny's house that morning.

"I felt so sorry for the family," she said. "It would be hard to get your head around a twenty-three year old guy dying, at any time, but I think the circumstances of Alex's death – being a murder – makes the whole thing surreal in the extreme. Murder is something that happens to other people and in other places. To people on TV shows. Certainly not here."

"How's Penny handling things?"

"She bounces between grief and a really measured sort of manner where she tries to maintain her composure. Back and forth. Oh, and sometimes she expresses self-blame. I wanted to say something to help, but there's no way words can do much. Except…well, you know…reminding her that she's not at fault and couldn't have changed anything."

"What would she be blaming herself for? For not stopping something she knew nothing about?"

"For not turning Alex off his new set of friends mostly. Self-blame makes no sense, I know. It might if he had committed suicide and you were chastising yourself for not noticing the signs, I mean, even when you shouldn't be blaming yourself…but Alex's life was so complicated that there was nothing Penny could have said or done to make it less so."

"Complicated how?"

"Well, he had a wife he hadn't quite split up with, a girlfriend he lived with, and he was in the arms of another woman when he was shot. And that's just his love life. I mean, what could Penny have done to change someone like that?"

"Nothing. So could it have been a jealous husband that shot Alex?"

"Could have been. That's one theory but there's others. Alex was apparently hanging out with some criminal types."

"So the police aren't saying if they have any suspicions?"

"No. They're interested in the store Alex bought, especially about how he funded its purchase with no job or credit rating. It suggests he may have borrowed money from some dodgy people and couldn't pay it back, and they killed him for it. Oh, and another possibility – which may or may not be connected to the business loan – is that Alex might have gotten himself involved with the biker gangs that have moved into PEI recently and are building up the illegal drug business. The woman that Alex was with when he was shot is the wife of a biker who's now in prison."

"Yikes. What does Penny's family think?"

"I don't know about her mother or sister but I think Penny is keeping an open mind. Her father's in denial about everything to do with drugs. He blames the husband of the woman Alex was in the lounge with for the murder, even though the guy is in prison and it was apparently the first time anyone had ever seen Alex and the woman together... Anyway, I'm going to get Penny in the morning at her parent's house. She's taken on the responsibility of looking after her mother. Penny seems to be the adult in the room. Her younger sister escaped the scene with her pal, and by the time I left, her father was sitting in Alex's old bedroom staring at his bed... I told Penny I'd help her any way I can so I'll be picking her up around ten in the morning and driving her to see her brother's wife... It's odd, the wife wasn't at her in-laws house like you'd think, where the whole family was gathering. It's like she's an outsider."

Hugh reached across the table and squeezed Heather's hand. He was worried about her. It wasn't that he thought that Heather shouldn't help her friend but she'd just come home exhausted and it was possible that this was only the first day of many.

The TV was on, with only Hugh watching it from his spot at the end of the couch.

Heather was stretched out, her feet on Hugh's lap so that he could massage them. Her eyes had been closed and had only opened a minute earlier.

"Why don't you get some sleep?" Hugh said. "You've had a hell of a day and tomorrow sounds like it could be just as draining."

"I'll go in a bit," Heather said. "By the way, I didn't ask you yet, how was your visit with the mermaid?"

"It was good. Most of the pictures in the photo album I took to show her were of women and kids at the beach. I thought Ellen might know who everyone was since the picture that she has, of her and Louise, was taken at the same time."

"And did she?"

"She knew who the women were. The identity of a lot of the older kids remains a mystery though. And Ellen didn't know the people who sent Great-Granny the Christmas cards. She thought they were probably friends from Charlottetown that Louise grew up with. And maybe some new friends from Montreal."

"Anything surprising in what she said?"

"A couple. One that stuck me was when I mentioned how close the women in the photos were. She said they were a mutual support group. Which isn't surprising, I suppose, given the isolation, I mean in that rural area, and being on an island. And she said the group was strengthened because so many men were away due to the war. Anyway, she referred to the women around her as a colony, you know, like seabirds that nest on an island. It made me think of the panels for your video that you showed me, and how your art group is a colony on the island of PEI. That, and you telling me you think that part of the siren myth comes from observations about birds."

"Yeah, giving the bird-women some of the behavioural traits of birds. I only have a bit of that in there but there will be more."

"I remembered you saying that. When I got home I did a bit of research. There's different theories about colony behaviour apparently. One of them is that it provides for mutual protection and mutual survival. And another is that same-sex pairings are very common, especially female-female. Not for procreation, but for raising young."

"And I think these type of birds usually pair for life. I'd like to meet your mermaid, like I said… She didn't talk about being called a mermaid did she?"

"No, but on the drive home I thought that I should have asked to borrow the photo she has of her and Louise so that I can get a copy made. I will, next visit. Maybe she'll talk about it then."

"So what else did she have to say? Anything?"

"A bit. She talked about the boy who was with Harry when he found the body of the murdered aviator back in 1943. It seems he's still alive and living in Charlottetown."

"What's his name?"

"Jack Eades. Ellen also told me something about the Nelsons – Harry's family. According to Ellen, the father was controlling and violent. He didn't want his wife to talk to her and she would flee when Ellen approached her… Oh, and Ellen said that Harry was really traumatized about finding the aviator and that when she approached him he would also run away."

"Maybe it wasn't just trauma. If his mother was told to keep away from Ellen it would make sense that he would have been too…and their reactions make it sound like both mother and son were terrified of the father."

"Or of being around a mermaid."

"Could have been the husband's reason, I guess. Ellen was reputedly a wanton woman so the guy may have wanted his wife to stay away from her. But then again, he may have wanted her to shut herself off from all the women in the area. I can't imagine that he would want his wife telling other women about what went on in his home…a violent guy like that."

"I wonder if my grandfather would remember Jack Eades. Ellen said that he and Robert were best friends for a time."

"You think there's any chance of it?"

"A slim one." Robert's short-term memory was poor and worsening. His long-term memory was much better but it was intermittent.

"You could ask him tomorrow when you phone."

"I will. You know, whether he does or doesn't remember,

I've been thinking about calling Jack and asking for his help. He might know who the kids in the photos are."

"Good idea."

"I'll see if I can find a number for him but he may not want to talk to me or even remember anything…"

"Are you planning to ask him what he remembers about the aviator's death?"

"I might. I'm curious. I don't care who killed the man, not really. I believe the results of the inquest. It was an accident. But knowing who killed the man would be good since it would completely exonerate my family in the public's eye."

"Do you think you could ever have a definitive answer about who killed the aviator?"

"Not without a confession. It would be futile to look. It would take a multi-year research project to track down everyone who was in the area at the time – including servicemen and women – and doing a ton of interviews. And even then there's no guarantee of ever knowing more than we know now."

Hugh was hoping he hadn't revived the discussion about the nature of history that he and Heather had conducted several times. Hugh looked to history as a set of facts to be ascertained whereas Heather saw it as a text to be read; to be interpreted differently by every generation and even by every person. History, she would argue, is always uncertain memory and reflects the teller's bias – even when there's data.

"Hopefully you'll find some closure," Heather said, "because I agree that the chance of getting an answer about what happened to that poor aviator is pretty much non-existent. On top of all the work involved in an investigation, the murder was over sixty years ago. People will have forgotten details and others will be dead."

"I'm still interested in knowing more about my family's history though, by talking to the few people who are still alive, who had a connection to them. I think that wanting to keep looking into the lives of my great-grandparents is a continuation of my attempt to chart my ancestry. I've been thinking about what Ellen said about my overemphasizing land when I think about the past. Maybe my family tree is less like a map of land and more like the charts a sailor uses to find his way. My interest in situating myself in the world comes from feelings of being adrift."

"So you're a sailor now, looking for home…and I'm not making fun of your feelings. What you said makes me think that being a sailor can be a metaphor for anyone who is trying to find home. And in this case a lost one."

And with that, Heather, once again, closed her eyes to rest them.

It was 2:00 a.m. when Heather woke up. Going to bed so early had taken the edge off her exhaustion.

She lay, for a moment, face to face with Hugh. She could feel his breath on her face and remembered her mother saying that she avoided sleeping close to her father's face so that she didn't breathe in his germs. Heather wondered if that sort of practical consideration would eventually override romance in her own life.

She lay there and thought about her day. One thing that struck her about the Callas family was the differing attitudes regarding the woman that Alex had been with when he was shot. She understood Hector wanting to blame someone for the murder and it didn't surprise her that he was focused on the woman that Alex was with, as if her gender made her the obvious suspect. The woman was a 'floozy', in Hector's words. A seducer. A manipulator. It was her fault his son had crashed on the rocks as he navigated the waters of life.

Penny though, had spoken of the woman sympathetically, as someone who might have sought Alex out from loneliness, because her husband was away. Since the woman was married it would make tactical sense to hit on someone who gets with a lot of women; someone always on the make, looking for a fling. The sort of person would be unlikely to become attached to her or mistake a one-night stand for a romance.

The difference between their perspectives strengthened Heather's commitment to follow in the path of those women artists who had done revisions of siren myth, imagining them from a woman's perspective, by doing something similar in the final segment of her video.

Strange, she thought, that there were parallels between the death of Hugh's aviator and the death of Alex. Both involved men who'd been murdered, and in both cases there were some who deemed a woman to be the one ultimately responsible for the death although they hadn't actually fired the murder weapon. They were accusations without evidence. Accusations, in both cases, that were based solely on entrenched, sexist ideas about women; that they are naturally immoral, engaging in behaviour on a continuum ranging from promiscuity to murder.

Events were affirming what she had already written about sirens. And she was anxious to write more.

Heather crept out of bed and went into the living room to read what she'd written so far. She did some editing. Reworked a couple of passages.

Then she began to write new material.

She worked for an hour before going back to bed.

Panel from Heather Bruce's Siren video

The Siren – cast as a woman – is knee deep in male corpses when depicted by men.
Their beauty – of their voices or bodies – is the basis of their allure and this is how they are imagined. Sirens are animals and ravenous. Man-eaters.
The femme fatale can still be, in our day, a viper or a feline. Inscrutable. Unfeeling. A cat toying with a mouse before killing it. Catwoman. Cat People. Panther woman. Cougar.
Like all sexualized women who reject or stray from domesticity – but unlike spiders drawing men into their web for sustenance – the Siren supposedly kills men for sport.
Nature is cruel and will kill you because it must. It doesn't feel compassion. Sirens are nature and not civil society.
The imagined Siren – in man-made myths – reflects an opposite view of nature to that of the feminine Pagan. An antagonistic view marked by mythic propaganda in a war between genders. One that is precipitated by men's fear of women's strength, sexuality, and society. Such myths view women-only collectives as uncivilized and a threat to men's dominion – so they must be destroyed.

15. Sunday

Heather was bleary-eyed, but when the CBC reporter, Rita Darling, phoned in the morning to ask about the siren exhibition, Heather instantly snapped to attention.

"The idea for the exhibition, *Siren's Island: Myth, Power, and Silencing Women in PEI*," Heather told the reporter, "began when we came across some graffiti on the front window of the storefront where we maintain an office and studio. It read, 'hell is this sirens island', which we took to be an attack on women having a voice and influence. It likened the voices of the women of PEI to those of sirens. The suggestion being that the very act of women using their voices, in a critical way, is an attack on men and is, in itself, an abomination that cannot be tolerated."

The reporter followed up with some questions about Heather's video, especially its intent and approach.

Heather replied, "The purpose of my video is to speculate on the reasons why some men wish to silence women's voices. I think that certain men, like those returning from war in *The Odyssey*, believe that free women have to be subdued so that men can maintain control of their homes and society. I think we can see that the characterizations of women from these ancient men's societies, like the military, still exist in men's society today. Men who resist and attack women who speak publicly – for speaking on certain subjects and expressing views those men disagree with – see themselves as soldiers in the cause, engaged in a power struggle. Their efforts at silencing women are so prominent now because women are taking on more leadership roles, exerting more influence, and able to live outside of marriage. The men who wish to silence them are fine with only a few people having voices, but they must be men's."

"So, in putting on this show, would you say that you are encouraging an island of sirens?"

"It wasn't us who said a sirens' island was a place where women express themselves. We only decided to co-opt the phrase. Sirens lived in a community and used their voices for protection. Their stories have been told by men and, in them, sirens have been characterized as evil, and a threat to men. In one way we see ourselves as a siren colony; as a group of mutually supporting women. A mini community where we use our voices rather than acquiesce to the demands of the powerful to be silent. The powerful control cultural production and we wish to challenge that by creating our own space where we can be heard."

"What would you say to a possible criticism of your video, that you are applying a modern feminist understanding of siren myth, and the authors of the myth wouldn't have been countering such views?"

"It's not that I think that siren myth was an attack on modern, feminist assertions about women's rights, but the myths convey certain attitudes about women and men that have become truisms, and feminism needs to debunk myths that are supportive of patriarchal power. In the original myths we are talking about soldiers in a society where men ruled. What, or who, threatened their power? Opposing groups. An outside army. A slave revolt. Women banding together. Women rejecting men's absolute authority. So keeping women in their place was important and to do that was to view them as a potential enemy of the state and of men's authority; and to silence them."

Later, Heather was pleased with the way that the interview had gone. It always helped her to clarify her thoughts when she explained herself to someone else.

She had a light step a short time later when leaving the apartment. She felt that she'd articulated her views clearly and that the publicity the interview would generate was a positive.

Penny's plan was to visit Hazel before they met up at the funeral home a little later in the day when it would be impossible to be alone with her.

On the drive to Hazel's, Penny shared some background information about her sister-in-law, prepping Heather for their visit. "Hazel is from one of the Channel Islands. She moved here in her late teens, along with her brother, and they both got jobs at my father's company. That's where she met

Alex. He liked young women who had jobs and their own apartments so his going out with Hazel wasn't surprising. But the two seemed infatuated with each other and got married. As I now know, Alex never saw the marriage as something that demanded his monogamy. I think he felt entitled. Like he was God's gift to women. That it was fine to have a wife and other partners on the side."

"Even if it hadn't been agreed to by his wife…"

"Yes. And I think getting women made him feel smug. Just another possession…conspicuous consumption for the up and coming executive. Like Dad."

"Why do you think Hazel didn't file for divorce? Or did she?"

"No she didn't. She's obsessed with Alex – or was – and while she talked a good game at first – like she wouldn't stand for this and that – she never acted on it. And she soon seemed determined to get him back. She plotted and planned… Obsession is so strange. The obsessed person can twist every action of the person they adore, every comment they make, and make them mean something else; something that doesn't shake the obsessive's view of the relationship but actually affirms it. Even strengthens it. So Hazel held out hope and wouldn't let go. She seemed to feel she was in a competition with the other woman, and would win, and that Alex would return to the fold. Nothing I said to her made any difference. I told her that things would never change, that Alex had always been selfish. He always put himself first and always would. It was just in his nature or because of the way he'd been coddled by my dad, and nothing would change him. She just made excuses for him and was baffled at the suggestion that he'd done something wrong. And, eventually, she would just get pissed off when I broached the subject."

"You said yesterday that she was trying to win Alex back with sex…"

"Yes, but it was more than that. I think that Hazel figured that marriage and family were central to Alex's life, like they were with her. He'd married her after all and hadn't left – not totally – so he clearly wanted a home… So she got pregnant; and now she's left with a baby to take care of on her own."

"They have a baby? How old is he…she?

"Two months. Damian."

"Two months? So, if Alex moved out a year ago and Damian is two months old it means…"

"… Yeah, that they'd been separated for a month before Hazel got pregnant."

"Hence, not only trying to lure Alex back with sex but with family, as you said."

"Exactly."

"And unfortunately Alex wasn't the sort who was into marriage and family."

"Oh no, he was in a way. Hazel had that right. I'm sure that he wanted to have a wife. It was just that it had to be on his terms: for Hazel to be there when he wanted her; to have a wife he could trot out for business reasons without jeopardizing his freedom to be with other women and his buddies; and to be able to roam and escape any bonds and responsibility. I heard him refer to marriage once as a potential trap. You know, he resumed his nocturnal visits to Hazel's for sex just days after she'd given birth. I told you he was a selfish bastard."

"Do you think Alex ever loved Hazel?"

"Oh, I think so, in his own way."

"I wonder what he would have done if Hazel acted the same as him and slept with other men?"

"Alex wouldn't have taken it well. I think he would have killed her lover. He was the centre of the universe and things had to revolve around him. Hazel's obsession for him would have made him feel like a star. If she had an affair it would have undermined his self-image. Feelings of jealousy would have left him feeling insecure and vulnerable. It would have killed him in a way."

"How do you think Hazel is taking Alex's death?"

"She's devastated beyond words apparently; as you would expect. She put the guy on a pedestal and made him her whole life."

Hazel's apartment was on the ground floor of a duplex. When Heather and Penny arrived they found Hazel in a bad way. She could hardly speak she was so upset.

So far as she was able to get the words out, she talked about how Alex was the great love of her life.

Heather looked down at the floor while Hazel spoke, but soon chastised herself. She shouldn't let her distaste for the man affect her empathy for Hazel. Of course Hazel had undergone something tragic and deserved sympathy. It's times in our lives of great upheaval when we most cling to our myths, sentimentalize, and develop amnesia about the person who is gone.

When Penny got up to make tea, Hazel went with her.

Heather stood up to stretch her legs and looked about the apartment. It was sparsely furnished, but neat and clean. Girly. Lots of pink. On top of the bookcase was a large framed wedding photo of Hazel and Alex. It was Heather's first glimpse of the dead man and she agreed that he was handsome. He looked a little embarrassed at the attention, smiling shyly in a boyish way that would have won many hearts.

A slightly smaller framed picture stood next to the wedding photo. In it, Hazel and Penny were sitting beside the Callas backyard pool where Heather had sat the day before.

She looked more closely at the image. The women were surrounded by large pink balloons. A birthday party perhaps. A slim Hazel, blonde hair and pink bikini, beside Penny, dressed in a pink blouse and sunglasses, perhaps having anticipated the colour scheme.

The top shelves of the bookcase held dozens of DVDs, but no books. Heather recognized the titles of some of the films; romantic comedies from the last several years and a few animated Disney films from Hazel's childhood – *The Little Mermaid* being one of them. Heather hadn't seen the film and made a mental note to do so. She wondered if there was a lesson in it about the need for womanly self-sacrifice or if Hazel had learned that elsewhere. Something occurred to her. In the fairytale the little mermaid's voice was taken away from her and she was in pain when she walked. Clever of Andersen to write it that way. Wilful loss of voice and mobility signalled the ultimate transformation from the siren to the mermaid; to a creature who loved a man and wanted to be married above all.

There was a mini stereo on the shelf below, and the shelf beneath that one was filled with CDs. Popular music. Phil Collins' love songs and the like.

Hazel and Penny came back into the room holding mugs of tea, one for Heather too, and they all sat down.

"I asked the police officer yesterday," Hazel began, directing herself solely to Penny, "if they'd spoken to…that woman." She struggled with the phrase, grimacing. Stripping the woman of her identity.

"You mean the woman at the bar?" asked Penny

"No, not the one at the bar. I mean the slut that Alex got himself mixed up with last year."

Penny exhaled slowly before speaking. "We talked to the cop. Well, Dad did all the talking, and he didn't mention that part of Alex's life. Maybe he felt it was up to you whether to tell the police about her, or not, since it could affect Alex's reputation."

"I thought so. I didn't make you guys out to be liars. I said that you probably didn't know about her. The policeman kept asking me where Alex got the money to buy his store. He made it sound like he had some underworld friends, like mobsters or drug dealers. I told them the money had to have come from the slut."

"Hazel, the woman is quite young, you said. It takes a lot of capital to buy a store which I doubt she had."

"Unless she was turning tricks."

"What? Jesus. She was a student scraping by. Forget her. Alex couldn't have gotten a bank loan without a long credit history so… Is there any chance that he was involved in anything ill…you know, something dodgy? He was hanging out with some shady people, you said. Sounds like the cops were confirming that."

"I knew that he started carrying a knife, so I knew that he wasn't hanging around with boy scouts, but Alex would never deal drugs!" Hazel shot back. "He hated them. He told me lots of times."

"I didn't mean drugs specifically, I just meant that

someone killed Alex and I was wondering if he'd gotten caught up in something dicey. Maybe through naivety."

"He hadn't. So there's only one possibility left isn't there?" Hazel looked triumphant, and was no longer listening, convinced that her logic was unassailable. "The money must have come from the slut."

"He could have borrowed it from some sort of loan shark. The sort of person who kills people who don't pay it back."

"No, not borrow. When I asked Alex who he borrowed the money from he said that he hadn't borrowed it from anyone. He said it was his… Which to me is further proof of where it came from. I'm not stupid. I know he wouldn't have been able to get a bank loan, or any kind of loan. But that means it had to have been a gift; a bribe from the slut to make him stay with her. Don't you see? It all makes sense. That's why Alex was with her. Women were always falling in love with him and he didn't do anything about it. There had to have been something for him to say 'yes' this time – and that was the money. She seduced him with it!" Hazel was becoming increasingly energized and angry. "And," she said triumphantly, "imagine how upset the pathetic slut would have been when Alex told her that he was coming back to me. I'm not saying that she killed Alex but she might have felt like doing it."

Although Hazel had often told Penny that Alex would return to her, this latest remark expressed certainty. "He was coming back?"

"Of course."

"He told you he was coming back?"

"He didn't have to."

The noise of a baby stirring could be heard coming from the bedroom. The mewling of a very young baby.

"Is he awake?" Penny asked, brightening.

"Not for another hour or so… See, he's settled already."

Sitting in her car with Penny, later in the day, in the parking lot of the funeral home, Heather said, "If you don't mind me asking, I was wondering… Do you think that Alex was helping Hazel out financially?"

"I really don't know. Hazel's getting maternity leave benefits, so she's scraping by. I doubt Alex gave her a cent, but I could be wrong."

"Maybe he wanted the business so he could support them."

Penny smiled at her friend's effort to cast her brother in a positive light. "Maybe…"

"Do you believe what Alex told Hazel; that he used his own money to buy the store?"

"I believe that Alex told Hazel that the money wasn't a loan. It doesn't mean it was though. If Alex was being honest for the first time in his life, then the obvious question is: Where did he get the money from?"

As Penny was opening her car door, she paused and said sarcastically, "Maybe Hazel is right and Alex got it from his new girlfriend; a young woman who works in a pub, and who just happened to have a hundred grand or so laying around that she would willingly gift to a shifty boyfriend. Because stuff like that, as you know, happens every day. I'm sorry to say it but Hazel's hate is making her delusional."

16.

"Hi Grandpa."

Silence.

"It's Hugh." The plan, as always, was to load information up front in case it was one of those days when his grandfather didn't remember who he was. It might stave off the awkward silence while Robert tried to identify who he was speaking to.

"Hi there Sunny Jim."

Hugh had long forgotten who Sunny Jim was – he'd once looked it up online – but hearing the words was a good sign: his grandfather remembered him.

Robert's decline had come gradually over the last six or seven years and was a source of much soul searching on Hugh's part about whether he was doing enough to help him.

The question had first arisen when he'd considered moving to PEI. It would mean visiting his grandfather less. Perhaps, he thought at the time, he should look for a teaching job in Quebec or eastern Ontario in order to be closer to Montreal. His mother and step-father almost never bothered with the old guy so it came down to his two grandkids to visit. In the end though, Hugh's decision to move to Charlottetown had come about at the urging of his sister, Laurie. She had lived in Montreal since university, worked from home, and visited Robert's nursing home every few days. She urged Hugh to live his life to suit himself. "Grandpa's well cared for. Keep calling him and visit when you can, just as you would if his decline hadn't happened. There's lots of stuff going on at the home and the staff are great. He's not lonely."

It was why, on this Sunday morning, like every other, that Hugh was on the phone with Robert.

In the past he would have spoken to his grandfather about the previous night's hockey game, but no longer. Even if Robert had watched the game he'd have forgotten about it by Sunday morning. He recalled things from the distant past however, on good days, and that's what Hugh was hoping for.

Hugh angled the conversation around to what he himself had been up to. "I went up to look at the old farm and farmhouse," he said.

A moment's hesitation on the line. "What old farmhouse?"

"Your parents' place in PEI, where you grew up."

"Who lives there? Are my parents…"

"No, sorry. Actually, no one lives there. The house is gone. A neighbour bought the farm but just for the fields."

"PEI. Rich soil there."

'Rich soil in PEI' was a common trope of his grandfather's. Whenever Hugh spoke about PEI, Robert always replied with a comment about the richness of the soil, like it was something he'd heard at school and was the only thing that he could think of to say about the place that he'd moved away from at ten or eleven years of age. Today though, Hugh wondered if the comment was a metaphor that alluded to family history; like the soil was rich with it.

"Yes. I met someone when I was there. An old woman. Her name is Ellen Comer. She said that she was a friend of your mother's. Of Louise. She said she remembers you and Edward."

To Hugh's surprise, Robert said, "Yeah, the Comers. They had a girl, much younger than me. Old Comer's daughter."

"I was wondering about Ellen."

"Who?"

"Ellen Comer, the lady next door who said she remembers you."

"Oh yeah. Is she still really beautiful?"

"Umm…okay…yeah. She said that she was friends with your mother. Sounded like they sorta had a mother-daughter relationship. But I was looking at your mother's photo albums that I have and I don't see Ellen in any of the pictures. Lots of your mother's other women friends and their kids are pictured, but none of Ellen. I was wondering if the two of them had a falling out. I mean, that you knew of."

"No." Robert suddenly sounded authoritative. Sure of himself. "No. I don't know if anything happened but my mother often talked about Mrs. Comer. They were close friends. There was no falling out."

"Ah… Oh, and I met a man too. An old guy who said you were friends with him: Harry Nelson."

"Harry? We went to school together. We used to go fishing behind the farm."

"In Sherman's Pond?"

"No. In the creek at the back of our east field. The pond was on Sherman's property, or behind it anyway… We used to go swimming there…" Robert's voice drifted off. He was remembering the times he walked the path that ran beside the creek. It led to the pond. He would tread silently along the hard packed ground of the trail beside the creek. Stealthily. A Mi'kmaw warrior. A scout. He'd clutch his slingshot watching for British New Englanders cleverly disguised as partridge. He would pass the charred remains of campfires where teenagers had come to socialize in the night, doing mysterious things he knew nothing about. And there was that one time when there was a body on the path.

"Grandpa?"

"Oh yeah, I remember Harry. His mother was nice but his old man was scary. When we went to their house you could feel that Harry was afraid of him."

"Harry had a buddy: Jack Eades. I think he was also friends with you."

"Jack? Yeah. he was in my class at school. We were chums at first but then he and Eddie became inseparable. They were both athletes. Loved baseball and hockey."

"Do you ever hear from him?"

"Jack? No. Never. He could be dead for all I know."

"Do you remember if Edward ever talked about him?"

"Sometimes, I guess. But just recalling memories about the past, I think. You should ask Eddie."

"Yes, I'll do that." Hugh didn't remind Robert that his brother was dead. It would only upset him, and for absolutely no purpose since Robert would soon forget the fact and go on speaking as if Edward was alive. Hugh and Laurie had decided to let his grandfather continue to believe it. It would be cruel to cause him to feel the same shock of death and loss, over and over.

Once again there was silence on the line. Hugh fought the urge to fill the space with small talk, having come to the conclusion that his grandfather's silences weren't necessarily signs of vacancy. Sometimes Robert just submerged himself in the waters of memory. He would return with a comment that indicated what had been playing through his thoughts.

Today, Robert was remembering laying on his bed in the farmhouse in PEI, in the room he shared with Eddie. It was illuminated by a light that hung two feet from the ceiling – like a suicide's noose, he often thought. It swung with any movement of air, making shadows slide up and down the wall when the door closed or opened, as if the room was tilting on an axis.

Once, his mother had removed a burnt out light bulb. She went to the kitchen to get a new one. Robert stood on the bed – he was only six years old at the time – and stuck his finger into the socket. He was flung across the room.

Hugh said brightly, "So Grandpa, did you watch the Canadiens' game last night?"

Back at home, Hugh went online, searching for a phone number for Jack Eades, thinking that if he didn't find one he'd call Ellen.

It was surprisingly simple. Jack had a landline and his number was quickly found.

A woman answered the phone. Hugh asked if he could speak to Jack and was told to wait a second. He heard the clunk of the handset being set down and the woman's voice calling, "Dad, the phone's for you!"

The wait for Jack to pick up the phone took almost a full minute. It got to the point where Hugh was wondering whether the man was ever coming, and whether he should hang up.

Jack, slightly out of breath, began with an apology. "Sorry to take so long. I live downstairs and I don't get around so well anymore."

Trying to pack as much background information into his call as quickly as possible to indicate that he wasn't a salesman or pollster, Hugh said, "Don't mention it. My name is Hugh Martin. I don't know if you remember the Martin family from Mount Pleasant but my grandfather's name is Robert. I understand you were friends with him and his brother Edward back in Mount Pleasant when you were a kid, back in the 1930s and 40s."

"Yes," said Jack, pleasantly and without hesitation, as if he'd known the call was coming. His tone altered to one of sympathy when he added, "I heard about Eddie's passing and I'm sorry for your loss."

"Thank you. I hope you don't mind me calling. I'm researching my family history, and am interested in their time on the farm at Mount Pleasant. Robert has dementia and his memory isn't what it used to be. Would it be possible to sit down and pick your brain? Maybe get you to look at some pictures of the people who lived around Mount Pleasant when you were a kid to see if you remember them."

"You want to meet me to…to talk about the old days?"

"And to look at some pictures. I'm researching my family history. I don't just want to build a family tree; I'd like to get to know something about my ancestors and who they associated with…if I can. I'm a historian… Anyway, if you'd talk to me I'd appreciate it very much."

"I'm not sure how much help I can be but I guess most of your other sources would have to be dug up." Jack laughed. "Of course I'll talk to you. It would be my pleasure. You could come over here. My daughter lives upstairs so I don't have to check with her about a time. How about tomorrow afternoon? My youngest daughter's family is coming over today for a Sunday roast and all that, so today's not great."

"Sounds perfect. We're going to a funeral tomorrow afternoon. I'll be just around the corner from you. Would something like 2:30 be okay?"

"Yes. So you know where I live?"

Hugh relayed the address he'd found with the phone number and Jack confirmed it was correct.

Hugh said, "Oh, and I don't know when this thing – the funeral I mean – will end so I'll call you if I'm going to be late."

"Don't bother. Just show up when it's over. I'll be here. Not much happens in my life."

That evening, at supper, Hugh told Heather about his plan

to visit Jack and asked if she knew how long the next day's funeral would last.

"I think they can differ a good deal," Heather replied. "I'd guess that things will be wrapped up by 2:30 though. I can't see it going on longer than that."

"Will you stay with Penny for the day again?"

"Penny will be fine on her own. She said that she's going with her family to her grandmother's house afterwards, so I won't be needed… I could come with you to meet Jack – if it's okay with you. It should be interesting."

"That'll be great!"

17. Monday

Heather lay in bed, mid-morning, awake but with her eyes closed. She was thinking about her meeting with Hazel the day before.

She was only mildly surprised to hear that Alex was desirous of having a home and family while still being able to roam free. It was straight out of *The Odyssey*. Her video, she thought, should focus some attention on Odysseus.

As she was getting dressed for the funeral, Heather was startled when Hugh stuck his head through the open bedroom door and said. "When you have a minute you might like to read this story on the CBC News website." His smile promised good news.

Heather, excitedly, went to the kitchen where Hugh's laptop was open on the table.

She read through the article and was happy with it since it provided a good summation of the exhibition.

The reporter concluded by writing that Heather's art collective was insisting that PEI become a sirens' island in some respects. One where there is mutual support among women to tell their stores and express themselves through their arts; as a means of empowerment.

Heather was pleased with the article. She looked up and smiled her approval at Hugh.

"Not bad eh?" he said, smiling back.

"Not bad at all."

Heather continued to scroll down the page having noticed that the article was followed by a comments section. Her demeanour gradually changed.

To her alarm, many of the comments were not only negative but aggressively so, and the names or pseudonyms of the posters were all men. Most misrepresented what she had said. They were, in fact, a validation of Heather's view, as expressed in the article, that a certain type of man sees relations between men and women as a war, and as confrontational.

One commentator wrote: "So it's a power struggle eh? Well, bring it on baby."

An irony and hypocrisy blind voice chimed in, "They're acting like PEI belongs to women and only they should have a voice. Well, they should shut up."

And the misunderstanding spread, with each negative comment moving further and further away from what had actually been written and characterizing the collective's upcoming show in a way that had nothing to do with reality.

"Did you read these comments?" Heather asked.

Hugh saw the concern on her face and moved closer to the screen so that he could read over her shoulder.

"It's almost all men who've commented," Heather explained, while Hugh read. "They make it sound like I'm suggesting that women should be in control… Look at this one." She pointed at the screen to a post that seemed to urge violence against the women in the art collective.

"This is our island too," it went. "We must fight these mouthy women who don't appreciate this society that men have built for them."

Together, Heather and Hugh continued to read as he scrolled down the page.

"Bloody feminists need to shut up."

"This Heather woman needs to get laid."

"Men in PEI have to fight back."

"This joker," Heather said, again pointing at the screen, "sounds like he wants to kill me; like he's engaged in a military conflict."

The comment read, "This is a declaration of war and I for one am ready to fight and to end this feminist!"

"It looks like most of the other comments are positive though," Hugh said, trying to find a silver lining. He read the CBC site regularly and added, "There's a mini-army of young men sitting in their mom's basements who take a break from watching porn and masturbating to rail about feminists, Natives, immigrants, and liberals; using these as derogatory terms."

"I know that some men try to intimidate any woman who says something they disagree with, or intrudes on a subject they consider to be men's terrain, like video games where men pretend to be warriors – trying to scare her into silence.

But it's still shocking when it happens to you. Do you think one of these idiots is going to show up at the door?" Heather looked alarmed at the prospect.

"No. These clowns are from all over since this is a national site. I'd be surprised if any of them actually live in PEI. Like I said, there's an army of them that comment on every political story or anything that smacks of liberalism. I think they're trying to create the appearance that they represent the majority view."

"They're bullies…ganging up on people because they're cowards. How long has this been going on on this site?"

"It's hard to say since I've only been looking at it since I moved to PEI."

"Why does the CBC let people do this?"

"I think they would argue that they're just allowing Canadians to discuss issues; like it's part of their mandate. But lots of other news sites allow comments too. They seem oblivious to the fact that their comments sections aren't a forum for discussion. That they've been hijacked."

"By reactionary men drowning out the voices of others by shouting over them. Foot soldiers in the cause. Little men playing soldier. Maybe they feel that silencing women is an assertion of masculinity; one that women have supposedly challenged by not following traditional gender roles."

"The sites have moderators so the most egregious posts get taken down; like those that threaten violence."

"But it still goes up online – at least for awhile after it's first posted – and that's when most people will read it. I didn't know this sort of comment stuff on CBC was going on. It's the first tactic of fascism, isn't it. Control the narrative, normalize hate. Make people afraid to speak out."

"If someone approaches the article with an open mind though, the comments will confirm your view that some men aggressively seek to silence women's voices rather than engage in discussion…"

"Yes, but the actual ideas behind the exhibition are drowned out by noise that describes it in incorrect ways. Job complete. Reinforce your point of view about what women are up to."

18.

When Heather and Hugh arrived at the funeral home their car was shepherded by the home's employees into the parking lot of a business up the street because its own lot was full.

As the couple walked back towards the home they observed that the line of cars waiting for parking was still three blocks long.

Alex had been a popular figure.

The funeral service was held in the home's chapel. Heather and Hugh were seated near the back, in a space packed mostly with young people, many of whom looked to be the age of college or university students.

Hazel emerged first, with a young man at her side. They found seats in the front row. Heather observed Hazel leaning on the man for support and concluded, based on looks, that this must be the brother she'd heard about.

Watching the scene unfold in front of her, it struck Heather how lonely Hazel must feel and how this might have influenced her dependency on Alex. Penny had mentioned that Alex never went out with Hazel – freeing him up to be with his other woman presumably. He always gave Hazel some reason or other why he had to be on his own: phony business meetings and the like. The picture Penny painted was one of a serial liar who thought only of himself; expecting his wife to stay at home waiting for him.

Heather again had the impression that Hazel was an outsider to the Callas family when Hector, Doris, and Alex's siblings did not take seats beside Hazel and her brother.

Heather wondered whether she was reading the situation correctly and if she was, whether Hazel was an outsider by choice or because the family saw her in that way. And if they did, could it be because Hazel was from the Channel Islands?

Heather recalled a woman, who had once frowned at her after hearing her accent, say that, "People on an island must protect their environment from invasive plants or animals because they will destroy the ecosystem. In the same way, we must guard against immigrants because they destroy our social ecosystem." It was a novel form of nativist bigotry, but essentially the same as you might hear on the mainland. Purity of the soil.

Heather quickly rejected the possibility that the Callas family were bigots. She'd seen no evidence of that.

The priest's sermon was a generic head-in-the-sand-about-reality-for-the-good-of-the-family type of speech about what a wonderful family man Alex had been. And what a good and loved friend he obviously was, as evidenced by the large turn out. And then, as if tired and wanting someone else to take the ball, the priest asked if anyone would like to come to the front and say something about Alex. "Anything," the priest emphasized in a pleading manner.

During the ensuing silence, two hundred eyes looked to the floor until the sermon was resumed by a now deflated priest.

Heather wondered if the man spent a good part of his life in this chapel giving this and a handful of other speeches with the names changed, and little else. The guy looked bored out of his mind. She wondered too if this sort of whitewashing speech helped normalize certain behaviour – like the selfishness engaged in by Alex – and maybe even enabled it.

After the service, the immediate family retired to a large room and formed a reception line.

Many of the mourners filed past, extending their sympathies, while exchanging hugs or handshakes.

Heather lined up with Hugh and other teachers from the school where they and Penny worked.

When Heather's turn came to hug Penny, her friend whispered in her ear, begging her to please not leave until they'd had a chance to speak.

One of the people from the school, in attendance, was the principal, Ellis Rice, who was twelve years older than Penny, and divorced. Heather felt that Penny was half in love with Ellis but couldn't decide whether or not she wanted a relationship with her. One day Penny spoke as if the two were a couple and the next as if they were the most casual of acquaintances. It was unclear to Heather whether Penny's reticence was because of Ellis's age, appearance, or that she was her boss. It was possible too that Ellis wasn't interested in a relationship with Penny and the realization of it had cooled Penny's ardour.

All Penny would say about the matter, when prodded for information, was that she and Ellis were 'just friends'.

Heather intently watched the interaction between Ellis and Penny as they met in the reception line. Penny shook with grief and clung to Ellis for much longer than she had with anyone else. It was as if she'd been waiting for her before letting loose her full grief.

All of the members of the art collective that Heather and Penny were part of had also come to the funeral. They congregated around Heather and were soon engaged in a whispered conversation about that morning's CBC online article. Everyone who'd read it was complimentary about Heather's interview and stunned by the aggressive response. Those who hadn't read the article were shocked with what they heard.

Gina Sorrentino said, "I did printouts of the comments before a moderator takes them down. I think we should consider using them in the show in some way." Some heads nodded affirmatively while others voiced their agreement.

"It validates the direction we're taking with the show," said Katarina Haigy, another collective member. "Nothing proves the point – that women who express themselves are still seen as sirens by some – more than those comments."

Heather didn't comment. She was thinking about her video and the ideas she was expressing in it. The men who'd attacked her online were bullies. They saw their relationship with women who speak out as an antagonistic one and they sought to put those women in their place. These cowards saw themselves as brave warriors in a gender war. They felt that testosterone conferred some special rights to them. Their vile words and threats were a form of violence; acts that gave them a sense of power. Creating fear was their objective.

The reception line was dispersing and the collective did as well, except for Heather. Penny soon approached, took her arm, and said to Hugh, "I hope you don't mind if I borrow our girl."

Hugh smiled companionably in response and said, "Of

course not."

Penny angled Heather into a corner.

"Well I survived that," Penny said, once they were alone. She looked about, ensuring there was ample space between them and those remaining in the room before saying, "Thanks for waiting, I wanted to catch you up on something before you left."

"What is it?" Heather asked.

"My sister Selene's friend, Sally, who is…oh wait, I think you met her at my parent's house…"

"Anemic looking…"

"Yeah, that's her." Penny pointed to a group composed of Selene, Sally, and a third girl. "The other one, the one who looks to be about twelve, but is sixteen like the others, is Megan Jones…" Penny's voice trailed off as she watched the three interacting with a well-dressed man who had his hand on Selene's arm. The guy – who appeared to be about forty years old – was talking and the three teens were listening intently. Penny felt disturbed by the scene for no apparent reason.

Heather, noting that her friend's attention had been hijacked, began to watch the interaction as well.

"Anyway, Sally's dad's a cop," Penny started up again, although her eyes remained on her sister. "She told Selene that she overheard her parents talking about Alex's case and her father was saying that the police think that Alex may have been lured to the upstairs lounge after the bar closed, by the biker's wife; to set him up. So she's now someone they're looking at very closely. They still don't know where Alex got the money to buy his store but because of this Bethany woman they now suspect it came from a biker gang."

The well-dressed man, who'd been chatting up Selene and her friends, was approaching Penny and Heather. His presence was smelled before he was seen. A whiff of expensive heaven.

He stopped in front of Penny who turned her attention his way.

"I'm very sorry for the loss of your brother," the man said.

Penny thanked him and asked if he was a friend of Alex's.

"Acquaintance. My name is Jason Hopkins. I'm the owner of the bar where Alex was on the night he died. I'm so sorry it happened."

"I don't blame you," Penny said politely. "It wasn't your fault."

"No… And I'm sorry we're not meeting under better circumstances. I knew Alex just well enough to know how much he thought of you. He carried a picture of you."

"Of me?"

"Yes. You and his wife. She was in an ultra-sexy bikini by a pool and you're beside her looking very…straight laced." The last words appeared to have put a bad taste into Hopkins mouth since he frowned slightly when saying them. In an apologetic tone he added, "A couple of gorgeous ladies enjoying summer. I can appreciate that."

Heather recalled the photo she'd seen at Hazel's where she was wearing a pink bikini. It was likely the picture that Hopkins had seen. No wonder he liked it. He was the owner of the business where pink-haired 'mermaids' swam in a giant aquarium behind the bar.

Heather hated this kind of man. She knew the type. All commentary on women was about sex; direct or implied. And, in this case, it was combined with an obviously phony sincerity. Not surprising a dirt bag like Alex Callas would have shared a sexy picture of his wife with this guy; they probably swapped brags about their conquests.

Penny appeared to be uncomfortable and said nothing.

Hopkins made an inane remark about the large funeral turnout. Size apparently mattering in all things.

After Penny agreed, there was a pause until Hopkins continued with several comments about the sermon.

Each received a one word response but Hopkins remained rooted to one spot in spite of it.

He next commended Penny's parents for their poise and strength.

She only replied, "Yes."

Heather studied the man. He was trying to strike up a conversation rather than just extend his sympathies. Men like this had approached her in bars. Their tactic was to keep the conversation going, the man filling in any silences so it doesn't end, thus normalizing his presence and inclusion. She had never seen anyone flirt at a funeral before. The man's fixations suggested a connection that Alex might have felt with him.

"I hope you'll drop by my bar some day," he said to Penny. "Everything will be on the house of course. Not that I think it will make up for anything…"

Penny hesitated, then said a polite, "We'll see."

Hopkins looked at Heather, his eyes running up and down as if assessing her at auction, and said, "And you, lovely lady, you're more than welcome too."

Heather stared back at him, saying nothing. Was the man subtly hitting on her now too? She wondered whether this was his modus operandi with all young women or specific to those he found sexually attractive. The distasteful thought crossed her mind that Hopkins might have just been engaged in flirting with the sixteen year old girls.

"Just a sec," Penny said to Heather, after Hopkins had finally given up and was walking away. She strode across the room and corralled her younger sister, herding her away from her friends.

"That man you were talking to," she began.

"Jason," corrected Selene.

"Mr. Hopkins."

"He said to call him Jason."

"What were you talking about?"

"Why?"

"I just wondered. He owns the bar where…you know… where Alex was shot."

"I know. He didn't say anything about that. He offered his sympathy. He was very nice. Megan's worked for him for a couple of years – she always has tons of money from tips – and she introduced us. He said if Sally or I was looking for a summer job that we should come and see his assistant. We couldn't work in the bar but there's lots of other things we could do; like work with Megan."

"I don't think you should be around that guy and working in a bar. Especially that one. There's some bad people that hang out there: criminals, bikers.”

“Well Alex liked him. Are you saying that Alex was a criminal?”

“No, of course not. It’s just that we know nothing about Hopkins. Plus he has a bad reputation…”

“Well, I like him.”

“And he reeks of insincerity.”

“So when he told me I was interesting you think he was lying?”

“I didn’t say that.”

“Well, unlike the people in my family, he treats me like an adult, and if I want to work for him I will!” Selene spun on her heel and moved back to the social embrace of her two friends who’d been watching.

Her sister’s response left Penny even more uneasy. She should have known that whatever she told her sister to do that Selene would do the opposite to prove her independence.

At Selene’s age, she’d been exactly the same: wanting to be treated as an adult. Also, like Selene, she’d wanted a job and to have her own money…and she’d made some stupid decisions because of her naivety. She could only hope that Selene didn’t make the same mistakes. The last thing that Penny wanted was for her sister to follow Alex’s path and make friends with the people who hung out in Hopkins’ bar.

Panel from Heather Bruce's Siren video

Odysseus wanted to go home. And, like any sailor, to return to land.

It's not a man's fault if he diverts from his trip home; it's blamed on women. He was lured. He became lost. The Siren myth is about men blaming women for a man's failure to find his way home. He was seduced by sexual allure.

Seeing women as seducers denies male agency. Men who made a choice to submit to erotic passion prefer to see themselves as victims of trickery; their reason having been stolen by seduction. Blame women. The remedy lays not with the men who act in certain ways but in forcing women to be be silent and draped 'modestly'.

Seeing women as seducers, and in sexual terms, just for living their lives, denies them full humanity, defining them solely in relation to men and to sexual service. Seeing women as incapable of reason, acting from more primal sexual impulses that need to be controlled inside a home. Tamed.

Of course.

19.

Jack Eades' daughter Matilda answered the door.

Heather and Hugh introduced themselves.

"Come in," Matilda said. "Your timing's perfect. I was out for a long walk and just got back. Dad's in the backyard. I'll take you through."

Matilda appeared, to Hugh, to be somewhere in her late forties. She was one of those people who he thought of as perfect. She dressed impeccably, obviously kept fit, and was very personable. Her house wasn't a large one but was spotless and beautifully decorated. Classical music played softly in a living room filled with bookcases. But there was a certain distance in her character: formality perhaps.

"I'll warn you about Dad," Matilda said with a smile. "If you get him talking about the old days you may not be able to stop him. He can be like an out of control train."

She led her dad's guests out to the back deck and left them with Jack, who stood up in greeting and pointed the couple toward deck chairs.

"What a beautiful garden," Heather said as she sat down.

"It's Matilda's doing," Jack replied. "If she isn't working she's always busy with something or other at home."

"The house is beautiful inside too," said Hugh.

"It is. This is the house where she grew up. Her little sister, Martha, got married and has four kids but Matilda stayed on here. I built myself an in-law apartment downstairs to give her some privacy. But she's not a social animal. Everything is family. I'd be lost without her… But you're not here to talk about me; you want to ask about Mount Pleasant you said."

"Yes, if I could," Hugh replied. "I brought one of my great-grandmother's photo albums that I was hoping you would look at." He handed Jack the same hefty album he'd shown Ellen. "I talked to Ellen Comer. She knew the names of the women in the pictures, but not those of the kids. That's why I was hoping you'd look at them."

"Certainly." Jack sat up in his chair. "It was Ellen who took me to the beach with everyone. Back then my own mother had bad migraines and spent most of her time laying in her bedroom with the curtains closed."

Jack began to flip through the pages of the album. The photos were glued to black paper pages by means of slip-on corners; six small pictures to a page. Jack closely studied each picture and had no trouble attaching names to the children.

"This is me and this is Harry," he said about one photo, "with Eddie and Robbie. The girl in the background is Cynthia Sherman. Her poor brother drowned about this time."

Hugh said, "I recognized Robbie and Eddie but, until this past week or so, I had no idea who the other kids in the pictures might be."

"Taken in August 1943," Jack said, pointing at the date stamp, which appeared in the white border along the right side of each photo.

"So it wasn't long before the time when that aviator was killed," Hugh said.

"No," murmured Jack, without looking up.

In most cases, his memory of the name of someone who appeared in one of the dozens of pictures, set off a recollected story about the person. His powers of recollection were impressive but, since he'd only lived in the Mount Pearl area until he was twenty years old, the stories were about things the kids in the pictures had gotten up to as teenagers.

"This fella is Arnold McCain," Jack said while examining one photo. "There was this one time when we were driving in his old Buick. Arnie, me and Harry, who was in the back seat. The car was on its last legs; smoking like crazy. It was burning as much oil as gas. Arnie asked Harry to light him a smoke and held up his hand with his first two fingers open in a v shape. So Harry lit up a smoke and reached over the seat, putting the cigarette between Arnie's fingers. Arnie didn't look at it and he sticks the lit end in his mouth. He yells and spits the thing out. It lands in his lap, so then he starts squirming, trying to find the burning cigarette between his legs. He was so absorbed with the cigarette that the car went into the ditch. We had to get a farmer to bring his tractor and pull us out. Once the Buick was out of the ditch and running we just drove off and waved thanks to the guy. We had no money to give him anything. We were just teenagers." Jack laughed heartily.

He went from one story to another, proving that his daughter's warning about her father's propensity to reminisce with long stories was prescient.

But it didn't bother Hugh or Heather. They were enjoying the often wild tales of adventures, and heard the sadness in Jack's voice when he mentioned that a friend's older bother or father had died in the war.

Eventually, Hugh steered the conversation in a different direction, saying, "I wonder if I could ask you about the aviator whose body you found on the trail to Sherman's Pond. If you don't want to talk about it, I understand."

"Oh no. It's okay. It was close to your family's fields."

"I understand that Harry was with you when you found the aviator's body."

"Yes. It was gruesome. Awful. A shotgun up close will do that. But seeing it was nothing compared to what many men saw during the war on a daily basis."

"Did you ever have any suspicions about how the guy got shot?" asked Heather. "They said it was probably an errant gunshot by a hunter."

"Hmm. I wouldn't be so sure about that," Jack said.

"Really?" Hugh said flatly, and defensively, unsure if his family was about to be implicated.

"Yes. I remember the damage to the guy's head. It had practically been blown off. I know the inquest decided that a hunter must have been walking through the bush, saw something close by that he mistook for a bird, and fired. But that's backwards isn't it? Whether he was shooting at a target or a grouse, a hunter would have been on the path and been shooting into the woods. Not vice versa."

"So you think the shot was fired by someone who was on the path?"

"I do. Judging by the damage the rifle inflicted, the two were almost face to face and the man with the rifle aimed at the dead man's head."

"Like someone despised him and wanted to destroy his face?" said Heather.

"Exactly."

"I wonder," Heather continued, "if that's what started the rumours that Thomas – Hugh's great-grandfather – killed the soldier after discovering the man with his wife, Louise. If a cuckolded husband thought the guy was a slick seducer, or handsome enough for women to want to seduce, then destroying his looks in an act of vengeance would make sense."

"Yes. Not that I think your family was involved," he quickly added, looking at Hugh. "Of course the rumours eventually changed and it was just the women who got blamed. I heard Freddy – that's Harry's old man – say that shooting a guy in the face was a woman's type of murder so Louise and Ellen must have killed the man."

"Louise and Ellen?" Hugh said, astonished.

"Yes. I especially didn't like it when Ellen was dragged into the stories. Like I said, she was very nice to me and took me to the beach. When my father joined the army, and went overseas, she would even take me to the dump to shoot skeet, using her shotgun. She was a crack shot. Ellen was like my second mother."

"Ellen didn't tell me about that rumour…"

"Maybe she didn't know."

"So what was the story about Louise and Ellen?"

"A nonsense story that the aviator was seeing one or the other of the women and they conspired to kill him because of something or other. I honestly can't remember…"

"So Freddy was the one spreading rumours you said," interjected Heather.

"Well, I know he was one of the people. He was the only adult I heard say stuff like that. I was a kid. I don't know what the other adults were talking about. But yeah, Freddy was doing his part, and I heard him blame Ellen and Louise. There were other farms in the area where women and teen-age girls lived but I never heard Freddy blame any of them for some reason."

"He sounds like he was a nasty man from what I've heard of him," said Hugh.

"He was: mean and nasty. He hated women and blamed

them for everything. They were all sluts – his word, sorry. He was a small minded and cruel bastard – excuse my French again. Men were pretty free with the belt back then but Freddy was something else. And probably was violent with his wife as well cus she left him."

"Harry stayed with his father though," Hugh said thoughtfully. "That seems strange. You'd think he would have wanted to get away from the guy and, at that age his primary attachment would have still been his mother."

"Harry didn't have a choice. So far as I remember his mother just took off without him. Harry was angry at her, and I don't think he ever got over it – but he never liked to talk about her so I don't know."

"Do you have any idea of who the aviator – Samuel Marsh – was supposedly carrying on an affair with, since it wasn't Louise or Ellen?" Heather said.

"I don't know. Speculating was nuts. There were lots of possibilities around there if you consider that the woman or girl could have lived in any direction from the air station. Lots of husbands were away and that meant there was opportunity. I heard it said that the guy was a stalker though. Used to go to the dances at the base and in town, and try to pick up women; even follow them home to see if there was a man there. So he could have been of those bullshitters – excuse me – and probably was. And he was stupid. Bragging that he was having an affair with a married woman was a very stupid thing to do. All the men in the area had rifles and he was shot in the face so it makes sense to think that one of the men believed the rumours and decided to put the guy in his place."

"Was there anyone you suspected?" asked Heather.

"I don't remember. It was a long time ago."

Jack returned to the back deck of the house after showing Heather and Hugh to the front door.

He sat for a long time, in thought, until finally getting up and going to the phone.

The person he called answered almost immediately.

"They asked and I did my best to put them off..." Jack

said, in answer to a question.

Pause.

"He was with his wife…his 'partner' he called her…"

Pause.

"Both. They both had questions. I didn't tell them anything. Said it was too long ago and I was just a kid… You won't be hearing from them again about this stuff…but, you know, I think it's time to stop all this silence, like I said…"

Pause.

"But what would it matter after all this time?"

Pause.

"Think about it, please. I think the kid should know the truth."

Pause.

"I'm leaning towards just telling him everything."

Jack hung up the phone. He'd done everything he could to lead Hugh and Heather to the truth of what happened without actually telling them; without betraying someone he was close to.

And now, on the phone, he'd stood up for the truth once again. But as he stood there, considering the matter, he was increasingly certain that it was time to go all the way and just tell Hugh what really happened.

Jack pulled the slip of paper from his shirt pocket and read Hugh's cell phone number. He stared at it, then folded the paper and placed it beside the phone.

Panel from Heather Bruce's Siren video

Women who seduce men are supposedly evil because they usurp male power.

In an early book, *Seduction*, written before he pronounced that reality had died, French philosopher Jean Baudrillard dismissed feminist's demands for their own sexual satisfaction and economic power. He argued:

*"They [women] do not understand **that seduction represents mastery over the symbolic universe, while power represents only mastery of the real universe**."* [emphasis in original] (Baudrillard)

('They do not understand', say the mansplainers over and over. Disparaging women's intelligence (as 'bird brains') is an age old argument that men make to justify their power and their deafening themselves to women's words.)

"The strength of the feminine is that of seduction." (Baudrillard)

This view of the feminine may derive from siren myth – that women's power comes through seduction.

20.

As Heather drove them home from Jack Eades' house, Hugh stared vacantly out the window, lost in thought.

Eventually he turned to Heather and said, "So what did you make of that?"

"He's a very nice old man. Some of his stories were hilarious – maybe more so because of the way he told them than because of the stories themselves."

"Yes… It was disturbing in a way though; I mean when it comes to the death of the aviator. I have had faith in the autopsy results, that the man's death was an accident. But now Jack is saying that it was an intentional murder. It changes everything if it was."

Heather didn't reply.

Hugh continued, "If Jack was right, and we never know who killed the man, my family may always be suspect… Oh, and I was surprised that there was a rumour about Ellen. Were you?"

"Not at all. Not when it's men who are inventing the rumours. Ellen's a woman. She kept to herself – other than her friendships with a few women friends I gather. Some of the men seemed to have had it in for her. Maybe their egos were bruised because she ignored them. And another thing, some people are suspicious of all outsiders and even hate them."

"I barely know her but I get the impression she's someone who wouldn't hurt a fly. And she seems to be kind."

"Yes. According to Jack she knew that he was on his own a good deal of the time so took him under her wing. Rumours don't care about facts. Besides, if Ellen did kill the aviator, maybe she had a reason to. I'd give her the benefit of the doubt. It sounds like all the men in the area fantasized about her…lusted after her. And the dead man was a possible stalker. There's likely a reason she keeps a rifle by her door."

Hugh was taken aback by Heather's comment. Did Heather now suspect that Ellen had killed the man? It was exactly what he was wondering – but he'd never confess it to Heather.

Hugh remained silent for the rest of the trip home; his thoughts racing. Had Ellen known Samuel Marsh? She was married in Summerside in 1942, at the same time as Marsh was stationed at the airbase there. Perhaps they'd had a relationship. Maybe Marsh had followed Ellen to Mount Pleasant and was making her life unpleasant.

Hugh's thoughts quickly shifted to Jack. Had the man been telling them that Ellen was a killer? Hugh had gotten the impression that Jack was trying to lead them somewhere.

It was Jack who'd told them the aviator's murder had been intentional, that Ellen was rumoured to have been involved, and that she owned a shotgun. It was solely because Jack had said those things that he – and seemingly Heather too – were wondering whether Ellen could be a murderer. Jack had put the idea of it into their heads.

For all he knew, Hugh thought, Jack may have told them what good friends he and Ellen were to disguise the fact that he was suggesting that she was a killer. Maybe Jack wanted him and Heather to arrive at the idea thinking it had come from themselves.

As they arrived home, Hugh said, "I know I go on about this stuff from the past but, like I've been saying, it bothers me that my family was suspected of a crime."

"I understand," Heather said, "but it's highly unlikely that anyone even remembers the rumours. Did I ever mention that my mother did some research into her family history? She discovered that her grandfather was conceived out of wedlock. His mother had become pregnant at age fifteen and married a thirty-year-old man shortly before she gave birth. My mother was struck by the question of whether her great-grandmother had wanted to get married or had been forced into it for financial or social reasons. And, given her age, it was possible that something inappropriate had happened... It's disturbing to look at history when it's personal but what's past is done, as cliché as that sounds."

21. Tuesday

Hector finally reached his office. He'd been waylaid while walking through the building by various members of his staff, hugging him, and/or offering their condolences.

He closed the office door behind himself, sat down at his desk, and immediately picked up the phone. He called Toby Harner and asked him to come to his office.

Hector had been thinking about Hazel, on his drive to work. Was it really possible that she had an older admirer when she was home with a new baby? And she'd told him that this man had…what?…proposed? Hector didn't know the exact nature of the man's approach but he'd apparently made himself clear enough: he wanted to marry Hazel… Or at least that's what Hazel said.

Toby Harner, the warehouse manager, was forty-two years old and divorced. He was well thought of by management; which was an opinion supported by results and not self-promotion, as was the case with many an incompetent manager. He was efficient at what he did, well-liked by his direct reports, and looked out for their interests. He'd been Hazel's boss for the past three years and she sometimes turned to him for advice; as a father figure, Toby assumed.

Toby had known Alex too. It was here that Hazel and Alex had met.

Hector's plan had been to have his son learn the business from the ground up. Maybe the boy would surprise him and show some initiative. Alex's first position, therefore, had been as a Warehouse Service Representative. Instead of being the first rung on a high ladder it turned out to be a small stepping stool. And it was Alex's only position in the company. He was too good for that sort of job he told Toby on his last day. He was going to buy his own company. Toby was shocked when, not so long after, he heard that Alex had indeed bought a store.

Toby was happy to see the back of Alex who he thought was lazy, and generally useless at picking and packing orders. On top of that, the guy was full of himself, always chatting up the young women he worked with. And he had a problem with female authority, continually trying to undermine Cora, his team leader, by running to Toby about everything she did and presenting it as a disaster. Toby figured that Alex was angling to be made team leader himself.

Toby knocked on the office door and Hector called for him to come in.

Toby closed the door behind himself and Hector directed him to sit.

He sat. Toby didn't offer his condolences since he'd done so at the funeral.

"I wanted to ask you something," Hector began. "I noticed that you and Hazel have always gotten along quite well. She told me last month that she has a close relationship with an older man who wants to marry her. I don't know if she's making that up or not. I can't see where this guy would have come from. She doesn't have much of a life in PEI. Her family's not here, except for her brother. Her parents are dead and she doesn't seem to have any friends. Is there anyone in the warehouse – any older man, I mean – who she might have developed a relationship with?"

"No..." Toby said before shifting uncomfortably in his seat. "I suspect this man is me, but," he quickly and firmly added, "there's absolutely no truth to it. Yes, we're friends, I mean at work. I think I may be a surrogate father to her... A couple of weeks after she had her baby she phoned and asked me if I wanted to come around to see him. I said 'sure', and I used the opportunity to help her out. I took her a present of some baby clothes when I went to visit."

He hadn't thought that Hazel's call had been unusual or objectionable. He didn't get involved with women from work, and especially not if they reported to him. And he'd never entertained any notion that Hazel's interest in him was of that sort. He was a paternal figure to Hazel – that was all – and he didn't mind since he knew she didn't have a father.

"And there was never any suggestion on your part that you wanted to marry her?" Hector said. "It wouldn't be any business of mine but I wanted to ask..."

Toby was suddenly on high alert and he shifted awkwardly in his chair. He wondered if Hector was thinking that the mystery man who wanted to marry Hazel may have knocked off Alex in order to achieve his romantic goal. He wished that he hadn't pointed the finger at himself by mentioning his dealings with Hazel. And he wished too that he wasn't still talking about it. It took an effort to control his voice when he said, "No. She may imagine I have feelings for her. She's pretty and a few of the guys in the warehouse have a thing for her – or at least that's what she says – but I wasn't one of them. I'm her boss, and an authority figure, so a relationship would be very inappropriate, even if she was single…"

"No, I'm sure you wouldn't have an affair with a direct report, but why do you think this man she said wanted to marry her was you?"

"Because she told Alex it was."

"She did? How do you know that?"

Toby again squirmed uncomfortably, again speaking about things he'd obviously rather not. "Because Alex told me. He was waiting for me outside work a few days after I was at Hazel's. He told me to keep away from her. He said that she belonged to him; one of several women who did… 'Belonged' was his word. Then he pulled out a knife and said I would regret it if I visited Hazel again."

"Jesus Christ. I knew he'd started carrying a knife but I hoped it was just to show off, like he was a tough guy."

"It was a rather large one."

Hector sighed. What had his stupid son been playing at? "That must have been unnerving."

"I can't say I was afraid." Toby wanted to say more but held his tongue. He'd said enough. Anything else he might add would just be his characterization of Alex and it may not go over well with the guy's father, especially at this time.

After the incident with Alex, Toby had thought about their meeting. The whole thing reeked of patheticness. Alex had gratuitously mentioned that Hazel wasn't the only woman in his harem. He was trying to show off in a kind of strutting peacock move. Like life was a pissing contest to collect cars, women, and money. Toby had noted, many times before, that the more misogynistic a man was the more likely he was to see women as property he had a right to control. And the more likely he was to find his way to women who let themselves be controlled by him – for whatever reason – and who shared the same ideas about men's and women's roles.

And what kind of ladies man, what sort of God's gift to women, needs to use a knife to threaten other men to keep away from his conquests? Surely not someone who wields hypnotic Svengali-like control over women; the sort of power that Alex Carras thought he had. Pathetic and desperate.

Toby thought that if Hazel had invited him around to see the baby, and then told Alex that he wanted to marry her in order to incite Alex's jealousy, it had worked. But Alex hadn't responded by moving closer to Hazel – as she may have hoped – to ward off other men. His response had been to threaten violence against the threat. Got a problem? The solution is violence.

22.

Heather closed her laptop. It was time to get going.

She'd been drafting some lines to accompany a possible new addition to the Siren exhibition, one that displayed the venom and threats of a few insecure men about the existence of the exhibition.

She'd written:

To silence people's voices requires power. For example, authoritarian regimes see opposing voices as threats to be squelched.

The men who seek to silence women usually have no political power so they revert to threats and intimidation. They act to defend patriarchy and the bit of power it gives them.

We see here the continuation of siren myth. Like Odysseus's men, these men deafen themselves to women's voices. And, like siren myth, they see women's voices as the output of deformed creatures (half bird of prey, half human) who defy the natural order, using seduction and beauty to make men lose control (in every sense).

Heather arrived at Penny's apartment in the afternoon, hoping to listen to her friend's recordings of the ocean.

She'd originally planned to listen to them the previous Saturday morning but that scheme had been aborted due to Alex's death.

Heather was shown into the living room, and took a seat on the couch, but, right on cue – like there would always be something to keep her from hearing the recordings – Penny's phone rang.

With a quick apology, Penny slipped into the kitchen to answer it in private.

Heather tried to ignore what was being said – and she couldn't discern much, in any case – but from the rise in the volume of Penny's voice it was evident that something had come up.

Penny soon returned to the living room. "Do you mind if

we head over to my parent's place for a bit," she said. "Hazel's there. My dad just fetched her from the police station. It sounds like the cops now think that she's a murder suspect; or at least, that's what Hazel told Dad."

As they drove, Heather took the opportunity to subtly prod. "So Hazel's at your parent's place." The comment begged an explanation.

"Yeah," Penny replied. "I was told she called and asked my father to pick up the baby when the cops were taking her to the station. Damian was sleeping when she called to get picked up after, so Dad brought her back to his place."

"Ah."

"Hazel doesn't have much to do with our family as a rule. I think it has something to do with being an obsessive. Like they want to shut out everyone in their life and focus their thoughts only on their adored one – or maybe to be always available. It's very sad. Like the person's lot in life is to be lonely. Of course it may have been that Alex wanted to shut her off from others. Or a combination of the two."

Hazel, Penny, and Heather were sitting in deck chairs beside the backyard pool at the Callas house, leaning forward, speaking in confidential tones as if there was someone in the empty yard who might be listening.

It occurred to Heather that she was tired of whispering; that she wanted to speak her mind without considering who could hear.

"Before the police hauled me down there for an interview, Hazel said, "I thought – because of what Selene's friend told her – that they figured some bikers killed Alex."

"So they've moved away from that?" Penny said.

"Now they think it was me! Courtesy of the lies told by that evil slut waitress who caught Alex up in her web. Constable Johnson said that Alex was afraid of me because I'd threatened to kill him… Can you imagine?"

"Oh brother," interjected Penny, leaning back and looking skyward in exasperation. Rocking forward, to her previous position, she said, "If the woman told them that it would just be her word against yours and anyone who knows you would know it's nonsense; that you wouldn't hurt a fly."

"I know, and I wouldn't be worried about it if that's all it was, but Johnson said that the slut has a note from Alex that he left for her one day saying that he'd be late and that she shouldn't be suspicious; that he wasn't going to my place later that day, and that he was afraid of me because I'd threatened to kill him."

"Bloody… Hah!" Penny scoffed and got to her feet, needing to burn off some of her outrage.

"I did no such thing," Hazel said indignantly.

"I know."

"So why did Alex lie?"

"I don't know. Is it possible that you said something that could have been misconstrued?"

"Along those lines? Never."

"Maybe…" Heather had been about to offer an opinion but bit off the remark, unsure if she should be saying anything.

"Maybe what?" Hazel said, not in an accusatory way but in a hopeful one, as if she was about to be thrown a lifeline.

"Maybe the most likely explanation," Heather said, "is that Alex was just saying some nonsense, lying to the woman to convince her that his marriage was over so she wouldn't know he'd been seeing you. It would save him the hassle of having to explain himself and having to deal with her jealousy."

Heather immediately wished that she'd said nothing. Hazel might only hear that Alex was being accused of having lied.

To her surprise, Hazel immediately nodded in agreement, as did Penny.

Hazel said, "Oh, and there was another reason that the police questioned me."

"What's that?" asked Penny, as she sat back down.

"That I have a permit to carry a gun."

"What? For real?"

"Yes. My brother, and I took the courses when I was nineteen. He said I might need protection, being alone in the city. I knew I wouldn't. I was planning on going home at the time and only stayed on eventually because of Alex. I just went to the class with Jeremy so he'd have some company."

"And do you have a gun?"

"A rifle. A .22."

"Which isn't the sort of weapon that killed Alex."

"No, but I guess my training shows that I know how to shoot." Her voice took on a pleading quality as she added, "I'm getting very scared now that they think I'm a suspect."

The back screen door was heard opening and heads turned.

The women saw Hector emerge from the house and watched him walk across the patio. He stopped in front of Hazel but remained on his feet, seemingly uncertain of how to proceed or whether to sit.

"Hazel's told us the whole story of what the cops said to her," Penny told her dad, "and that they now suspect her of murder."

"I know what they said to her but it sounds to me like they just had to ask her some questions to clarify things. I doubt they suspect her."

Directing himself to Hazel, Hector said, "I have to ask you if you have any interest in keeping the store. We might be able to get some money out of it for you… I mean if you want me to wrap it up."

"Please do that," Hazel said. And, with vehemence, she added, "I don't want the damn thing!"

"Fine. Right. Do you know if Alex ever made a will?"

"He did, when we got married. We both made them."

"Good. The bank will need to see Alex's will before we can do anything. It will give you power over his estate. If we don't find a buyer for the store I'd suggest trying to return all the product we can, then trying to find a buyer for the rest of the stock and the fixtures. Oh, and someone to take over the lease."

"Yes, thank you. I'll get the will from my safety deposit box." Hazel's eyes were immediately filled with tears "It was Alex's dream to have that store."

Silence from everyone followed Hazel's softening on her position of not wanting the 'damn thing'.

Hector, who was still standing, looked about before seizing a nearby deck chair and placing it beside his daughter-in-law's. He sat down, looking like he was about to have a father-daughter talk.

"Hazel," he began, "you said that there's an older man in your life that wants to marry you. Who is that?"

"Just someone I know. We aren't involved."

"I understand, but can I ask you the name of this man?"

"Why?"

"I thought we should pass his name along to the police. They should speak to everyone who may have wanted something bad to happen to Alex."

"He wasn't involved. Absolutely not." Hazel was firm.

"But maybe the police should be the ones who determine that."

"No! Just leave it."

Hazel stood up. "I need to use the bathroom," she said, and walked off, escaping the confrontation.

Hector watched her go and, as soon as the house's back door closed behind her, he turned in his chair to face Heather and Penny. "There's a likely reason that Hazel won't say who the mystery suitor is," he said, "because she made it up and doesn't want that to come out."

He proceeded to tell the women about Toby Harner; that Hazel had invited him around to see the new baby, that Toby had gone, and that he had taken things for the baby. Hector concluded with, "And she then told Alex that Toby had visited and wanted to marry her."

"Could it be," Penny said, after her father concluded the history, "that Hazel made up the story to try and make Alex jealous so he'd stick around?"

"It's what I think," said Hector, "and maybe why she invited Toby in the first place – to have a story. But I wonder if she maybe thought there was some truth in it."

Or maybe Hazel just saw Toby as her friend and decided to act without getting Alex's permission, Heather thought. Would it be surprising if Hazel needed to imagine that Toby was in love with her to soothe her ego after dealing with a dirtbag like Alex Callas?

Hector continued, "It must have gotten Alex all riled up because he waited for Toby after work one night and threatened him with a knife. Told him to keep away from

126

Hazel."

"Jesus," Penny said, shaking her head, "I wonder if Hazel knows. It might be another reason why she just wants the whole episode to be water under the bridge. Anyway, I was just wondering, do you want me to be the one to wrap up Alex's business? I know you have a lot on your plate."

"Well… Are you comfortable doing that?"

"Of course. I have a degree in business and I teach it. And I'm off for the summer."

"Right. I just thought you might not have the time to do it, what with your music… But okay, if you're willing. It would be helpful. I'm a bit like Hazel in that I don't want anything to do with the store, although my motives are entirely different. I'm afraid I'd get all sentimental being at the place since I know it was Alex's dream… Oh, and I've been meaning to ask you. The woman that Alex was shacked up with. Do you know anything about her?"

"No; only what Hazel told us about her. She's a college student and a part-time waitress in a pub where Alex liked to go to before he started hanging out at The Sailor's Roost…"

Allowing him to hit on women without being seen, Heather thought. And maybe he then began to hang out at The Sailor's Roost to further his career aspirations.

"So the woman is poor," Penny added.

"Which doesn't mean that she doesn't have contacts that could have loaned Alex money," Hector replied.

"I assume the cops have asked her about all that and rejected the idea."

Once they were alone, Heather asked Penny if Hazel would really have made up the story about Toby Harner.

"Does Toby's version ring true, you mean? Yes. I know Toby and trust him. Hazel thinks that all the men where she works are in love with her. She told me that and that she's the most beautiful woman there. It's obviously self-affirming for her to think that; so something she needs. She and Toby were on friendly terms – he's nice like that, and supportive of his staff – but she could have read his kindness in a personal way. Maybe – if she did – it was Alex who put the idea into her head. He saw everything nice that any man said to Hazel as attempted seduction, so a threat to his interests, and he tried to convince Hazel to treat any man who was nice to her as if they were an enemy and only wanted one thing from her. I heard him say stuff to her along those lines."

"Robbing her of friends because of his insecurity."

"Yes, and maintaining his control. He probably believed that other men were like himself; incapable of seeing women as friends. He always played the expert and Hazel deferred to his judgement. Who knows if she believed what he told her or not? I suppose that she must have understood that Alex was insecure. It would explain why she spun a tale to Alex about Toby wanting to marry her. She knew it would ignite his jealousy. Bloody selfish thing to do, putting Toby in danger like that. That Alex would respond, not with returning to her but with violence toward Toby, was entirely predictable."

Heather had heard that Alex had begun carrying a knife sometime recently and now wondered exactly when that was. It was assumed that Alex had begun carrying a knife because of the company he was keeping, but the thought now crossed Heather's mind that he may have been thinking that he would use it to keep men away from Hazel. Maybe even convey to her what might happen if she looked at another man.

Panel from Heather Bruce's Siren video

The ancient mythic fight for home continued even after men returned from battle. Once there, they had to fight against their wives and their wives' suitors. The suitors of Odysseus's wife Penelope were slaughtered.

A man's aggression towards other men who interact with his wife isn't only an alpha male battle to see who gets to mate with the female. It's an attack on a woman's autonomy and ability to socialize. It tells men that if they approach a married woman that they should be afraid. And it tells a woman that any entertaining of men will lead to violence against the man and possibly her as well.

The thought of a woman's freedom undermines this type of man's self-esteem and he responds with violence because it is a question of dominance in, and ownership of, home.

A wife's fidelity must be ensured by violence – since it is seen as the ultimate crime against home, family, and property – as a sign to others of a man's power and dominance, and of his ability to protect his own home and possession of his wife. And to soothe his ego.

This violence is an unintentional signal of a man's insecurity that exists today among men with a certain mindset and weakness.

Panel from Heather Bruce's Siren video

The Mermaid, as described by men, is a complete inversion to the Siren; as he imagines her. An opposing pole.
The Mermaid is a hybrid Siren. Half human, half fish. The Siren's wings were clipped. As a Mermaid she sank to the bottom of the ocean.
The Mermaid does not lure the sailor to his death. She is not out to kill men. She is not the enemy of home.
She watches human life. Falls in love with a man. Is filled with longing to be in his world to complete herself.
The Mermaid is often pictured sitting on a rock, basking, gazing into her mirror, brushing her hair. Mindless. There to be admired and looked at. If she sings, her song is lovely but not deadly. She does not seduce for evil purposes.
She is longed for by sailors who seek her out and dream of her. She is the ideal of men. She is a virgin who can save a man but still grant him total control.

23.

The pair stood just inside the front doors of The Sailor's Roost, their eyes searching the room. There was a drone of chatter and wallpaper music but nothing at the level one would expect in a bar. The place seemed more like a restaurant. Many of the tables had plates of food on them.

"If I'm going to deal with Alex's finances," Penny had told Heather, back at her parent's house when the two were finally left to themselves, "I need to know where Alex got the money to buy his store."

"Why?" asked Heather.

"Because he may have borrowed it from criminals. And he may have been murdered because of it. Isn't that what the police think? I'm not going to sell the business and then hand over the money to Hazel just for someone to show up at her door and demand it back, and threaten her with violence if she doesn't pay up. If a mobster or money-lender – or whatever you want to call him – murdered my brother then she would be in real danger…"

"Can't you ask Alex's friends?"

"I've been trying to reach his best friend, Dave, but all I've done so far is to leave unanswered messages."

"So you're going to ask Jason Hopkins if he knows who loaned Alex the money to buy his store?"

"Yes. And if he doesn't know, to find out."

"So you think he'll poke around at the bar, asking questions? Unless he's a total fool, he'll figure out that the person who loaned Alex the money may have been his murderer, and he won't want any part in identifying him."

"Well then, what if I ask him to just put out the word that I'm closing up Alex's business and looking for a creditor? In that case, the person will contact me when he hears."

"The guy will be outing himself to call you."

"Outing himself about being the one who loaned Alex money but not that he's a killer. I don't think it's necessarily the case that the money and the murder are connected; or, at least, provable that they are. The guy can just say that he loaned Alex money because they were great friends and he was trying to help a young guy out. It would still be up to the cops to prove that this person was the killer… And you know, it just occurred to me, that if I'm that guy, I keep my name out of it and have my lawyer call and say that Alex and I simply had a business deal."

"Are you going to tell the police what you're up to?"

"Not now. They'll try to talk me out of seeing Hopkins. I'll definitely talk to the cops if I have a name to give them – and hopefully I will. But I'm going to proceed on my own. I'm Alex's sister so people will be more forthcoming with me than with a police detective. If I find out who loaned Alex the money I can protect my family and – best case scenario – also discover who killed Alex."

"And what about your father?"

"You mean, am I going to tell him what I'm doing? Not on your life. He'd worry about me. Plus, I want to spare his feelings if I find out his son was involved in something really bad."

The downstairs bar was surprisingly upscale – not at all the sleazy dive that Heather had imagined: a sort of modern version of a smuggler's den filled with salty criminals and bikers. If Alex Callas had become chummy with a biker gang could it really have been here?

The place was nautically themed, in a cliché way, and in all likelihood intended for downtown hotel staying tourists. She'd heard about the mermaid aquarium behind the bar but hadn't pictured it being as enormous as it actually was. In it, she observed a scantily clad woman, dressed in a pastel mermaid costume, with pink pastel coloured hair, twirling and rolling languidly in the water. Her show was being silently watched by a group of three men perched on stools in front of the bar. A sad group in Heather's opinion.

She wanted to leave, but couldn't, since she was here as Penny's back-up. Looking around, Heather spotted a set of stairs, off to the right and wished that she'd been more aggressive when trying to discourage Penny from coming here. This was where Alex had been murdered and those were the stairs the murderer had crept up. Surely they would trigger some awful feelings.

There was a velvet rope blocking the entrance to the stairs. Heather wondered if it was because the lounge wasn't open at this time of day or if it was being cleaned up. She noted a sign above the stairs that read, *The Mermaid Lounge*.

"Let me talk to the bartender," Penny said decisively – like she had to act quickly before she lost her nerve – and headed off in that direction. Heather followed.

The bartender, a scantily clad young woman with green hair, and dressed in a skimpy mermaid-like costume, turned her attention to Penny and asked if she could get her something.

"Not right now. I'm looking for Jason Hopkins. He told us to drop by. Can you tell me where I can find him?"

"He may be in his…"

"Never mind, there he is," Penny cut in. She had spotted Hopkins slipping under the velvet rope guarding the stairs; a leather laptop bag in one hand and a cellphone in the other.

Hopkins seemed to be entirely self-absorbed and on his way to the front entrance.

Penny strode across the room, to head him off, with Heather scrambling to keep up.

Hopkins only spotted Penny after she'd stopped a couple of metres in front of him, blocking his way. He halted, looking confused, but his reaction changed when Penny said, "Jason."

"Well, well, Ms. Penny Callas," he said, his face brightening into a plastic smile of recognition. "I'm glad to see you took me up on my offer to visit. I'm only sorry the timing isn't better. I'm just on my way to the airport on a business trip."

"I won't keep you then," Penny said. "I was hoping to chat."

Hopkins' smile continued. "I'll be back on Saturday night – late. Why don't you swing by at 10:00, no, make that 11:00 in the evening, and I'll be all yours." If he was curious about why Penny wanted to meet up he didn't show it.

"Oh, lovely. I'm wrapping up my brother's affairs and closing his business. I wanted to talk to you about it."

"Me?" Hopkins appeared to be genuinely surprised. "I…I know anything about his business."

"I'd rather leave the details till we have the time to go over them, but I'm hoping you might be able to point me in the right direction. When it comes to business…"

"Oh, of course. Don't worry dear lady," Hopkins cut in, paternally laying his hand on Penny's arm and gently squeezing it while staring into her eyes. He then looked towards the bar. "Jennie," he called and the young bartender looked his way. "Please give these lovely ladies whatever they want – on the house." Turning back towards Penny he said, "I'm sorry. I have to rush off now, but I look forward to getting to know you – to knowing the two of you I should say – in a more relaxed setting." There was a subtle but flirtatious tone to his voice.

The women stood aside and watched Hopkins go as he rushed away.

"It's okay Jennie, we're leaving," Penny called to the bartender who waved her acknowledgement. "Shall we?" she said to Heather, pointing towards the door.

"Yes," Heather said. As they started off she added, "It sounds like he wants to turn any meeting with him into a social event." Having noted the helpless female tone in her friend's manner when Penny had been speaking to the bar owner about needing his help, she added, "What was that about needing some direction when it comes to business?"

"It's nonsense is what it is. I have no interest in his business judgements. I just wanted to appeal to his ego so that he would agree to talk about Alex's business."

A common and proven method of seduction, Heather thought: play to a man's ego. A siren's call to manipulate a man. Play to this sort of guy's sexist ideas: in this case that women aren't too bright. But she didn't say so.

Panel from Heather Bruce's Siren video

There is still an element of danger for a man from the Mermaid however. A threat to his essential nomadism.

If a man unites with a Mermaid, giving way to temptation and love, and embraces her, she may pull him down to **her home** at the bottom of the ocean, unintentionally killing him with her love. Smothering him with it. Stopping his breath. Ending his mobility. The Mermaid is described in a way to appeal to men's fantasies but it still reflects a fear of women. Mermaid myth also reflects gender power. Men are entitled, goes the myth. They are admired. Women will follow them. It is now only a man's home and family that matters; meaning one where he is in control.

Sailors all over the world scanned the seas for Mermaids and myths about them spread; including to the Maritimes after Sir Richard Whitbourne said he'd spotted one in St. John's harbour, perhaps to lure colonists to the area.

1943

Jimmy Sherman took another swig from the bottle of Canadian Club Whisky he'd swiped from the store in Summerside on a trip into town with his dad. He'd hidden it in the back of his sock and underwear drawer with this occasion in mind.

Jimmy climbed up onto the large flat rock on the south side of the pond. It was an ideal spot for sunbathing, given its size and smoothness, but he'd only ever used it as a diving board. The drop off was dramatic since the rock protruded far out into the pond to a point where the black and still water was a good eight feet deep.

He took another drink from the bottle and grimaced, beginning to feel the effects of the warm, bitter liquid.

Jimmy had been been thinking about this day since the trip to Toronto at the end of the school term. He was an exceptional artist his teacher Mr. Skelton had said: someone with a future. Skelton had taken Jimmy with him to Toronto, on the train, when he made his annual summer trip back to his family's home. He said it would inspire and help Jimmy's career as an artist for him to see the masterworks at the Ontario provincial art gallery. Once there, Skelton had looked on approvingly as he watched Jimmy study the art. There was even one work that Jimmy had twice returned to and stared at.

Jimmy sat down on the rock and stretched his legs out in front of him.

When he'd passed near Ellen Comer in the grocery store, earlier that day, she'd avoided looking at him. She stepped back when he sidled up beside her, repulsion showing on her face; but Jimmy didn't get it. The mermaid was playing cat and mouse, he told himself.

Jimmy had then drifted away from his father, while keeping an eye on Ellen, and when he spotted another opportunity – a moment when she was alone and Larry wouldn't hear what he said – Jimmy approached and whispered, "I'll be at the pond at 2:30. I expect to see you there. It'll be fun." His smirk was back.

Ellen scowled hatred back at him.

Jimmy screwed the cap onto the whisky bottle then sat it down on the rock, as carefully as possible. It was still half full.

He looked off to his left, to the trail that meandered through the bush beside the creek; it ran all the way to Martin's west field.

The path was the route the mermaid would take on her trip to the pond. Of course she'd come, Jimmy thought. He imagined how she'd look walking toward him. She was the most beautiful girl he had ever seen.

Fumbling slightly from the drink he undid the buttons of his shirt before removing it and laying it out on the rock, as if spreading a blanket.

Jimmy sat and leaned forward to remove his shoes and socks. A mild and brief wave of nausea swept through him with the motion. He was quick to sit back up.

Next came the pants. Jimmy got himself up on his feet, swaying with the effort. He undid his belt and slid the pants down to his ankles. He extracted his right foot but when he tried to do the same with his left foot it caught hold and wouldn't come loose. He stepped on his pants with his right foot to hold them down so that he could pry his left foot free.

And that's when he saw the mermaid, in a summer dress, walking along the trail, heading in his direction.

Jimmy was mesmerized.

He tugged his left foot furiously upward, cursing his pants. With a mighty effort, Jimmy freed his foot, but he was off balance. He lurched and then teetered, knocking the bottle of whisky into the water before following it in.

Jimmy got his head above the water and took a deep breath. He dove down. He found and scooped up the whisky bottle off the bottom of the pond. He planted his feet on the bottom to push himself upwards, but when he did so he discovered that one foot had became caught by something. He tried to tug it free to no effect. He tried again and again with panic setting in. It was like a powerful hand had taken hold of his foot and wouldn't let him move.

24.

Hugh sat in the easy chair in the living room, headphones on, listening to music, and thinking about how little he knew about Ellen Comer.

Before commencing, he self-consciously glanced towards the bedroom door to ensure that Heather wouldn't know what he was up to: invading the privacy of a woman who wished to be left alone.

Hugh retrieved his laptop and, after propping it on his knee, continued his earlier research into the life of Eleanor Comer (nee Lange), born in Moncton. He searched Ellen's name in the city where she'd lived when she was young.

An old news item, that he stumbled upon, upended everything he thought that he knew about the old woman he'd been dealing with in Mount Pleasant.

Research made her more mysterious rather than less.

Eleanor Lange, 'Ellen', as she was known, had drowned at Parlee Beach in Shediac, New Brunswick when she was fourteen years old!

The article gave the names of the dead girl's parents so Hugh returned to the ancestry site he'd been using and looked them up. The couple's dead daughter had the exact same name, birthplace, and date of birth, as the woman who had married Lawrence (Larry) Comer in Summerside, PEI, four years later.

Hugh stared at the computer screen, and considered the matter. In a short time he became annoyed with himself. There was a flaw in one of the stories Ellen had told him. Why hadn't he seen it?

He recalled her saying that his great-grandmother Louise would welcome Acadian storytellers and singers into her home. Ellen had said something like, 'us Acadians' or, 'we Acadians'... But Lange wasn't an Acadian name. It was of German derivation, as was her mother's maiden name: Bauer. And a bit of further research revealed that Ellen's husband, Lawrence Comer, wasn't Acadian either.

But his Ellen – the one who didn't want her picture taken – **was** Acadian. And she shouldn't have been.

Hugh continued his online search of Eleanor Lange and found a newspaper story about her death. It said that she was in the ocean, laughing and calling to her friends when they saw her suddenly get dragged under the waves. The police told the newspaper that the group of girls had gone into the water immediately after a large storm and there had to have been a strong undertow dragging water back into the ocean from the still high waves breaking on the shore. "It was like she was pulled under by an invisible hand" the police spokesman said.

Ellen – his Ellen – had stolen the dead girl's identity. Had they been friends? Enemies? Had the two girls been together at the beach or was Eleanor's death just an event that Ellen knew about?

Had Ellen been hiding in Mount Pleasant for some reason? Since she'd already adopted a false name by the time she was married in Summerside at age eighteen, she may have been hiding from something that had happened in New Brunswick – or from someone.

Hugh searched Ellen's daughter Leona's birth certificate and discovered that Ellen wasn't her birth mother. It explained why his grandfather had referred to the girl as 'Larry's daughter'. But the facts of her parentage suggested nothing to him about Ellen's true identity.

The big questions about Ellen, Hugh decided, were these: Where did she come from and who was she? The men of Mount Pleasant had been right, it was like she'd been hauled out of the water by Larry Comer.

25. Wednesday

Heather had initially been surprised at the ugly online response to her interview with CBC News even though she knew – well before the interview and article – that threats were becoming a common response from some anti-feminist men against any woman who publicly used her voice in a critical way, or to comment on any subject these men considered their own.

As a result of that, Heather had an image of the guys responsible for the invective. They were likely young men, isolated, going nowhere. They were outraged about their own social and political impotence and wanted to restore the world to the old status quo, where men ruled and women knew their place. They needed to vent, and to feel powerful and masculine. They posed as tough guys, warriors in a battle for their own relevance and entitlement, pitted against people like Heather who were supposedly stealing their privilege and places in life. These women had to shut up. Taking away their voice is a means to enforce men's power and control; a restoration of the masculinity that the men thought had been taken from them by women.

On the other hand, it had been heartening to read the many comments that attacked the attackers and called them out for their misogyny.

Heather didn't think that the response to the CBC article was anything other than nasty words.

She was sitting at the kitchen table with a mug of coffee in front of her when she opened an envelope that had arrived in the mail. Inside the envelope was an 8X10 page of printer paper. Scrawled on it, in large letters, were the words:

Cancel your man hating show or you will die.

Heather dropped the paper onto the kitchen table, stood up and backed away. She rubbed her hand against her hip as if trying to erase the filth of the letter.

She called Hugh.

"Look at that," she said, pointing to the table, when he walked into the room, "that…thing."

He picked up the paper, read the line scrawled on it.

"Gutless coward," he said, setting the paper back on the table while shaking his head.

Heather said, "I thought the crap those people were spewing online was just hot air...but this. This is of a different nature than basement wankers who hate women and want to sound off against them."

"Is it?"

"Of course. This is an actual threat of violence."

Hugh looked uncomfortable. He spoke cautiously, in a way meant to reassure Heather – and calm her fears – without discounting the validity of those fears. "There was stuff in the comments after the CBC article, from men, that said things along these lines. Somebody called your show a 'volley of war' I think the phrase was, and another said that..."

"But this is a direct threat!"

"Yes, that's true... I'm not saying that this isn't shocking or that you shouldn't be upset, but I'm thinking that whoever did this might just be trying to scare you enough to stop the exhibition without actually..."

"But who might also be someone who doesn't know the difference between empty threats and real actions."

Hugh picked up an envelope off the table. "Is this what it came in?"

"Yes."

He studied the postmark. "This was sent from Regina."

Heather stepped forward and snatched the envelope away, to look for herself. She confirmed the source of the letter before remembering that it, like the letter, had been touched by the hands of the person who sent it, and she threw the envelope on the table. "I'm not sure that makes a difference," she said. "Someone could easily fly here from Regina."

"Are you going to call the police about this? I'd say that you should, if you think there's any chance that it's a genuine threat – but, of course, it's your decision."

"I will, and I have to talk to my group about it too. We're all potential targets. Everyone involved in the Siren exhibition needs to know about any threats, and any decision about what to do – like whether to make a public statement or not – should be made as a group. I doubt that anyone will want to cancel the exhibition but everyone needs to have their say. I think that, by now, all the artists have seen the original article and read the comments, and no one has come forward to suggest that we not go ahead. I hope they'll all still feel the same after they hear about this poison letter."

"So, is there a change in today's plans?"

"What? No. I'll make some calls tonight and set up a group meeting at the studio – or maybe a conference call – hopefully for tomorrow."

A short time later, as they were leaving the house on their planned outing, Heather said, "Gina took screenshots of the original comments and suggested we do something with them as a part of the exhibition. I'll have to give her this page – after I show it to the police – to add to her collection. I think it should be included in any stand alone piece. I've already been coming up with some potential text for it."

Panel from Heather Bruce's Siren video

A prominent influence on the young Jean Baudrillard was the guru of the television age, Marshall McLuhan. McLuhan's position was anti-feminist, as is Baudrillard's.
Both he and Baudrillard argue that women's lack of power is, in reality, their strength in a world of mediated reality.
How self-serving for men to argue that real world power does not shape mediated reality but only vice versa.
But while Baudrillard prefers the (Siren) seducer as an ideal, McLuhan – that good Catholic boy – opted for the (Mermaid) wife. A woman's place is in the home; influencing her family. (Another instance of how even intellectual men want to control women's voices.) No need to seek more power in the world, McLuhan said, women have all the power they need.
"Women are experts at it [wielding power through role playing] because their role through the ages has been to submerge the private self and submit. That gives them a tremendous advantage in the TV age..." (McLuhan)
It is the wife at home who actually has all the power, he said.
"The Mafia is run by godmothers – not by godfathers." (McLuhan)

143

26

Heather, Penny and Hugh drove north from Charlottetown, heading in the direction of the beach. The canoe that Penny used, when doing her sound recordings, was strapped to the car's roof racks.

The trip was part of Penny's sound art project for *Sirens' Island*, the part of her work that would consist of recordings of the ocean in various locations around PEI. The beach had been added to her itinerary after Heather mentioned that she and Hugh planned to drive there because Hugh's family had a connection to the place and he was anxious to visit it.

Heather was happy for the reprieve from the drama of the last few days – and especially that morning. On the drive north she'd convinced herself that the threatening letter she'd just received was a sign of someone's impotence, so not an actual threat of impending violence, and it relieved her sense of imminent danger.

It occurred to her that Penny – whose life had been taken over by the murder of her brother – would also benefit from the trip. It would provide a break from what she'd been going through and get her thinking again about her recordings; and hopefully becoming distracted by them.

Heather was pleased to see how animated and engaged Penny was when explaining how her recording equipment worked.

Penny was not unaware of the potential mental health benefit of the trip either. Like Heather and Hugh, she'd turned her cell phone off, then stashed the three devices in the glove compartment. Penny had promised herself that she would refuse to give in to the temptation to turn hers back on and check for messages.

As they drove through the national park, towards the beach, Heather turned her head to look at Hugh in the back seat. Like a kid, his face was crammed up to the window, taking in his surroundings, clearly relishing the act of following a route that some of his ancestors had often taken.

"So Hugh, did I understand Heather correctly?" Penny asked. "I think she said that your ancestors used to visit this beach."

"Yes. My great-grandparents had a farm near here – well sort of – and my great-grandmother would come here with her friends and all of their kids."

"And this is your first visit to the beach?"

"Yes. My parents never brought us to PEI and the only relatives I still have here are very distant ones."

"So your family moved from PEI to Toronto."

"Just my father's family. They first went to Montreal. My parents moved us a few times then settled on Toronto – where my mother's family lives."

"So your family, on your father's side, is still in Montreal then?"

"Just immediate family. Most of the extended family also left PEI over time, but scattered all over Canada."

"Heather said that you're really getting into studying your PEI ancestry. Is it just your paternal side you're looking into?"

"At this point. My father died when I was seventeen and I was left with this profound sense of…I don't know what to call it…loneliness, I suppose. It's like an absence that needs to be filled."

Heather cocked her head to listen more closely to what Hugh was saying. She was surprised by his revelation. He'd never told her that losing his father had led to his obsession with the past of his paternal line. It now made more sense to her.

"Sorry about your father," Penny said. "I didn't realize. I thought you said once that your parents lived in Toronto."

"My step-father and my mother. She re-married when I was nineteen. It was after I'd moved to Montreal, for university, and to spend time with my grandfather. I don't actually know the man at all well."

"And you moved here after university. Is you grandfather still alive?"

"Yes. My sister moved to Montreal even before I did. She urged me to move out here because she knew it was something I wanted to do more than anything. I know there's likely an element of her taking care of her little brother, and sacrificing her freedom for the family, but she said that she'd gotten into the habit of visiting our grandfather and planned to continue to do so regardless of what I did. She told me to call him on the phone every week, just to keep in touch – and I do – although it's sort of fifty-fifty whether he knows who he's talking to. When we visit in person he always recognizes our faces but sometimes thinks we're his brother and sister. When it's our voices on the phone he hasn't a clue."

The conversation fell off.

It was Heather who broke the silence. "You know Penny, there's something about this beach that pertains to your project. There's a sirens' island aspect to it. An historical moment in sirens' island history." She laughed lightly. "And Hugh has pictures of it that he might let you use. He told me that the women his great-grandma hung out with would come here with their kids during World War 2. They probably did it every year, but during the war a lot of men were away so apparently the women developed a stronger support network."

"I spoke to an old woman who said that they formed an island colony, the way birds do," Hugh added.

"A siren's island colony," added Heather.

"I'll have to look at your pictures then – if that's okay," Penny said. "I don't know if Heather has told you Hugh, but I plan to record women from different parts of the island. The idea of sirens suggested to me that I could overlay women's voices talking about different things so it would be like a musical composition, like a sirens' song, bringing out the variety and beauty of the voices. And I also want to get some women's stories recorded because their tales and myths are also part of our culture; of everyone's history and culture for that matter. Silencing women and only listening to men's stories and voices denies our culture and hurts us all. When it comes time to record women it sounds like your old lady might make a great subject – if she's willing."

Nearing the beach, people could be seen moving towards the water, drawn by it, exemplifying the magnetic pull of the sea that Melville talks about in the opening to *Moby Dick*.

Some of the walkers that the threesome drove past were

wearing light jackets. Although it was the start of summer holidays, the temperatures were still cool in the mornings: perfect for walking. By mid-day, it might get up to thirty celsius or higher, and when it did the strolling pedestrians disappeared and the beach bunnies emerged.

With a little navigational assistance from her passengers, Penny found the parking lot and then a launch site for her canoe.

The three friends unloaded the boat from the roof rack but left the bag of picnic things they'd brought on the back seat. Sandwiches. A bottle of wine. Plastic wine glasses. They would be for later.

The canoe was taken to the water's edge and Heather stayed with it while Hugh helped to carry Penny's recording equipment from the car.

Penny went to work setting up her equipment in the middle of the canoe, saying little. During the car ride, she'd explained to her friends what a hydrophone was, how it worked, and the difference between recording on land and under the waves because of the water's increased density.

With her equipment eventually in place, Penny situated herself behind it.

Hugh – at the back end of the boat – gently pushed it into the water, and climbed in as it slid forward.

As her friends paddled, Penny prepared to drop her hydrophone into the ocean when they reached a sufficient depth.

As they travelled, the three silently listened to the water rhythmically swishing from the paddles.

Having gone out deep enough for Penny's purposes, Hugh angled the canoe's path eastward, aiming it towards a quieter recording spot, away from the beach. Off to the right the three could see kids playing in the sand and couples strolling hand in hand. After the beach ended, the view consisted solely of grassy dunes.

It was absolutely perfect on the water, fresh and serene.

At that exact moment of tranquility the first rifle crack echoed across the bay.

A chunk from the bow of the fibreglass canoe flew off in

the direction of open ocean. Heather ceased paddling, baffled about why a piece of the canoe had suddenly taken flight.

Then, in rapid succession, came two more shots.

"That's gunshots!" screamed Penny. "Bail!" She dove over the side of the canoe, toward open sea.

Heather half stood, planning to follow suit. She had one hand on the edge of the boat and was leaning forward.

At that exact moment, Hugh, keeping low, rolled out of the canoe to his left. And his weight forced that side of the boat down to the water level.

Heather violently pitched downward. Still holding tightly to the side of the canoe, her forehead crashed against the side of the canoe as it forcefully bobbed back upwards. Unconscious, she crumpled and slid lifelessly into the water, head first.

A fourth bullet tore through the beach side of the canoe. Then all was silent.

On the beach, kids were snatched up. People yelled. Fingers pointed out to sea. Or to the dunes beyond the beach where the shots had emanated from. The shooter had apparently found cover there and fired at the canoe when it was directly in front of them.

Under the water, Hugh twisted, searching out his companions. He discerned the blur of Penny beneath him, swimming upwards.

He did the same, desperate for air. His eyes burned. When he broke the water surface he ran the back of a hand against them, to little effect. He looked about. Twisting in a complete 360. Where was Heather? He shouted her name.

He swam ahead. To the spot where Heather must have gone into the water. Diving, Hugh tried to look about but it was just painful blackness. Closing his eyes, he reached ahead, waving his arms from side to side, like antennae. Searching. But still nothing.

When he emerged from the ocean, Hugh saw Penny treading water.

"I don't see Heather!" she shouted.

The pair gulped in deep buckets of air, preparing to dive again when suddenly, halfway between them, Heather shot out of the water, like the ocean had spit her out, or some force had thrown her upwards.

Hugh reached her first. Heather's eyes were closed and she was still unconscious.

Hugh cupped a hand under her chin, and held her face above the water. Then came a welcome, loud, and surprising inhalation.

Penny called Heather's name and coaxed her to wake up.

Heather did, looking languidly and confusedly about.

Hugh's eyes, meanwhile, sought out the canoe. It had drifted off and was sinking.

Let it go, he thought. There were no gunshots. No need to hide behind it.

"We have to get her to shore," Penny said.

"Right," Hugh agreed.

He and Penny each placed a hand under one of Heather's arms and they set off.

Ahead of them, two people could be seen running through the shallow water near shore. They plunged forward, where the water deepened, and began swimming to the rescue.

27

"They said it's because of a muscular spasm of the larynx," Heather explained to Hugh.

She was sitting on an ER bed, her legs dangling over the side, with Hugh sitting on a chair in front of her, reaching up and holding her hand.

"Your airway automatically closes when the first bit of water enters the trachea," Heather continued. "It makes me think of the Nirvana album cover with the baby swimming underwater. It's instinctive."

"You just shot up out of the water like a cork," Hugh said, repeating a story he'd already told Heather twice before; the first time being in the ambulance. "I'll never forget it."

"The doctor looked dubious when I told him," Heather said, "but he didn't say it was impossible. Well, I mean, he can't can he?"

The pair had already been interviewed by the police, but individually because they'd been separated at the hospital after a paramedic noted that Hugh was in shock.

Now, two hours later, reunited, they were waiting for the go ahead for Heather to leave.

"I started to tell a policewoman about the threatening letter you got but she cut me off," Hugh said. "She already knew about it."

"Of course. And I also told her about the article and the vicious comments. She wants the letter and its envelope. And she said that she'll talk to CBC and see if they have a record of any comments that the moderator deleted for being threatening – I mean if there were any… Have you seen Penny?"

"Not since the beach. She said she was going to look into getting her recording equipment back and that she'd drive herself here after that. She gave me our phones before we left in the ambulance though, so I'll call her."

As Hugh reached into a pocket with his free hand he asked Heather if she'd told Penny about the threatening letter.

"I didn't have a chance."

"Should I tell her to be on the alert?"

"I assume the person with the gun was aiming for me…but okay, warn her, Penny is part of the collective and we were all threatened online. You know, now that I think about it, it's possible that Penny was the target. Maybe it's unlikely, but she did make it clear to the owner of The Sailor's Roost that she has questions about her brother's business affairs. If Jason Hopkins has already mentioned that to people in the bar, then every one who hangs out there may know about it by now. The person who killed Alex might figure that there's something in his files that will identify him and wants to keep Penny from finding it."

"Did you mention to the police what she's doing?"

"No. I want to talk to her first. She told me she doesn't want them to know about her plans to visit the bar and I don't want to betray her confidence. But I plan to do everything I can to convince her to speak to them."

"But what if she finds out something that she thinks might lead to Alex's killer?"

"In that case, she'll talk to them. Her aim is to keep her sister-in-law and nephew safe. She thinks she can get further on her own. She doesn't want to get the police involved unless she finds out who loaned her brother money."

"So at this point we don't even know who was being targeted today," Hugh said, summing up the obvious, then left it at that. When he was laying down, after being diagnosed in shock, he'd considered the possibility that the bullets could have been meant for him – he'd been asking around about a murder – but he soon talked himself out of the idea. He couldn't see how anyone could take his casual questions about a sixty-year-old murder as a threat to them. He had zero evidence against anyone.

He phoned Penny and got no answer. He left a message asking her to call him and begging her to please keep her head up since there was no way of knowing who had fired the shots at them or why. Or who was the target.

A nurse walked into the curtained off bedroom and smiled at Heather. "The doctor gave you the all clear to go home. Remember what I told you," he said to Hugh, "there's no need to wake Heather up at regular intervals. That advice on concussions is no longer accepted protocol." To Heather he added, "And no alcohol!"

"Just shoot me."

Back home, Heather indicated that she wasn't experiencing any of the possible symptoms she'd been warned about: dizziness, headache, nausea.

The pair ate dinner and had just moved into the living room when there was a knock at their front door.

Hugh went to answer it and soon returned with Penny trailing behind him.

On spotting Heather, starting to stand, Penny rushed to Heather's side saying, "Np, no, don't get up." She sat down on the couch, and took Heather's hand. "How are you?" she asked.

After being assured by Heather that she was doing well, Penny said, "I just spoke to the cops. They came to my place. They told me you received a threatening letter this morning. You didn't say anything…"

"I planned to, on the drive home. My idea was to set up a meeting with the collective, probably for tomorrow. I didn't think anyone would show up here anytime soon – and likely never. The letter was postmarked Regina."

"I probably would have agreed with you – this morning. But not now. Don't worry about the meeting, I'll set up a conference call. I'd like to get my hands on the bastard…"

"Me too. Hopefully the police will sort it out. They said they'd talk to the CBC since the shooter may have been one of the online losers who threatened me – us – about the siren exhibition."

"It's hard to imagine that anyone would go so far as to kill people over an art exhibition."

"Can you grab that letter?" Heather said to Hugh, pointing to the desk on the other side of the room, "and give it to Penny. But just hold it by the corners in case there are fingerprints on it. We've likely already mucked it up."

Hugh retrieved the piece of paper and passed it along.

"Jesus," Penny said after reading it "There's some real sickos out there. Well, if the person with the rifle was this guy, I guess we both could have been targets."

"Right," Heather said. She'd overheard Hugh when he'd left the phone message for Penny. He'd asked her to be careful since there was no indication of who the bullets were meant for. So, without saying so, he had put it out there that Penny may have been the target of the shooter because of her visit to The Sailor's Roost. It seemed however, that Penny had decided – even before seeing the letter – that the gunshots had definitely come from someone upset about the siren exhibition. It likely meant that she would continue with her insistence on a late night visit with Jason Hopkins. The woman did not seem to realize her own vulnerability.

Changing the subject, Hugh said to Penny, "Oh, did you get your equipment back?"

"Not yet, but I hope to. I found an amateur diver who'll head out there in the morning and give it a go. He's a little dubious about the prospect."

"Is everything waterproof?"

"The hydrophone is, of course, but I'm not sure how safe the recorder is. It's in a waterproof case though, so hopefully it's fine… I waterproof everything. The first rule of underwater recording."

"Well we weren't in very deep water," Heather said. "Maybe that'll help the diver to locate everything."

Panel from Heather Bruce's Siren video

Hans Christian Anderson's fairy-tale, *The Little Mermaid* is a horrifying, and at times reactionary, moral fable for children.
In it, the Mermaid is a loving stalker and voyeur. She falls in love with a handsome prince. Saves him from drowning. Then longs to be with him in the human world. She leaves her home, hoping for a new, human one.
She comes to understand that only the love of a man – and marriage to him – can give her a soul and for that she sacrifices all. She gives up her voice, home, and mobility.
For the Mermaid, to walk on human legs is to experience excruciating pain with every step, yet she dances for the prince's pleasure.
Her life is constant agony in many ways.
She comes to realize that she can never have the man she loves, no matter what she does. He loves another woman, who he thinks is the Mermaid who saved his life, and the real Mermaid lacks the voice to tell him it was her. Fantasy will always supersede reality.
The real Mermaid will die soon – when the prince marries – and she will disappear forever.

28

At 9:00 o'clock that evening, Hugh's cellphone rang. He answered it and heard a woman tentatively say, "Hello, Hugh?"

"Yes." He recognized the voice but couldn't immediately place it.

"This is Matilda Eades, Jack's daughter. You were here on…a couple of days ago."

"Yes, Matilda, hi" Hugh said cheerily.

"I have some really sad news. My father died this afternoon…"

"Oh my God."

"He was out for his daily walk and was run over by a hit and run driver."

"Jes… I'm sorry."

"Thank you."

"It's shocking."

"Yes. I'm devastated…" Matilda was struggling to control her emotions, so Hugh waited. She continued, "The reason I'm calling you is because last night my…Jack…told me that he was going to phone you today because he had something he wanted to tell you about that concerned your grandparents…no, your great-grandparents. He said it was important and that you deserved to know it. He even left a piece of paper with your name and number on it by the phone. He didn't speak to you last night by any chance did he?"

"No, only on Monday."

"Then I'm sorry. I don't know what Dad was going to talk to you about. I hope you do."

"I don't. We spent most of our time looking at an old photo album and hearing his stories about the past. Apart from that though, we did talk about the death of an aviator behind my great-grandparent's farm in 1943. There were rumours about who was involved – including people in my family – but the inquest came up with no names. Jack was one of the boys who found the body of the dead man and I had the impression he had some ideas about who the murderer was but he didn't say so... Did he give you any idea of what he wanted to tell me, apart from saying that it was important?"

"No, I'm sorry. It was none of my business. I always figured that if he wanted me to know about something he would tell me."

Hugh asked about the funeral home where Jack would be laying, and promised to visit.

After ending the call, Hugh walked into the living room. Heather was no longer on the couch.

He found her dozing on the bed in their bedroom, on top of the covers. He stood beside the bed watching her sleep and thought about all she'd gone through already that day. His feelings were overwhelming. He'd almost lost her. The thought of that was unbearable. Life could be so bloody short and uncertain.

Returning to the living room, Hugh sat on the couch for a long time, engaged with the question of what Jack had been planning to tell him. It had to have been something regarding the death of the aviator in 1943 and the rumours involving his family's involvement. It was something he 'deserved' to know, so what else could it have been about?

If Jack had known – or strongly suspected – who was responsible for the murder, and why, that information was now lost and the identity of the murderer would forever remain a mystery.

Eventually, Hugh picked up his phone, checked the time, and set the alarm to vibrate. Post-concussion protocol may no longer be to wake the sufferer up at regular intervals throughout the night but that didn't mean he couldn't wake himself up and check on Heather.

29. Thursday

"Of course I'm coming to the funeral home," Heather told Hugh. "That poor man."

As she got up from the kitchen table, where they'd been having breakfast, and put her dirty dishes in the sink, Heather said, "I have to phone in to our conference call."

She walked into the bedroom and closed the door.

After doing the dishes, Hugh went to the living room, sat on the couch, and opened his laptop.

His curiosity about Ellen Comer was like an itch that he couldn't ignore, no matter how much he told himself to respect her privacy. He set to work scratching.

Over the next hour he made no headway in his effort to discover the actual identity of the woman he knew as Ellen Comer, the mermaid, and he had no idea of how to proceed.

The real Eleanor Lange was from Moncton and drowned at Parlee Beach when she was fourteen. The beach is a fifteen to twenty minute drive from Moncton and is one of the places that people from the city travel to on hot summer days; especially families with kids, and groups of college students.

Hugh suspected that his Ellen had, originally, also come from Moncton. It would explain how she had settled on Lange's name for her new identity. The girls may have even known each other (although he now had no idea of how old his Ellen actually was).

He eventually found a second news story about the drowning – a follow up to the one he'd already seen – but there was nothing of consequence in it that he didn't already know. It unfortunately didn't include the names of Eleanor Lange's friends who were at the beach that day.

Hugh unsuccessfully searched for any mention of missing children or adults, both in New Brunswick and PEI during the approximately four year span between the death of Eleanor Lange and his Ellen's marriage. Nothing. His Ellen had left home in her late teens – assuming she had taken the identity of a girl who was the same age as her – and that was when she had taken Eleanor's identity. But why had she done so?

In spite of her recent experiences, Heather was shocked by the messages that had been posted on the art collective's Facebook page. She'd forgotten about the thing's existence. The commentary was vile. There were no overt threats, but they were there, just veiled.

When Penny set up the conference call she had told each collective member, individually, about the events of the previous day, when she, Heather, and Hugh, had been shot at. And she'd described the threatening, poison letter that Heather had received.

After kicking off the meeting, by making everyone aware of the messages that had been posted on Facebook, Penny made it abundantly clear that they all might be in danger.

After several inquiries about Heather's condition, the group came to a consensus that the threat wouldn't deter them from staging the siren exhibition. The poison letter vividly demonstrated an importance to the show that wasn't just about analysis or personal expression. To continue on with the exhibition was an insistence that women – in the face of attempts to silence them – exercise their right to speak, to be creative, and to tell their stories. When women could be murdered for speaking, the stakes were high, and the need to change attitudes was significant. They couldn't let the man who'd threatened them win!

"Are the police investigating?" Myrna asked Heather.

Heather told the group about her conversation with the officer at the hospital, concluding by saying, "She said they were going to approach CBC about any comments that might have been taken down by a moderator."

Katarina said, "I'm wondering, Heather, what do you think about getting in touch with the CBC reporter who did the online article about the exhibition and bringing her up to date? It could lead to another story."

"I'd be happy to ask her, but at this point we don't know…" Heather said. She hesitated, uncertain about how to proceed without betraying something Penny had told her in confidence.

Penny understood. She said, "We aren't certain at this point that the shooting is connected to the letter. It's probably best to hold off until we are sure so that any future article can not only cover the threats that women using their voices might receive, but also the extent that those making the threats may go to."

There were some tentatively stated objections until Penny explained that she was engaged in closing up her brother's business affairs and it may have spooked his murderer. "Maybe there's something in Alex's business records that someone doesn't want me to discover and the gunshots were meant for me. After all, we went to the beach in my car so I was the one who was followed there. We – the collective I mean – could be accused of being alarmists if we go to the press and say that we were attacked and it turns out the incident had nothing to do with the exhibition."

There was a tentative enquiry about exactly what Penny was looking into but Katarina cut it short. "That has nothing to do with the collective. It's Penny's business. Of course you're right then Heather. You need to hold off going to the press, or releasing a statement, until this ugly business plays itself out and we know more. And hopefully, who was responsible for the shocking events of yesterday is in jail."

The group quickly agreed that they'd take a wait and see attitude before going public about the threats.

Panel from Heather Bruce's Siren video

The Little Mermaid – in Anderson's tale – is told that if she kills the prince she will become a Mermaid once again, and live under the sea. But the Mermaid refuses this path; of killing, like a Siren does.
So she dies. But she does not disappear. She becomes a spirit. She learns that if she lives a life of good deeds for three hundred years that she will gain a soul. A lesson for all little girls perhaps. They have two options in life: to be a murderous Siren or to be a good Mermaid and live forever.
I do not criticize the little Mermaid for her choice.
She refuses to be a murderer and instead honours love.
She refuses to kill the man she loves to save herself. It is laudable, even though it can be read as reactionary.

30.

Hazel took a knife from the kitchen drawer and walked into the living room. She knelt in front of one of the power outlets: the one that Alex had disconnected. He'd capped the ends of the three wires inside and wrapped them with electrical tape.

Hazel loosened the screw that held the plastic faceplate and removed it. After gingerly extracting her safety deposit box key, she reattached the faceplate and returned the knife to the cutlery drawer.

Forty-five minutes later Hazel sat in a room at the local bank branch, alone at a table – Damian asleep in a stroller by her side – and opened the box in front of her.

She carefully removed the photographs of her parents, taken in the Channel Islands where she'd grown up, and the bit of jewellery that had come to her after her mother's death.

She avoided disturbing the handgun that was wrapped in a plastic baggy.

Hazel had been shocked to find it the previous month. She'd gone to the bank to retrieve one of her mother's rings to sell. She needed the money. Hazel hadn't seen Alex in a month and he wasn't answering her calls so she had no choice.

Her visit that day was the first she'd made in a year; since around the time that Alex began to use the box. He told her that, henceforth, if she needed anything from it that he would retrieve it (even though the box was hers). And Hazel had complied, never asking Alex even once why he took the key and headed to the bank every month.

Hazel didn't understand why Alex had bought the handgun. If he was afraid of his store being robbed then why did he leave the gun at the bank rather than keep it under the store's front counter? She hoped that the gun – like the knife he'd taken to carrying since he made new friends – wasn't an indication that he might get into some tricky situations.

The more stunning discovery that Hazel made that day was the money. Wads of it inside multiple, clear, plastic food storage bags!

That night she had sat in her living room, after the baby was put to sleep, and soberly considered the possible sources of the cash, legal and illegal, and what she should do about the find.

Her assumption – since Alex had told her that the money to buy his store was his own and not a loan – was that the start-up money had to have come from his girlfriend.

But what about the money in the safety deposit box? Where did it come from and why hadn't Alex deposited it in his bank account?

The likeliest reason, she decided, was that the money came from his store. It had to be doing well. If Alex was selling some product 'under the table' for cash, to avoid paying taxes – like she'd heard some Canadian businesses do – then he wouldn't want to deposit the money in his bank account because if the store was audited he'd be found out.

It was the best answer to her questions she could come up with.

During her ruminations the shock and fear of finding the money had gradually given way to intense anger. While she'd been struggling with money, since the weeks before Damian's birth – and especially after – Alex had been sitting on tons of cash and given her nothing.

It made her furious! Once again she was faced with her ambivalence when it came to Alex. She loved him more than herself, and would do anything to have him back, but sometimes she felt an overwhelming hatred towards him and a desire to strangle him and be free.

She didn't mention to Alex that she knew about the money.

When the police and Alex's family had questioned her earlier this week, Hazel had told them nothing. And why should she? The money was hers now and she deserved it.

She would take what she needed and keep some of the cash as 'escape money' – a phrase she'd heard her mother use in a half-joking way to refer to an emergency fund.

Hazel extracted $500, locked the box, and left it on the table for bank staff to put away.

She and the baby then headed for the grocery store.

31

That morning, Penny had been exhausted from the events of the day before and slept late as a result.

She'd gotten up, prepared herself a cup of coffee, and dialed in to the art collective's conference call.

The result was that almost another hour had gone by before she got around to listening to the message her father had left at 7:00 a.m. that morning. In it, Hector asked if she'd seen a story on the CBC News website about a friend of Alex's and – if she hadn't – would she please read it then call him back.

Penny immediately went to her laptop and found the article. It concerned a man named Rufus Jones. She knew the name although she didn't know the man. He was the father of Megan – her sister Selene's pal – and the late Clive Jones, a lifelong friend of her brother Alex.

Clive had committed suicide the previous summer.

Mr. Jones had called CBC to tell them that he knew who had killed Alex Callas.

Penny's pulse quickened and she leaned into her laptop.

Jones went on to say that his son Clive had died from a gunshot wound to the head at an ocean front cottage on the south shore of the island. His death was ruled a suicide.

Downstairs, two of his friends, Alex Callas and Dave Seaver, were doing some work for the cottage owner. According to Rufus, Dave was visiting the basement bathroom when he heard a gunshot, so he stayed there. Alex though, went upstairs and was the one who called police.

During the police investigation, no gun could be found. Callas and Seaver swore that they hadn't removed it.

Penny knew about the suicide but not about the absence of the gun. If the story was true, it struck her as extremely odd that the police concluded that Clive Jones had killed himself.

According to the news article, they refused to say where they thought the missing gun had gotten to, although it seemed obvious to Penny that someone had to have been with Clive, and that this person had walked off with the gun.

And it wasn't Alex or Dave since the police obviously had

a reason to believe that they hadn't taken it.

"Clive's best friend, Carl Conroy, struggled with his death afterwards," Jones told the reporter. "He began seeing a psychiatrist, and was soon hospitalized for several weeks. I talked to him at Clive's funeral and I had the distinct impression that Carl was convinced that Alex Callas had killed Clive. And now Carl has disappeared. I believe he shot Alex for revenge and then fled."

The news reporter indicated that he had been unable to contact Carl Conroy. He also said that the police wouldn't comment on Conroy but completely rejected Rufus Jones' theory out of hand. They told the reporter that they couldn't talk about the matter but they were certain that Clive Jones' suicide and Alex Callas's death were not connected.

Penny leaned back in her chair and took a deep breath. According to Alex, when Penny had spoken to him after Clive's death, there was no suicide note. That fact was a reason to give credence to Rufus Jones' conclusion that his son had been murdered. The possibility that Carl Conroy had killed Alex was also a reasonable assumption.

Before she followed up on her father's request to call him, Penny scanned the news site to see if there was a report about the gunshots that had torn her canoe apart the day before, but found nothing. It would make her phone call to Hector easier. The last thing she wanted was for him to hear about the incident. Her parents didn't need a reason to worry about another one of their kids.

"I was getting worried about you," Hector said when he answered Penny's call.

"Sorry for not answering your message earlier. I slept late then had a conference call with my art group."

"Not a problem. So, did you see the CBC article I mentioned?"

"I did."

"And what did you think?"

Penny was suddenly very nervous. If she told her father she thought that Rufus Jones seemed to have a legitimate theory, would it sound like she was suggesting that Alex had murdered his friend Clive? After all, Alex was surely the strongest suspect if it was a murder. He was first on the scene and the gun was missing. There wasn't any proof that he had only gone upstairs after the shot was fired. He'd been left alone by Dave, who was in the bathroom.

Is that why her father had called, Penny wondered; to be reassured that Alex wasn't a killer?

Penny proceeded diplomatically. "I think that, on the face of it, Rufus Jones' theory that it was Carl who killed Alex sounds reasonable. The fact that the handgun was missing suggests that someone was with Clive when he died. Someone who assisted with the suicide and then walked off with the gun most likely. We know it wasn't Alex or Dave. They didn't even know Clive was there, plus I'm sure the police examined their hands for gunshot residue and whatever – and Clive's too. If Carl felt that Alex had shot Clive then, in his mind, he would have had a motive to go after Alex."

"I had the same response. Did you ever talk to Alex about what happened? About the missing gun maybe?"

"A bit, but not about the gun. Today was the first I've heard of it. He said that Clive wasn't supposed to be at the cottage that day; that only he and Dave were. They were doing some work for the owner; a guy that all three of them did work for sometimes."

"So Clive knew about the cottage."

"Um, yeah, I guess he would have. Alex said that he'd talked to Clive a couple of days before he died, and that Clive was really bummed out about something but wouldn't say what it was. But he didn't leave a note."

"But his state of mind supports the idea it was a suicide."

"It does. Alex never questioned it."

"Anyway…why I wanted you to call me was because, after I read the story, I phoned Constable Johnson. He told me that Clive killed himself and that was that, and that he couldn't answer my questions. He asked me if I knew about something that happened at the bar the night that Alex was shot, involving Dave Seaver." Dave had been Alex's best friend for a number of years. Everyone in his family knew him.

Penny was instantly on the alert at the mention of Dave's

name, wondering if her father had heard that she'd been trying to contact Dave. She hoped not. She wanted to be left alone while she closed up Alex's affairs.

"Well, according to Johnson, Dave and Alex had a falling out the night of the murder." Hector loudly sighed. "It seems that Alex had slept with Dave's wife Nicole, and she'd told Dave about it."

Penny could discern the emotion in her father's voice and wondered if it was a commentary on Alex's behaviour or fatigue about, once again, having the subject of Alex's extra-marital affairs brought up.

"Dave was furious with Alex," Hector continued. "They started to scrap at The Sailor's Roost lounge."

"Alex and Dave?"

"Some of the guys Alex was with had to separate them. Apparently Dave even threatened to kill Alex. Johnson said that they need to find Dave – that he's gone missing, and so has his wife. You know Nicole…"

"Of course."

"Johnson said that he has his doubts about Dave being involved in Alex's death – for various reasons – but the fact that he can't be located is disturbing, so finding him has become a priority… Oh, and there's something else, something that Johnson did seem okay with telling me; forensic tests showed that Alex and Clive Jones were killed with different guns which may be why they think that…"

"That Alex's killer didn't also kill Clive."

"Yes."

"So Johnson said that Dave isn't a suspect in Alex's death," Penny began thoughtfully, "yet he's missing. I wonder if they're afraid that whoever killed Alex also killed Dave."

"Jesus. It would make sense. They were like twins. No wonder the cops are looking for him and Nicole."

"And one way or another it could lead them to Alex's killer… I hope that Dave and Nicole are okay. It seems that every one of Alex's friends has gone missing in action."

32.

It was past lunchtime when Penny arrived at Alex's now shuttered store, planning to go through his business affairs.

Penny found a laptop, printer, and two cardboard boxes of material that the police had returned. They were sitting on a desk in the back room.

She sat down at the desk, plugged in the laptop, and flipped it open. Fortunately, for her and the police – who'd made copies of the files – Alex had seen no need for privacy. He'd attached a piece of masking tape over the laptop's camera and had written his password on it.

Alex managed his business using commercial software that, given the time span of the documentation, had been set up by the previous owner. It provided a simple record of all aspects of the business and was easy to read.

Sales and receipts had been input into the program, which automatically updated the inventory.

Penny managed to print out a spreadsheet that provided a complete and up to date store inventory.

The financial records were current as well, and detailed. They showed that sales were weak and not sufficient to cover expenses.

Alex's initial tax filing appeared to accurately reflect his actual income; declaring a loss.

Penny had no idea of whether he'd been keeping the store open to match the times given on the placard on the door that stated its opening hours. She decided to assume that he'd done so, which left her pondering the reasons for the store's apparent continual demise since Alex had taken over ownership.

One reason was glaring. Stock levels had dwindled and many products were out of stock all together. Few new products had been added since Alex took over, meaning the store's core clientele – weightlifters and athletes – had likely begun to shop elsewhere.

There was no indication of where the money to purchase the store had come from although it was listed as a 'personal loan from Alex Callas' in the amount of $70,000. The same 'loan' designation was given for monthly cash deposits, in the hundreds, sufficient to cover all outstanding costs. It was clear that no other creditors, other than inventory suppliers, were receiving money, so no one was being paid back for the loans – at least on record.

Penny found the bill of sale for the store and discovered that – besides the seventy thousand – that Alex had assumed responsibility for all outstanding debts that the store carried. Paying those made for an impossible strategy for the store's survival. The cash infusions kept the store afloat but the store was in a death spiral with declining revenue.

On the face of it, Penny thought, buying the store had been an idiotic move: a losing venture.

Apart from what she saw on the books, there was no indication that Alex had been taking any money for himself. It was the opposite in fact.

Penny wondered if the monthly infusions of money had come from the same mysterious source as the seventy grand. The monthly deposits may have come from his new girlfriend's tip money, but not the purchase money.

Penny's next step was to do her own inventory of stock to ensure that sales weren't being hidden to avoid sales tax. Looking about, at the product on the shelves, it seemed likely that everything had been accurately accounted for, but this required verification, even though she assumed that the police had carried out an inventory of their own and she didn't expect to find anything new.

Using the inventory list she'd printed out, showing current item quantities, Penny began to count.

There wasn't a huge number of products because of the inventory decline, and it was still relatively early in the day, so Penny judged that she'd be able to do a complete inventory by late afternoon. She wrapped up her count by 4:00 p.m.

Penny placed the inventory list on the desk. There were a few minor discrepancies in stock levels – as you would expect in any store, from theft and damages – but, other than that that, the stock quantities in the system were accurate.

Penny made some adjustments, based on her count, and

printed a new document that she could use when she attempted to sell off the store's assets – or the business.

Going through a file folder, Penny spotted a lease agreement and set it aside. This was something she would have to read and then deal with. Hopefully someone could be found to take over the lease if she didn't find a buyer for the store.

Another file folder, in the box the police had returned, contained waybills. She didn't know if there was any need to go through them but she did a quick scan anyway. Most of the stock was coming from one British Columbia company, and shipped with one trucking company. It arrived every Monday. As well, a number of much smaller shipments came regularly from a company in the US. There was no obvious reason to question the accuracy of the shipping documents.

Penny needed a break.

She hadn't eaten all day so she pilfered a protein bar from a box beside the cash register and walked out the back door of the store to get some air in the paved space out back.

After downing the bar, and looking to dispose of the wrapper, Penny lifted the lid of the dumpster that stood beside the store's door. To her surprise, inside the bin, on top of the cardboard and plastic garbage bags, were what looked to be a few dozen large white plastic bottles. She fished one out and immediately recognized the label. The bottle had once contained one of the products that the store carried; a brand of organic protein powder.

She opened the bottle. It was empty and clean. Pristine. She checked the expiry date on the label. There was no reason, based on that information, for the contents to have been disposed of. Penny sometimes bought bottles of protein for her smoothies and knew that, when empty, the bottles always contained some residue. The only way this bottle could be so clean was if it had been washed or if whatever had been in it had been in a bag.

Back inside the store, Penny went closely through the waybills, and then the sales and inventory records. Alex had inherited only two bottles of the product. In total, during his time here, the store had received an additional 24 bottles.

Fifteen had sold and there were eleven in stock. Everything accounted for.

She returned to the shelves of overstock storage in the back and scanned the same locations she'd counted earlier. If the bottles in the dumpster had contained bags of protein they weren't here.

But something else was. When Penny lifted a box, to glance behind it, she discovered it had been sitting on top of a pile of waybills.

She took the batch to the desk, sat down, and began to shuffle through the documents. Each of them – one for each month of the store's operation – was for one item only, and it matched the description of the empty protein powder bottles now resting in the dumpster. None of the product listed on these bills had been entered into the system, and none of it had shown up on Monday along with the other bottles of the product that were on the store shelves. She observed something else as well. According to the waybills, the weight of each mystery shipment had been confirmed by the carrier and it far exceeded the weight it would have been if the boxes were filled with empty bottles. Penny felt certain that this proved that the bottles had been full of something on arrival. Something that had since been removed.

She cursed under her breath. Her worst fears were confirmed. Alex had been involved in the illegal drug business – at least no other explanation immediately came to mind. And he hadn't been doing this on his own. Penny felt certain that the seventy thousand and the monthly deposits were connected to the drug business.

The store was a front and nothing else. Apparently, a warehouse for drugs arriving in the province. It certainly wasn't a viable store. The money that Alex had 'loaned' the company every month – to sustain the business – was probably a cut from drug sales.

Penny felt sick and immediately thought of Bethany Yeats, the woman that her brother had been with when he was murdered. Bethany was the wife of Butler Yeats, a career criminal and biker, who was new to the area. According to the news and Constable Johnson, biker gangs were now invading

PEI and bringing in illegal drugs. Had Alex gotten caught up with them? Is that why – according to her sister's friend Sally – the police thought that Bethany had knowingly lured Alex to his death?

But why was Alex killed? Had he been ripping off his partners? Had he gotten himself in the middle of a drug war? Was the seventy thousand a loan that he wasn't repaying?

And what about Dave? He was missing. Had he fled or had he too been killed? The two pals were inseparable. If Alex was selling drugs then Dave likely was too.

Penny guessed that the police hadn't found the empty bottles in the dumpster or the stash of waybills. If they had, they would have taken them – and a lot more – as evidence.

Telling them about what she had found might help their investigation so she should call them immediately.

But it wasn't that easy. She didn't want to out her brother to the cops. Her father would never forgive her. Yet the police had to know about what she'd found because it showed that Alex was probably killed by someone connected to his illegal activities. She had no choice.

Penny cursed under her breath.

She couldn't think straight and told herself to make a calm and rational decision. She considered calling Ellis Rice, the principal of the school where she taught, and her potential romantic partner. But she didn't. The ambivalence pendulum swung back and forth when it came to her feelings for Ellis and it was one of those periods where she wanted to cool their relationship rather than fuel it.

Instead, she phoned Heather and asked if she could come by her apartment later. "I'd like to talk to you about something and get your thoughts about it," she said.

Heather replied that she had plans to visit a funeral home with Hugh that evening, after supper, but offered to come by Penny's after that.

"No, no, spend the time with Hugh, but if you could drop by in the morning I'd appreciate it."

They agreed to meet at 11:00 a.m.

Panel from Heather Bruce's Siren video

Although the Mermaid is the opposite of the Siren, and together they mark a polarity, the Mermaid was born of the Siren so has certain of her abilities; not always in latent form. She maintains the ability to seduce. She's been luring colonists and tourists to Copenhagen and Newfoundland since the 18th and 19th centuries. And, in our world of media and commodities, it is this skill that she's continually employing – scantily clad – to hawk products.

The modern Mermaid unites the ambitions of both Baudrillard and McLuhan. Both equally reactionary. She can manipulate symbols to sell a variety of items as a sexual object and icon of beauty for adults, while, at the same time, reinforcing traditional attitudes and values for girls.

the sharp shells of the ocean could not harm their dainty fingers. The "Tips" of the

**"KAYSER PATENT
FINGER-TIPPED" SILK GLOVES**

are made so that there is no **wear through** to them; they wear as long as the gloves, and should they not, the **guarantee ticket** that is in each pair is good for a new pair **Free.** The genuine have the word "Kayser" in the hem. **50c., 75c. and $1.** If your dealer hasn't them, write to

JULIUS KAYSER & CO., New York.

33.

Matilda Eades stood just inside the entrance of a visitation room in the funeral parlour, greeting arrivals. Her sister Martha was close by, doing the same.

Jack's closed coffin sat at the opposite end of the room.

Matilda was composed as she voiced her appreciation of everything positive about Jack that the visitors mentioned but said little beyond, "Thank you."

The brevity allowed the mostly seniors a chance to visit the coffin and then quickly find a seat.

Following their wait in line and then offering their condolences to Matilda, Hugh and Heather walked to the back of the room to stand briefly in front of Jack's coffin.

They then moved to one side of the room where they stood against a wall. There was a row of chairs in front of them which they left for the seniors and those accompanying them. Their position offered a view of everyone coming and going.

Hugh bent his head close to Heather's and softly said, "That's Harry Nelson," while nodding in the direction of the old man who'd just come through the entry door.

Harry was shaky on his feet, bowed over, and looking lost. This was a marked difference in demeanour from what he'd demonstrated when Hugh had seen him at his fruit stand. Harry was even shakier on his feet than that day – by a considerable margin. Jack's death had clearly hit him hard.

Hugh noted that Harry was alone. It was astonishing, he thought, that this shaken old man had presumably driven to Charlottetown and the funeral home by himself.

Matilda paid Harry more deference than she had to the others who'd arrived and personally led him to one of the sofas near her. She bent over, speaking to him for a full minute while those in line waited.

Hugh returned to scrutinizing the lines of people waiting to speak to Jack's daughters, craning his head because the lines now ran out the door. He was curious about whether Ellen Comer would make an appearance. Jack's death had been all over the news so she would certainly have heard about it.

"Should we see if Harry wants to stand in front of the coffin," Heather whispered in Hugh's ear, "and assist him if he does? He seems to be bewildered, and no one's helping him."

"Yes, let's do that."

Together they walked to the old man's side.

Bending down, Hugh said, "Hello Harry, I'm very sorry for your loss."

Harry looked at Hugh and then Heather, his eyes conveying confusion and surprise, perhaps at hearing his own name. "Thank you," he said.

"Would you like to stand by the coffin?" Heather said.

"Um, yes, yes, I would."

Hugh helped the man to his feet.

"I'm sorry. I'm not this helpless really," Harry said, "but this has just knocked the wind out of my sails." He reached out a hand and gripped one of Hugh's arms.

"I understand," Hugh answered, while wondering if Harry remembered him.

Side by side they began a slow shuffle towards the coffin, with Harry leaning on Hugh's arm. Heather moved to Harry's other side and lightly slid a hand around his free arm.

"Did your daughter bring you?" Hugh said.

"No, I drove myself," Harry replied with a defiant tone, as if the act was a testament to how much Jack meant to him, or perhaps to his own toughness.

In front of the coffin, Harry loosed his grip on Hugh's arm and took a step towards the coffin, laying his hand on it. He softly spoke to Jack, in a conversational tone, while Heather and Hugh made a conscious effort to not listen in.

Harry turned around and, as he began to shamble away from the coffin, Hugh and Heather moved to, again, take up positions by his side.

"I'm okay," Harry said, "but thank you both. I'll be heading home now. I don't know any of these old people here and I have work to do."

He walked out of the home under his own power, but with Hugh and Heather – one remaining at each side – ready to offer support if needed.

They accompanied Harry to his car.

As they watched him drive off Hugh said, "Jack's death really hit him. He wasn't like this when I saw him."

"How's he different?"

"He was stronger before…less frail…a little shaky but less so. He even seemed younger. I'll check in on him when I go to see Ellen."

"You're going to see Ellen?"

"I thought I'd call her tomorrow morning and see if I can stop by on Sunday – or another day if you'll be needing your car. I want to offer my condolences to her about Jack's death. They were very close. She told me she doesn't have people to talk to – apart from her family I guess."

"Yes, that's a good idea. I won't be needing the car."

Hugh and Heather returned to the funeral home and said their good-byes to Matilda.

"If you don't mind me asking," Hugh said, "did you happen to call Ellen Comer in Mount Pleasant? I know she and Jack were friends."

"Yes, I let her know about Jack. She'll be here tomorrow."

"And I wanted to ask about the funeral."

"It will be the next day, Saturday, but it will just be a service for the family before cremation."

34. Friday

Hugh woke up at 5:00 a.m. and didn't immediately fall back to sleep. He was thinking about Harry Nelson and wondering how he was doing.

It was nearer to 6:00 when Hugh eventually gave up on the idea of getting more sleep and slipped quietly out of bed. He went to the living room, sat on the couch, and reached for his laptop. It semi-permanently lived on the coffee table but today he perched it on his knees and logged on.

He immediately went to work making ancestry inquiries about Harry; a benign activity in Hugh's mind.

It was easy enough to find public records about the man's birth and baptism. Harold Nelson was the child of Frederick Nelson and Lorelei Fischer – another woman of German origin Hugh noted – but this one had been born in Alberta.

Hugh recalled the picture of Lorelei from his great-grandmother's photo album. She was a beautiful woman. A girl-woman, according to Ellen. Sweet and quiet, a songbird apparently, and married to a brutal and intimidating bully.

Ellen had mentioned that Lorelei fled to escape her very violent husband, leaving her son at his mercy. It was extreme behaviour that spoke of a need for self-survival.

Hugh searched the name Lorelei Nelson and soon came upon a story in a weekly PEI newspaper, from early in 1942, about a singer in Summerside who performed at local dances. The story noted that the dances were frequented by the airmen from the local base and that Lorelei was their favourite performer.

The gist of the story was that Summerside's loss was Mount Pleasant's gain because Lorelei and her husband were moving to the latter area so that they could take over the family farm.

What caught Hugh's eye was the headline for the article. It read: *Summerside Loses A Siren*. A funny coincidence given the project that Heather and Penny were working on.

Hugh was surprised at the dates mentioned in the article. Harry had told him that his family had moved to the Mount Pleasant area and that his mother had left soon after. Hugh's impression was that this had been when Harry was small. After all, Harry had chummed with Hugh's grandfather and great uncle. At the time of the aviator's murder, Harry would have only lived in the area for a year – if that.

Hugh sat back and considered his finding. It wasn't just Ellen and her husband who had been in Summerside in 1942, and may have known Samuel Marsh. Lorelei, Freddy, and Harry had been there too.

The aviator was stationed at the RCAF base and Lorelei sang there, at the base dances. Wasn't it more likely, if the man had known any woman in Mount Pleasant from his time in Summerside, that it would have been Lorelei and not Ellen?

Could Lorelei and Marsh have been having an affair? Or were the rumours about Marsh true; that he was a stalker? Perhaps he had even followed her from Summerside.

A whole bunch of other people had also made the move to the new RCAF station at the same time as Marsh. But it suggested that the roots of whatever led someone to kill him in 1943 stretched all the way back to Summerside. Did 'the siren' murder him? Or, more likely, had her violent husband done it?

At 9:30 a.m. Hugh went into the bedroom. Heather was laying on her side, facing the door, and opened her eyes when she heard him. She half smiled and murmured, "Hello," but otherwise didn't move.

It was enough of a response for Hugh. He dropped onto the floor, on his knees, and leaned forward so that his head was level with Heather's.

"I found an old news article online," he said and launched into the story about the siren of Summerside.

Heather watched his face, and listened, but Hugh couldn't read her expression.

"I know you're sick of hearing about this but please hear me out... I remembered a couple of things," Hugh said. "During the Samuel Marsh autopsy it was mentioned that he was first posted to Summerside and had asked for a transfer to Mount Pleasant. He went there in 1943. And the other thing I remembered was Ellen telling me what a fine singer Harry Nelson's mother Lorelei was. Anyway, I just came across a news article from 1942, concerning Summerside and Lorelei. It mentioned that she sang at the RCAF base dances but was moving to Mount Pleasant. According to Ellen, Lorelei also sang at the dances in Mount Pleasant after she moved there."

Heather's eyes opened a little wider. "Her name was Lorelei?"

"Yes."

Still laying on her side, Heather raised her head, and propped it up with a hand. "And you think," she said, "that Marsh was carrying on with Lorelei?"

"Oh I don't know, but it is possible that he was having an affair with her in Summerside and didn't want it to end so he followed her to Mount Pleasant. But it's just as possible that she wasn't involved with the guy. I'm thinking of what Jack said…"

"That Marsh was possibly a stalker and wasn't having an affair with anyone?"

"Exactly," Hugh confirmed.

"But Lorelei was never the subject of rumours…"

"If you had mentioned that yesterday I would have said, 'Of course not.' Harry told me that she left home shortly after they moved to the area so she didn't even live there when the man died. I assumed she'd left years before, when Harry was small. But I now know, because of the article I found, that she only moved to the area in 1942. She was probably living there when the aviator was killed. Stupid me! I didn't pick up on it after Ellen pointed out that a picture of Lorelei was in my great-grandmother's photo album. It was taken only a few weeks before the aviator's murder. Maybe even days before."

"Well, you weren't investigating who may have killed the man…"

"No. I was assuming the soldier had been killed by accident. I wasn't considering the possibility that Marsh's bravado (that he was seeing one of the local women on the sly) was true, and that he may have been shot because of it."

"Until Jack said…"

"Yes. And now I'm wondering – since Freddy was likely the one making up rumours – if he was just trying to point the speculation, about who the aviator was seeing, at any woman in the area who wasn't his wife."

"Because, among other reasons, if the guy was seeing Lorelei it would make Freddy suspect number one for his murder."

"Indeed. And he should be. And is. Do you think It would be okay to ask Ellen about Lorelei?"

"I don't see why not…but tread carefully. She and Lorelei were friends. Maybe just try to nail down when Lorelei left, if you want to dig into this."

"I wish I knew what Jack was going to tell me."

Heather rolled onto her back while shaking her head. "Shit," she whispered softly. Turning to look at Hugh she said, "I didn't know that Harry's mother's name was Lorelei. Jack never mentioned it. Did you look up anything about the name Lorelei?"

"You mean, like, its meaning?"

"Right."

"No."

"There's a character in a German fable named Lorelei. She's a siren who lures ships against the rocks causing the sailors to drown. Like other such myths, a story invented by men in order to blame women for their own foibles, and to present women as heartless murderers."

While Hugh was absorbing the information, Heather added, "So you're still planning on phoning Ellen to see if you can visit?"

"Yes."

"Sunday works for me, if she doesn't mind meeting me."

"Matilda said that Ellen will be here in Charlottetown today to visit the funeral home, so I'll hold off calling her until tonight. I'll ask if the two of us can stop by, and I'll offer our condolences."

35.

As Heather stepped over the threshold of Penny's apartment, later that morning, expecting to talk about the previous day's news story involving the death of a young man named Clive Jones, she noted the obvious agitation in her friend's manner.

Penny stepped back and waved her hand to beckon Heather inside. Immediately after the door closed Penny said, sputtering in anger, "They burned it down!"

"What?"

"They burned down Alex's store."

"Who?"

"The drug gang."

"The drug gang?"

"Yes."

"A drug gang burned down Alex's store?"

"Yes."

"When? Why?"

"Last night. To destroy the evidence I found yesterday when I was cleaning up. The fire was sometime in the night; sometime after I talked to you on the phone. My father just phoned to tell me about it. The store was burned and the stuff in the dumpster behind it too."

"You used the word 'evidence'…"

Penny paused and breathed deep to regain her composure. "Yesterday, when I was in the store – starting to wrap up the business – I found evidence that Alex was involved in the illegal drug business and now the gang, or whoever it was he was working with, has burned the store down to destroy it."

"The evidence you mean?"

"Yes."

"And what was it?"

"Waybills and inventory reports that don't match up. Alex was receiving regular shipments from a supplier out west, of what was supposed to be protein powder, but he wasn't putting it into inventory."

"Can't you get duplicates of the waybills from the carrier?"

"Yes, but they are irrelevant now. In the dumpster behind the store I found dozens of empty plastic bottles that had labels on them saying they contained protein powder – but the bottles were empty. And they were so clean it was evident that whatever powder had been in them had been in bags. Everything was burned or melted."

"In the dumpster?"

"Yeah. The empty bottles. Physical evidence that's not replaceable. Even if I did get copies of the burnt waybills it would prove nothing. All they would say is that the store received some protein powder. Alex may have ordered it for a client and just not reported it. A wee bit of tax fraud."

"So you're now confident that Alex was involved in the drug business…"

"Yes. He deposited money every month, hundreds of dollars. His deposits said they were personal loans, even though he had no income from the store, and the money deposited each month was the exact amount he needed to break even; meaning that he must have been getting more money than what he deposited. He needed some to live on…"

"So he was a dealer?"

"I wouldn't say that, but maybe. The evidence I found makes it clear that the store was a drug warehouse."

"Was he smuggling drugs?"

"I don't know, at least not yet. The stuff I found came from Canada."

"And the seventy thousand Alex had to open the store… where do you think it came from?"

"I don't know. The store was in his name so it may have been a loan. It suggests, pretty strongly, that Alex was working with some people who had deep pockets."

"Were they laundering money through the store?"

"No, at least I don't think so. The store belonged to Alex so I think he likely borrowed the money to set it up as a drug warehouse to get the drugs into the province. I've been thinking about it and I'm wondering if he anticipated eventually bringing in drugs from the States and that's why he set up the store as a cover. It's possible, I think, that the money came from a silent partner – someone who didn't want to be associated with the store. My guess is that whoever Alex was working with had to have some connection to the company out west that's selling the fake protein powder, or at least the company distributing it."

"So. Alex would receive the drugs and what? Distribute them?"

"He was getting too much money for that. He had to have been selling the drugs. I suspect he was a middleman. Selling to street dealers. Alex wanted to be ultra wealthy and I heard him say a few times that the legality of something or not wasn't an issue for him."

"Laws are for other people sort of thing?"

"Exactly. He was certain he was brilliant and could con anyone."

"Any chance he was smuggling the drugs out of the country?"

"I hadn't thought of that but there was no paperwork to suggest he was."

"Penny, do you think it's possible that the containers you found actually did contain protein powder? Maybe Alex was selling it under the table to avoid charging tax on it. Like the cigarette sellers you hear about."

"The tax on them wouldn't be exorbitant, like it is on cigarettes, plus, if you're selling the stuff under the table there's no reason to put it in plastic bags. You would sell whole bottles. You only put the contents into small bags if you want to cut up what's in them into smaller quantities."

"Did you tell the police about this?"

"No. Since they suspect that he was lured to The Sailor's Roost to be killed by bikers they already know he was involved in the drug business. I have nothing new to tell them… Oh, my dad left me a phone message. He said the police arrested Dave Seaver. He apparently threatened Alex on the night he was killed."

"And did you tell your dad about what you found?"

"No. I have no reason to do that."

"Why not? I understand that you don't want to sully Alex's name but…"

"But why tell him at this point when I can't prove it? I've

been thinking about what to do and I've decided to go through with my visit to The Sailor's Roost."

"What? Why? The idea was a dangerous one before and it's even scarier now you're certain that anyone who approaches you is a criminal."

"But that person doesn't know that I know. They burned the store so they'll think they're in the clear. I can stick with my plan to look for the person who loaned Alex the money to buy the store. I can even put it out that I know nothing about the store and the money; that I just want to do what's right. That should disarm whoever burned the store and make it more likely that they will approach me."

"But seventy grand may be peanuts to them and they will just let it go if you walk away and do nothing. They may have killed Alex as a lesson to others not to do whatever…"

"Yeah maybe, but we will only know if that's the case if they don't contact me or Hazel. I want to be proactive, to protect Hazel and I want to find Alex's murderer, if I can. I don't want the killer to let the money go. I want to lure him to me. I will never forgive myself if I don't try."

The two friends were still standing in close proximity to each other in the entryway to Penny's apartment.

"Sorry," Penny said. "I've kept you standing here in all the excitement. Come into the kitchen." As they walked in that direction, Penny added, "There's been a change of plans, if you don't mind. Do you want to come with me while I check in with my father? He just texted me that he's heard something about Dave Seaver. I want to head over to my parents' place so I can also check on my mother, in person."

36

Heather trailed Penny into her parent's house, through the side door, up the stairs, and into the kitchen. She held back after seeing Doris in the kitchen, washing dishes, allowing Penny time to hug her mother and ask how she was doing.

"It's pretty rough," Doris could be heard saying, "but each step helps. I felt better after going through the funeral."

"Heather's with me," Penny added, stepping aside out of Doris's line of vision.

"Yes, I saw. Come in Heather." To Penny, Doris said, "I suppose you're looking for your father."

"He called me this morning and said he was working from home."

Doris smiled. "Is that what you call it? Well maybe he is. You'll find him in a lounger by the pool."

Penny and Heather left through the back door.

As soon as Hector spotted them he stood and waved. He was on his cell but signed off.

"I guess you came to ask about Dave Seaver," Hector said,

"Yes," Penny replied, taking a seat. As she and Heather sat she added, "Any news?"

"Yes. Dave called me this morning. Said he'd been on a camping vacation with his wife. Said he'd already spoken to the police. He asked if he could drop by sometime and I said of course. He and Alex were best friends for most of their lives."

"So you're presuming that the cops have ruled him out as a suspect."

"Yes. That's what Dave said. Like I told you, Johnson said that he didn't think Dave was involved in the murder and they were worried about him. It seems he has an alibi for the time of the murder and the cops apparently believe him; according to Dave."

"Well, we should be going," Penny said brusquely, although to whom she'd spoken was uncertain.

It was at that moment, however, that the back door opened and a young man emerged from the house. He began walking in the direction of the pool.

Penny and Hector stood up.

Heather saw the chill in the faces of the two Callas family members. Not knowing what to do, she stood as well.

The young man approached Hector and held out his hand saying, "Hello sir."

"Carl," Hector replied, shaking hands with the newcomer. "I see you're not missing after all."

Carl? Heather quickly placed the name. Carl was the man named in the CBC article as a prime suspect in Alex's murder, at least if you listened to Rufus Jones. Jones's son Clive, had supposedly shot himself on the upstairs floor of a cottage while Alex and Dave Seaver were on the floor below. According to the news article, Dave was in the bathroom and hid there after the shot. Alex told police that he went upstairs, saw no one, and no gun. According to Rufus, his son Clive's best friend, Carl Conroy, felt that Alex had killed Clive. Rufus believed that Carl killed Alex in revenge.

Carl turned towards Penny and took a small step towards her but apparently changed his mind after seeing her cold expression. He nodded in her direction however, glanced at Heather, and did the same.

Turning back to Hector, Carl said, "I thought that I better come to see you after reading the news story where I get blamed for Alex's death. I wanted to let you know that none of what Rufus Jones said happened actually did. Alex was my friend and Clive killed himself. End of story. Clive was my best friend and for a week or so before he died he was off in some other world in his head. He was drinking heavily, sometimes swearing at no one in particular, and saying things, like he was a terrible and blind person, that he'd betrayed his family and had to stand up for them. I told the cops all this at the time and I guess others confirmed it cus, well, you saw the news article; the police believe that Clive killed himself."

"It said you'd taken off, and I recalled that you weren't at Alex's funeral" Hector said.

"I suffer from anxiety and depression. Have for years. The day after Alex died I checked myself in to the hospital to get my meds adjusted and to talk to someone. The cops came to see me in the hospital to ask me a few questions; so I wasn't in hiding. I guess the cops didn't tell the news reporter where I was to respect my privacy. Being in the psych ward was the sole reason why I didn't go to the funeral. I just checked myself out today after seeing the news about being a suspect."

Heather glanced up at the kitchen window and saw Doris's face, watching the proceedings. Had Carl told her what Hector and Penny were now hearing? Likely not since he'd appeared in the back yard so soon after her own appearance there.

Heather was suddenly very angry on Doris's behalf. Why was Doris not included in these family discussions?

Heather could no longer contain herself. "Did you tell Mrs. Callas what you just told us?" she asked Carl.

"Um, oh no. I will."

"I'll do it," Hector said uncomfortably. Before he headed to the kitchen he thanked Carl for his visit.

As soon as they were out of earshot, Penny turned towards Carl and said, "Who do you think killed Alex?"

"I don't know."

"Do you think it was because of his involvement in the drug trade?"

"So he was selling drugs then. I thought he might be but I wasn't sure."

"He didn't confide in you?"

"No, not about that. I'm sure Dave knew. You should talk to him. Do your parents know about the drugs?"

"No, and please say nothing to them, or to anybody. What about the money that Alex borrowed to open the store and the money he was getting every month? Do you know where it came from?"

Carl stared at Penny, obviously drawing a blank. "I heard that he'd saved up to buy the store from money he got working for your father – and I believed it, I mean, your dad's rich… But the monthly money…Alex would have been getting money every month from selling drugs wouldn't he?"

"I actually don't know what his role was. Maybe he was selling. Maybe the store was a front of some sort. Maybe for money laundering.”

“I see.”

“Do you have any idea of who the players are in the drug scene in Charlottetown that Alex may have been involved with?”

“I wish I could help, but I don’t know.”

Penny looked at Carl sceptically, frowned, and sat down.

Heather followed suit but Carl remained standing, looking confused about what to do.

“Can I ask,” Penny said, “why weren’t you at the cottage the day Clive committed suicide?”

“What? Oh. I had no reason to be there. So far as I know, Dave and Alex were up there doing some work for Jason.”

“Jason? As in Hopkins?”

“Yeah. I assumed you knew it was his cottage. Anyway, Jason wasn’t there. At Clive’s funeral I talked to Dave about what happened that day. He said that Hopkins ordered some massage tables and some other stuff… I don’t know what all. Dave and Alex were at the cottage to set the tables up in exchange for an afternoon of swimming and free use of the massive sauna… Dave told me that Jason’s staff were coming up later that night when he and Alex would be back in town.”

“So Alex and Dave must have been friends with Jason.”

“I doubt it. I know they’d never been to the cottage before. They were too poor to be the sort that Jason invited. Lots of kinky stuff went on or so I’ve heard. Lots of booze and drugs…and girls. Alex and Dave were just at the cottage to work.”

“Did you know Hopkins?”

“We all did, through Clive. He worked in the kitchen at The Roost and we all picked up a bit of work there, especially Dave and Alex. That was before Alex bought the store though. A lot of people came to the place through Clive, even his little sister, who’s a dishwasher. He told me that Jason and his assistant rewarded him for bringing in new people.”

Penny seemed to have finished her questions but suddenly added, “So Clive was at the cottage, but not with Dave and Alex. And since he worked in the kitchen of the bar he wasn’t part of Hopkin’s circle?”

"Yeah, that's right."

"So any idea why Clive went all the way out to Hopkins' cottage to commit suicide?"

"Maybe he was part of the kitchen staff but came up early. Or, I guess, he may have just wanted a place away from home where he could kill himself and didn't know that anyone would be there."

37

Penny had had enough. As she was leaving her parent's house she announced to Heather that they were going to her sister-in-law's. "I'm sick of Hazel's mousy ignorance act," Penny said. "She must know something about what Alex was up to at his store, and she's taking a big risk by being in denial."

Heather said nothing, knowing that Penny was possibly just aiming her frustration and anger at Hazel. So far as she could tell, Hazel didn't appear to be someone putting on an act about being naive. It did seem possible though that Hazel's naivety was more like wilful blindness due to her obsession with her late husband. No matter how awful Alex treated her, and no matter how much he lied to her, she found a way to rationalize it and exonerate him. He remained the perfect person who did nothing wrong.

The moment Penny turned her car on the road and accelerated, her phone rang.

"Dave, yes, hello," Heather heard Penny say. "No, don't mention it. My father told me that you were away."

Heather picked up bits of what was said over the next few minutes but looked out of the car window in order to appear not to be listening.

Penny was telling Dave about the fire at Alex's store when she said, "Dave, I'm going to put you on speakerphone because I'm in my car."

"Okay," Heather heard him say.

"Dave," Penny said, "I'm going to come right to it. Who do you think killed Alex?"

"I don't know. Honestly. It wasn't me!"

"I know. Do you think it was because of his involvement in the drug trade?"

Dave wasn't evasive, immediately replying, "I've been thinking about it, and I can't come up with any reason to think that; not from what I know."

"What about the money that Alex came up with to buy the store and the money he was getting every month? Where did he get it? Was he missing his payments?"

"Penny, I honestly know nothing about any money Alex had. He told me he'd saved the money to buy the store and he never talked about any monthly money."

"Who was buying from him? You? Carl? Clive?"

"No, no, and no. It was small timers for the most part, or so I understand. Street dealers. Alex sold some directly to his contacts though. Like there was apparently one businessman who bought loads of ecstasy."

"So that's all you know?"

"Sorry."

"Do you know who the big players are in the local drug business? I heard that biker gangs are moving in."

"Could be, I guess. I hope Alex wasn't involved with them but I honestly don't know."

Hazel was surprised when she found the two visitors at her threshold. Rather than throwing open the door and being pleased at the sight of them she blocked the opening and said, "Hello?"

"Can we come in?" Penny asked. "There's something I'd like to talk to you about."

Hazel glanced up and down the street, appearing to be anxious about who might be outside, and only then did she step back and hold the door open.

Soon the three women were seated in the living room. Heather sat on the couch beside Penny, while Hazel perched on the front of an easy chair, facing them expectantly.

Before Penny could utter a word, Hazel said, "The police were here first thing this morning to tell me about a fire at Alex's store... They say it was arson. Everything just goes from bad to worse. I don't even know if the place was insured or if it's just gone."

"It was insured," Penny said. "Do you have any idea who would do such a thing?"

"That's exactly what the police asked me, and I'll tell you what I told them: I have no idea."

"You must know that Alex was involved in the sale of drugs and that the fire burned up any evidence of it, which is certainly a reason why someone would want to torch the place."

"He had nothing to do with drugs. I told you," Hazel shot back. "Alex hated gangs and drugs."

"I can't believe anyone could be as naive as you're acting," Penny said aggressively. "You have to know, at least a bit, about who he was working with, and what his role was."

Hazel stood up, angrily, searching for words.

Heather, speaking to Penny, offered some assistance by asking, "Didn't you discover something at the store yesterday that prompted your conclusion and questions?"

Following the lead, Penny said, "Yes."

"What did you find...?" Hazel challenged.

"I found discrepancies. I looked at the total amount of a brand of protein supplement that was regularly shipped to the store. It arrived on Mondays and was taken into inventory. There were monthly shipments too, supposedly of the same protein powder, but from another company, and those weren't entered in the books. I found the waybills stashed in the back room and the empty bottles in the dumpster out back of the store. I believe that, whatever was in the plastic bottles originally, was drugs – cocaine, ecstasy, whatever."

"Or there was a problem with the protein and Alex dumped it. So what?" said Hazel.

"The bottles were spic and span clean. Whatever powder had been in them must have been in plastic bags and then removed."

"Or the bottles arrived empty."

"No they didn't. Transport companies confirm the weight of every shipment on the paperwork and it only would have been accurate if the bottles had been filled with something during their transportation. Something with a similar weight to protein powder. The store was obviously a good front because no one would think it strange that boxes of bottles labelled 'protein powder' were arriving at a store that catered to weightlifters. The business was a bust but all the bills were paid every month because Alex covered them with deposits of cash that he labelled as 'loans'."

Hazel didn't immediately respond but her fierce

expression said that she was far from convinced. And she wasn't going to explain that Alex – in her opinion – had been bringing in product to sell under the table.

"I talked to Dave this morning…" Penny said.

"He's back?"

"So you knew he was away…never mind…and I asked him if Alex was selling drugs. He confirmed that he was. Alex was bringing it into the province and selling to small time dealers and businessmen."

"Well Dave would say anything, wouldn't he, because he had a fight with Alex the day he died?"

"He's never been a suspect. Alex was buying the drugs from someone and I suspect it was the same person who gave him the seventy grand; either to be a partner or as a loan. And I suspect – until proven otherwise – that that person was behind Alex's murder. Alex maybe wasn't repaying the loan or was ripping off some of the drugs."

"The seventy grand came from the prostitute; maybe she was selling drugs."

"What? Huh? We're talking serious criminals here. Biker gangs maybe. Organized crime. People that don't fuck around; that kill other people. I'm worried that whoever gave Alex the seventy grand will come after you, looking to get the money back. You and Damian could be in danger."

Hazel, still standing, remained silent but her expression had transformed from anger to alarm. "You think he was killed for the money?"

"Yes. Hazel, you're both in danger now."

Hazel sat down and glared at her sister-in-law.

"But you could be wrong."

"About some things? Possibly. But probably not about the fact that Alex owed a criminal seventy thousand dollars and he will want it back. My brother was a serial liar who admired gangs. I've been thinking about all the stuff he joked about, like how he could get away with anything because he was convinced that he was oh so clever. I always put everything he said down to boyish fantasy but lately he was hanging out with criminals, had armed himself with a knife, as you know, and I think he was trying to make his fantasy real: to be a multi-millionaire without the work. I think getting away with crimes would have confirmed his feelings of superiority – I mean, to himself. Pulling the wool over the eyes of the suckers would have made him feel powerful. Anyway, all that aside, you have to consider your options in case people come looking for the money. Go to the cops and report them, or, if you don't like that, and you want to protect Alex's reputation, see what money you can cobble together from insurance and other assets to offer his associates."

"I have to protect his reputation at all costs," Hazel said, now dabbing away sudden tears with the back of her hand. "I need that money in the safety deposit box."

"Alex has a safety deposit box with money in it? How much?"

"The box belongs to me. I don't know how much is there – thousands and thousands. It's my emergency money."

"I think we know where it came from."

"I assumed it came from store sales. It just made me angry."

"Because he had a stash and never gave you money for the baby?"

"Right."

"Jesus," Penny said quietly. "I've seen the books. The store was losing money. There were almost no sales. It was kept afloat with cash deposits of a lot of money so it had to have been drug money. I figured that Alex was getting more money but that he'd spent it on day to day stuff. And now you're saying there was a lot more."

Hazel didn't appear to be listening. "I knew nothing about the store… You're scaring me, and it's not just because of the money. It's because of the gun."

"What gun? Alex had a gun?"

"It's in the safety deposit box. I thought that he bought it in case the store got robbed but maybe it was for protection against…"

Penny felt as if she was going to be sick. "Do you have any idea when Alex got the gun?"

"I don't. Maybe last summer. That's when he took over my safety deposit box and told me I couldn't touch it."

Penny looked towards the heavens. 'Last summer'. Was this the missing gun from Jason Hopkins' cottage that Clive Jones had used to kill himself? Or had her brother also been a murderer?

Hazel said aggressively, "The drug gang won't know where Alex's money is since it wasn't anywhere in his name."

"Jesus, Hazel… Leave the money alone – at least for now – and for God's sake don't touch the gun!"

"Something occurred to me when we were talking to Hazel," Penny told Heather when they were back in her car. "Alex left behind a lot of money that can help her and the baby. If the cops know about it, and think the money came from the sale of illegal drugs, I assume they'll confiscate it as the proceeds of crime. I want Hazel to have it."

"Meaning what?"

"Meaning, if I get some information and go to the cops, I won't be able to hide the fact that Alex was involved in the illegal drug business, but I don't have to tell anyone about the money that Hazel has."

Heather wanted to say that having the cops confiscate the money immediately would be the best way of protecting Hazel but she could see that her friend was maxed out on the amount of stress she could handle and that it was time to back off.

As they drove away from Hazel's, Heather made the decision that she would no longer try to convince Penny to keep away from The Sailor's Roost, despite the danger. Hazel needed help and Penny wanted to provide it. Penny was the one person in the Carras family – that she had seen – who was offering genuine kindness and support to Hazel. Including Hector. His refusal to acknowledge his son's behaviour amounted to condoning it. It had likely been an enabling factor. From what Heather had heard, Alex Carras was a cruel, violent, and manipulative person who abused the fact that his wife would go to any lengths and endure anything to win his affections and to keep their marriage.

Panel from Heather Bruce's Siren video

The Mermaid, as a modern object of beauty, is one sign of the death of the idea that she is a creature of nature, and that is what guides her actions. Nature is supplanted by mechanical control, and the standardization of beauty is shaped by economic power.
This also signals the end of the Pagan Siren. The Mermaid is an advertisement for conformity and conventional beauty.
She helps to give birth to the timid consumer par excellence.
Advertising is the further containment of the Mermaid, by the appropriation of her voice.

38. Saturday night

"Selene told me," Penny said to Heather, "that she has an appointment to meet Jason Hopkins' personal assistant, Bethany Yeats, about working for Hopkins over the summer. Her and her pal Sally."

Heather was surprised to hear that Yeats worked for Hopkins at the bar. It explained why she had after-hours access to The Mermaid Lounge on the night that Alex was killed. "And Selene knows that Yeats is the same woman who was with her brother when he was murdered?"

"She does, and she doesn't care."

"She doesn't care?"

"I don't mean about Alex's murder, of course, but she couldn't care less that Bethany was with him. Her friend Megan seems to like this Bethany and made the introduction. Swears by her. Selene tells me that Megan says she made a ton of money in tips last summer bussing tables. I think Selene is just so hopped up about getting a job that she's convinced herself that there's no way that Bethany was involved in what happened to Alex."

"But her friend Sally said that the police suspect that Bethany lured Alex to the lounge!"

"Yes. And Selene doesn't believe it. And – I don't know – she could be right. Bethany has an obvious connection to bikers – through her husband – but that doesn't mean that she's involved in whatever he's up to. She has a job after all. Someone like that isn't likely to also be an assistant to some low level thug, is she?"

"I suppose being assistant to a high level dirt bag is probably enough work."

"And offers a degree of respectability – oddly enough."

"Do you think the police know about her connection to Hopkins?"

"Yeah, it's no secret. I looked at the bar's website and there's a picture of the two of them together – Bethany and Jason I mean. It even gives her name under the picture."

The taxi arrived.

"Do you think I'm on a pointless mission?" asked Penny

once they were in the car and on their way to Hopkins' bar.

"Well, I doubt Hopkins is going to tell you anything…"

"But he can start the ball rolling…"

"As long as you don't play drug detective."

"I won't. I'm just going to say I'm looking for the nice guy who loaned my brother money to start his business. I don't want it known how much I discovered about Alex's life. The person who loaned Alex the money may have killed him and then burned his store. And maybe tried to kill me in my canoe."

"So you're definitely going to play dumb when it comes to the drug business then?"

"Please rest assured. I'm only going to say that I'm handling the liquidation of Alex's store and ask Hopkins if he'll ask around the bar to see if he can find out who was bankrolling the business."

As the taxi neared their destination, Heather said, "Be careful. For all you know, Hopkins may be the person you're looking for and he may not take kindly to you poking around into his activities; especially if they're illegal."

Penny caught Heather's eye, then nodded towards the driver as a way of telling her to stop talking about such matters.

Both lapsed into silence.

On arriving at The Sailor's Roost, Heather and Penny observed that the barrier in front of the stairs leading up to the lounge was gone. They headed up.

Penny walked brusquely, weaving between love seats and lounge chairs, that surrounded low tables, and headed for the three-sided bar.

The large aquarium, behind it, was smaller than the mermaid pool on the main floor and, unlike that one, its only inhabitants were some aquatic plants waving in the water.

The bartender though, was similar in some ways to the woman behind the bar on the main floor who they'd previously met: young, hair dyed a pastel colour, and wearing a skimpy mermaid costume.

Penny asked where she could find Jason Hopkins.

"He's not in… Are you Penny Callas?"

"Yes."

"He's expecting you. I'll text him to let him know you're here. I don't think he'll be long. Please have a seat while you're waiting." She pointed to the swivel bar stools.

Penny and Heather dutifully climbed onto stools.

The bartender walked to the end of the bar where she retrieved a cellphone. Returning, a short time later, she said, "Mr. Hopkins advised that he'll be arriving in a few minutes and that I'm to get you drinks – on the house."

Both women ordered gin and tonic.

Soon after they'd been served, when the bartender was out of earshot and engaged in banter with a middle-aged man who she appeared to know, Penny said, "I think it would be best if I speak to Hopkins alone."

"Why? I thought you wanted me here."

"I do, but I'm thinking now that Hopkins might be more forthcoming if I approach him alone."

"Forthcoming? You're just going to talk about business."

"I am, although you never know what an egotist and flirter might reveal unintentionally. Maybe shoot his mouth off, bragging about people he knows. I'll have the small recording device I brought, turned on, so I want to get him talking."

It donned on Heather that Penny had come to her decision to meet with Hopkins on her own well before this moment. Penny was wearing a tight, short skirt, a low cut top, and red lipstick. Not business attire. Was the stupid woman going to ask about the drug business? "Won't he think that you just want to be alone with him if I disappear?"

"Exactly. Let him try to impress me. The great seducer. You know what guys like him are like. They want to show off."

"Yeah, I do know…" Heather didn't have a chance to complete her reply before the bartender reappeared in front of her and Penny.

"I've had a further text from Mr. Hopkins," she said. "He asked me to show you into his office." She pointed to her left.

Penny and Heather both looked in that direction but saw only a group of three men sitting in loungers around a low table in the corner of the room. They were silently drinking and staring back.

As Penny got up out of her seat to follow the bartender, Heather said loudly, "I'll wait here."

At the end of the bar, where the three men sat, the bartender made a u-turn into a hallway running behind the bar. Penny trailed along. At the door to Hopkins' office the bartender removed a key from her pocket, unlocked the door, stepped aside, and pointed into the office. "Please have a seat and make yourself comfortable."

In front of Hopkins' desk was a low, round coffee table. A semi-circle of three chairs were positioned around it. The bartender left Penny on her own and closed the office door.

Penny took a seat in the closest of the chairs, then shifted to the middle one so that she was directly facing Hopkins' desk.

She opened the small bag that she'd been carrying and removed the minuscule recording device inside. She turned it on and returned it to the bag, which she then set on the coffee table, leaving it slightly open.

Sitting back, she took a look around the room. It was sparsely and elegantly furnished. Behind the large glass-topped desk was a black leather chair, and beyond that was a bureau. There were three framed photos perched on it. On the wall above them was a metre long photograph of an ocean-front cottage. Penny guessed that it was Hopkins' cottage.

She stood up and glanced in the direction of the closed office door. Hearing nothing, she walked behind the desk and, one by one, studied the three photographs atop the bureau.

All of the pictures appeared to have been taken at the cottage. One of them depicted a smiling group of men; fortyish like Hopkins, or older. And all of them wealthy if Carl Conroy was to believed. In the second picture, Hopkins stood in the middle of another lineup of men, but this time, with Bethany Yeats at his side. They were arm in arm. The third photo was the largest of the three. Hopkins again stood in the centre, but on each side of him was a row of five, very young looking women, all with variously coloured dyed hair and dressed in the same skimpy pseudo-mermaid outfits as the bartenders. The women looked like participants in the Coney Island Mermaid Parade. Penny presumed they were servers.

Hearing voices outside the office door, including that of Jason Hopkins, Penny quickly returned to her seat.

The door opened. Hopkins stepped inside the room, closed the door and smiled at Penny who had stood up.

"Please sit," Hopkins said. He glanced about the room and added, "I thought you were coming with a friend."

"I did. She's waiting at the bar…" Penny replied and left the sentence hanging as if she didn't want the reason to be stated.

Hopkins' smiled broadened.

In response to a knock, he called, "Come in."

A waitress from the lounge opened the office door, and entered. Her free hand supported a tray holding a pitcher of lime margaritas and three glasses. She set them out, with coasters, on the round coffee table.

"Thank you Emma," Hopkins said, with a big smile and a lingering look at Emma's backside as she left the office.

He'd been standing beside his desk but now circled the coffee table to sit beside Penny. Appearing to treat her presence as a social visit, he moved his chair closer to hers then poured each of them a margarita.

Penny hesitated briefly before taking the glass that was held out to her.

"Cheers," Hopkins said, and they tipped glasses.

Hopkins again adjusted his chair, moving it closer still to Penny's.

She pointed to the photo on the wall above the buffet and said, "Is that your cottage?"

"Yes." Hopkins flashed another broad smile.

"And the picture on the buffet, on the right… Are they supposed to be mermaids?"

"Yes. They're servers. Mermaids is a theme of the Roost, as I'm sure you've noticed. You likely saw the gorgeous mermaid swimming in the tank behind the bar downstairs. The servers here and at my cottage wear similar outfits." Abruptly changing the subject, he said, "But you're not here to talk about my bar.”

Penny hesitated. Something had occurred to her which she was trying to sort out. She put it aside and carried on the conversation. “I wanted to talk to you about my brother’s business…”

“Which I know nothing about.”

“Yes. I’ve been wrapping up Alex’s affairs and…well, the first order of business… He paid seventy thousand dollars to buy the store. He listed it in his books as a loan from himself. I suspect he borrowed the money from someone whose name he didn’t want to put on record. I don’t want to close out the business and then have someone showing up who says that Alex owed him seventy grand or more. If I knew who Alex borrowed the money from – and the person wanted it back – I would try to get it for them.”

“So you’re not even sure this money was a loan?”

“He listed the deposit as his own money but no, I’m sure it was a loan. He was twenty-three and the only paid labour he’d done was a low level job at my dad’s company. He wouldn’t have managed a loan from a bank and there’s no record of one. Nobody in my family loaned him money and none of his buddies has any money to loan.”

“His wife?”

“She’s young too, and only ever worked in a warehouse.”

“Interesting. I have no idea of who might loan seventy thousand to a kid with no collateral. Could it be that Alex had a silent partner? Isn’t that more likely?”

Penny feigned credulity. “I never thought of that. Could you ask around? I’d appreciate it very much. I don’t know who Alex was associating with, but you might. His store was burnt last night and all his records are gone so I have nothing to go on but I want to do what’s right.”

“Is that true about his store?”

“Yes. It appears to have been arson.”

“I’m sorry to say it but Alex may have been involved in some sort of business that was… I don’t know…well paying but illegal?”

Penny tried to sound astonished when she said for the benefit of whoever might later listen to her tape recording of this conversation, "Like street drugs? Not Alex."

"I did hear talk. Nothing concrete. So what is it you want me to do."

"To get the word out that I think Alex got a loan from someone he knew, or had a silent partner. Don't mention the amount though."

"If there is such a person they may not want their identity to be known – they might be a silent partner for a reason. Something to do with taxes, for example."

"If the person contacts me and can give me the money amount and date details that align with Alex's bank deposit then I will try to settle the debt or give them their share back – assuming I have the money after I get the insurance payout for the store. I know you don't know who the person is but the people who hang out here know you and will trust you. If you ask around people are more likely to direct you to Alex's friends than me."

"Why do you assume the person you're looking for frequents here?"

"Because Alex only quit his job and bought the store after he began hanging out here. I could be wrong but here is the place to start."

Hopkins placed a hand over Penny's hand, resting on the armrest of her chair, squeezed it, and said, "Of course I'll try lovely lady."

"That's very generous of you. I'm ready for whatever I hear," Penny said.

"I will even volunteer to intercede for you. If it turns out the person who loaned Alex money is a little shy, but wants it back, I will volunteer to receive the money from you and pass it on."

Penny was surprised at the offer, and uncomfortable with it. Hopkins hand on hers suggested he expected a quid pro quo. She moved her hand away.

Hopkins smiled and placed his hand on Penny's back, between the shoulder blades, saying, "I'm sure everything will be great," as he massaged the spot.

There was a knock on the office door.

Hopkins immediately halted all contact with Penny, sighed

in frustration, and called, "Yes, come in!"

The door opened, just enough for the head of a man to fit into the opening and say, "Really sorry to bother you boss, but I think you need to come out here for a moment. We're not sure how you want us to handle this."

Hopkins got up and said to Penny on his way out, "I'll be back in a minute." He closed the door behind him.

Penny stood up, exhaled deeply in relief, and stood up. She walked behind the desk to take a closer look at one of the photos on the bureau. It had been distracting her while she was speaking to Hopkins.

Her eyes ran along the line up of young women in mermaid costumes and sporting brightly dyed hair. She was right. One of the them was Megan Jones!

The photo had to have been taken the previous summer, which meant that Megan would have only been fifteen at the time. Penny took another, closer look, at the photo, her eyes running from one end of the line of women to the other. The mermaids all appeared to be teenagers.

Would serving Hopkins' cronies at the cottage be the summer job that Selene and Sally were after? Did they know what the job entailed or were they just dazzled by the 'ton of money' that Megan had told Selene about?

Carl Conroy had told her and Heather that Hopkins paid people to recruit others to work for him. Had this been why Megan was helping Bethany recruit Selene and Sally as mermaids for this coming summer?

Had Megan's 'ton of money' been paid out for 'tips' from a group of much older, affluent men? Men who apparently had a thing for much younger women, and whose visits to the cottage required the installation of more massage beds. The work that had taken Alex to the cottage.

Penny made the instant decision that she would speak to her parents if Selene accepted the job. Girls working in skimpy clothing at a secluded cottage with a group of much older, well-heeled men, was not acceptable summer employment.

Penny returned to her chair and sat back down. As she looked, once again, at the large picture of Hopkin's cottage, a thought crossed her mind. Dave Seaver had told her that Alex was providing big quantities of ecstasy for a wealthy businessman. Was that businessman Jason Hopkins? Were the drugs intended for his parties at the cottage?

Her thoughts then turned to Alex's friend Clive. The cottage was where he'd supposedly turned a gun on himself. She remembered Carl saying that, before Clive killed himself, that he was extremely upset and talking about having failed his family. Could he have been referring to his sister? Had Clive found out about Megan's work at the cottage? Carl said that Hopkins, his friends, and his staff were expected at the cottage that day. Was Clive at the cottage to retrieve Megan? Or was it to confront Hopkins?

The door opened and Hopkins slid inside. "Sorry about that," he said. "It seems your friend got a little rowdy with one of the regulars. The guy's a bit of a lout when it comes to women. Doesn't understand the word 'no'. The staff called me because they know your friend is a guest of mine."

"And where is Heather now?" asked Penny, alarmed.

"We got her re-settled at the bar. No worries." Hopkins walked to Penny's side, moving back into her personal space, sat down, and returned his hand to her back. "Where were we?"

"I was just looking at some of your photos."

"Ah yes. My cottage." Hopkins smiled at the photograph on the wall, looking on it proudly.

"Is that where Clive Jones died?" Penny asked.

"What? Oh, yes. Killed himself, poor boy. Not on the day this picture was taken though."

"No, I figured that. A few weeks before, I assume."

Penny got to her feet and retrieved the photo of the 'mermaids'. She held it in front of Hopkin's as she sat down. "And is this his sister?"

Hopkins appeared to study the photo. "Yes, yes, I believe it is. She was working as a server that day."

"She was fifteen years old, I believe."

"Was she? I'll take your word for it. She was bussing then. I like to help out students." His voice trailed off as he pushed his knee up against Penny's.

She moved her knee away. "What did Clive think about his sister going to the country with you?"

"I have no idea."

"Why did he go to the cottage on the day that he supposedly committed suicide? Why did he go there specifically to commit the act?"

"I don't know. Privacy maybe. To punish me maybe. I'd fired him the day before. He was obviously suffering from serious psychological issues. He'd come into the office here and was talking wildly; threateningly."

"Did he object to his sister being at your cottage with a man who is famous for his sex parties?"

"Please. You shouldn't condemn something until you try it. And Clive was fine with his sister working there. He'd even been paid for recruiting her."

"No wonder he felt guilty. The Clive I knew would have been protective. He would have been distraught knowing that you'd been using him and others to get girls like his sister to work for you – to provide massages and God knows what else for a bunch of older men. I think you invited Clive to the cottage pretending you were going to show him the place and relieve his fears but I think you ended up shooting him to stop him from telling others what he'd discovered – and made it look like a suicide. Probably managed to get gun residue on Clive's hand. And you then left the gun there. You didn't know Alex and Dave were downstairs working. Bethany saw to such things."

Hopkins abruptly stood up and blurted, "Did Alex tell you that?"

Penny stood up as well; facing him. "He heard your conversation with Clive and knew what happened didn't he?"

Hopkins reached out and took firm hold of her arms. "He leave a note or something?"

Penny didn't answer. "You couldn't know that Alex took the gun and heard everything."

"I see," said Hopkins, angrily, tightening his grip on Penny's arms. "You want money like your brother did."

"I didn't say that."

"Your brother was a weasel who said that the seventy k

was a one time thing so he could buy a store, but he soon started pushing for more money – every month! And look where it got him. And now you want to follow the same path.”

“You paid off Bethany Yeats to seduce Alex so that you could kill him; so the cops would think he was murdered by drug dealing bikers.”

“Your brother followed his dick. He’d been chasing Bethany since they met last year.”

“And you burnt Alex’s store to also make it appear that it was drug dealers who killed him.”

Hopkins pulled Penny towards him. “And now, you frigid bitch, I don’t have a choice about what comes next.”

He cupped a hand over her mouth, still holding her with his other hand.

Penny planted both her legs and lunged forwards. They went over Hopkins’ chair.

Landing on the floor, on his back, with Penny partially on top of him, Hopkins’ grip loosened.

It was enough. Penny pushed herself upwards and managed to get on her feet.

She reached behind her. Grabbed the pitcher of margaritas – a solid, heavy glass pitcher.

Hopkins was climbing to his knees when Penny crashed the pitcher against his skull.

She snatched up her bag from the coffee table. And she ran. Out of the office. Along the short hallway.

Heather had heard the loud voices coming from Hopkins’ office and the thud of falling bodies.

The bartender apparently had too. She was on her cellphone, and looking alarmed,

Heather was on her way to Hopkins’ office when she came face to face with Penny, rounding the corner of the bar.

“Let’s go!” Penny said, and took Heather’s arm. She marched towards the top of the stairs with Heather in tow.

Two burly men were sprinting up the stairs. They brushed past the two women making their way down.

At the bottom of the stairs, Penny said, “Run!” and the two friends fled for the street.

Late Summer, 1943

The noise shouldn't have been there since it was mid-morning and she was the only one at home.

Louise Martin froze at the kitchen doorway, on high alert.

The noise had come from the boy's bedroom at the back of the kitchen; the converted former porch.

With only the slightest of a tremor in her voice, in spite of the rush of adrenaline, Louise called out, "Is that you Robbie? Eddie and Dad are out front, waiting with the rifles."

Eddie and Robbie were at the creek. Tom was at the gravel pit. Ginny was at a friend's.

The noise from the bedroom immediately ceased, as if someone's breath was being held.

Louise backed into the living room. Her eyes remaining on the bedroom door, which was slightly ajar.

She took three backwards steps, slowly. It was an animal lowering of the head. She posed no threat.

Spinning on her heal she hustled across the room to the front door. Stomping her feet as she went. Grateful for the loud complaints from the floorboards.

She slipped outside without banging the door.

She didn't cross in front of the farmhouse, taking the path to Ellen's. The usual route back and forth. It was years before the undergrowth and trees created a wall that blocked the view and the access.

Louise wanted the dirt road out front. It would take her well away from the house.

She didn't look back as she ran to the road, as if an unseen threat can't hurt you.

At the road, she turned right and continued her sprint. Ellen's place was a hundred feet away.

A woman running on a country road in Mount Pleasant, in 1943, was never good. Not for the recalcitrant boy being chased by his broom-wielding mother. Not for the mother, whose son was in the armed forces, clutching an unopened letter from the government that she was afraid to open, and heading for her neighbour's.

Louise knocked on the side door of Ellen's farmhouse. A rapid tattoo. "Come on, come on," she whispered under her breath.

She heard Ellen inside, speaking to Leona, Larry's daughter with his late wife.

The door opened and her young friend Ellen's face appeared, breaking into a smile when she saw who was there.

"Can I come in? I need to call the police." The words flew out of Louise's mouth and were barely discernible.

"Ah, of course." Ellen stepped back. Her expression had changed to wide-eyed incomprehension. "What's the matter?"

Louise squeezed past her friend, saying, "There's someone in my house." She paused and looked at Ellen.

"Yes, yes, the phone is there," Ellen said, pointing.

As Louise dialed the police, Ellen locked the house doors and went to her kitchen window – which faced Louise's farm – to watch.

Three-year-old Leona sat on the floor with her toys, silently taking in the scene.

He arrived almost immediately having been just up the road when he got the radio message.

Louise was out the front door as soon as she saw Constable Winters step from his vehicle.

Ellen, still at her front window, watched Louise gesturing towards the Martin house.

Winters was nodding. He punched his finger aggressively towards Ellen's house as he spoke, obviously directing Louise to return there, then hustled back to his car.

Ellen opened her front door and stepped out onto the porch.

Louise walked towards her but stopped and turned when Winters called, "Louise! Where's Tom?"

"Off with his rifle, to the old gravel pit."

"Right. I'll be right back."

Louise joined Ellen at the kitchen window.

They watched Winters park his car in front of Louise's house. Watched him enter through the front door. And they stared intently while nothing happened.

Winters eventually reappeared. He walked sedately to his car and drove back to Ellen's.

Louise went out to greet him.

Winters rolled down the window of his car. As always, when he was at work, he spoke in what he deemed to be cop formal: authoritative and calm. "Didn't see any intruder inside. Can you get in the car? I want you to take a walk through the house with me."

Louise looked back at the front window of the Comer house and waved at Ellen in thanks.

Back at home, Louise toured the house while Winters stood in the kitchen, waiting. He'd already checked out all the rooms in the house, looking for the intruder, but now wanted Louise to tell him if anything was missing.

It didn't take long. Nothing to see in the living room and dining room. Same with her and Tom's bedroom at the front of the house. Ginny's room hadn't been touched either. The bathroom only merited a glance, as did the kitchen.

Louise hesitated in front of the boy's bedroom; the site of the noises she'd heard. She looked back at Winters and said, "That's where he was." She didn't move.

Winters understood the cue. He walked past Louise and reentered the room he'd been in minutes before. She followed.

They paused, a few steps inside. Clothes were strewn across the floor and the dresser drawers were open.

"What the heck?" Louise said.

"The boys didn't leave the room like this?"

"No. Certainly not."

"The intruder came through the open window."

"You don't expect someone will climb through an…"

"No, of course not."

Louise stepped forward, carefully avoiding the clothes on the floor.

"They were looking for clothes," said Winters.

"I can't think why."

"He was probably a deserter from the air station, looking for civies, and didn't know this was a kid's room till he went poking around. You must have scared him off."

The nearby RCAF Station Mount Pleasant had recently been expanded from a relief landing field to a full RCAF training station. Some men had been shipped up from the Summerside base while others were arriving from all over Canada and Europe.

There had been two recent reports of deserters stealing clothes from farms.

The inspection concluded, Winters headed for his car and Louise walked beside him She looked all about, still apprehensive.

"Oh geez!" she said suddenly, pointing towards the clothesline running from the side of the house to a nearby tree. An empty gap on the line was clearly evident. "Some of Tom's clothes are missing."

"So they got what they came from after all. Well Louise, I don't think that whoever was here will be back. If they came from the direction of the base they wouldn't have seen the clothesline until they left. Guy must have headed back to the Sherman's pond trail. He could have taken this path here or cut through the bush and followed the path along the side of your eastern field. Either way, once he gets to the trail he'll head to the highway where he can hitch."

From off in the distance, somewhere in the bush beyond the farm field, or maybe the gravel pit, the sound of a shotgun echoed around the pair.

"And that would be Tommy," Winters said with a smile.

But Louise was distracted with another thought. "The boys are fishing in the creek by the pond," she said.

"The man will avoid them – he won't want to be seen. I'll drive around to the spot where the trail meets the highway and walk back to the pond and the creek – just to be on the safe side."

39. Sunday

Harry Nelson had tears in his eyes when he walked out the side door of the farmhouse that he shared with his daughter and her family. It wouldn't do to have one of his grandchildren find him; it would scar them for life the same way that he'd been affected after his father killed his mother.

With a rifle in hand, Harry walked toward the road where he'd be visible to passing motorists. They often slowed down when they drove by the fruit stand to check out what he had for sale or to wave.

A passerby who spotted his body on the shoulder in front of the stand might think he'd had a heart attack and stop. Surely young Vezina would, she was a cop after all, and, if everything went the way that Harry hoped, it would be Leona's daughter who found him. It was why he was here, well before she would pass by at her usual 6:00 a.m..

Harry had left a note on the kitchen table. It explained that, in 1943, when they were ten years old, he and Jack Eades saw his father, Freddy, walk out of the bush with his shotgun against a shoulder. It was only seconds after hearing the shot that killed a deserter from the RCAF station.

The way that Harry and Jack later figured it was that the guy had to have been walking up the side of Martin's east field, on his way to the trail, while they were walking beside the west field, so they hadn't seen him. Freddy must have been out with his shotgun, walking the trail on his way to the bush or the old gravel pit, when he came across the aviator near his land.

Harry explained in his note that he and Jack had kept quiet about what they'd seen because they were afraid of Freddy, and with good reason; the man had no restraints when it came to violence. Harry knew that better than anyone, being Freddy's son and having dealt with the man's explosive temper for his entire life.

Harry went on to say that, even after Freddy was dead, he and Jack had agreed to remain silent. It was what he wanted and Jack had gone along with it out of loyalty. Harry told Jack that he wanted to protect the family name, and that no one would do business with the son of a murderer.

Jack kept his word all this years. But things had recently changed.

Several days earlier Harry had called Jack to tell him that Robbie Martin's grandson was nosing around and asking questions about the dead aviator, and might approach him. Harry reminded Jack of his promise to say nothing about Freddy, and Jack had agreed to keep their secret. And he did when he talked to young Martin and his girlfriend. But afterwards Jack phoned and made it clear he thought that the time had come to tell people what really happened in 1943, saying that Robbie Martin's grandson had a right to know.

Jack appeared to have left the decision with Harry, but the next day he called again to say that he would no longer keep the Nelson family secret and planned to phone young Martin.

Harry wrote.

"I mulled things over before I packed a rifle into the trunk of the car and drove to the city. I knew Jack's routine. Where he walked every day. When I saw him I acted. I then tried to wipe what had happened from my memory. The Martin couple were next on my list. They had to be dealt with because I figured Jack had already shot his mouth off. I had the kid's address from the farm's mailing list. I sat in my car outside Martin's place, getting up my nerve to knock on the door when a car with a canoe strapped to it drove up. Martin and his girlfriend got into the car and when it drove off I followed."

Harry went on to explain that he saw his chance to shoot Heather and Hugh when they set out in the canoe. All he needed was to find a place away from the beach where he could take cover – and he 'got lucky'.

"God or luck spared them," Harry wrote, *"but I can't live with myself. Jack didn't deserve to die."*

He whispered an apology to the sky in the hopes that if Jack was looking down, and heard, that he would forgive him.

Maybe killing people was in his genes, Harry thought.

Before he'd set out for the road he'd looked at the spot where his mother Lorelei was buried and apologized.

Of course he hadn't always known that she was dead.

For years he'd hated his mother for deserting him. Over and over his father had railed on about how Lorelei had left them because she was a whore who was undoubtedly shacked up with some clown she'd met while singing. And by now, she was busy raising a bastard by her new lover.

It was one night, many years later, when Harry was struggling to fall asleep, that the truth suddenly dawned on him. It was a random memory of the night after the murder of the aviator. Harry had gone to his bedroom window on the second floor of their farmhouse after being awakened by a noise. He saw his father digging near the maple tree and Harry guessed that he was burying the shotgun he'd used to kill the aviator. But Harry was suddenly certain, without needing to be told, that Freddy was also burying Lorelei. Freddy had killed the man he imagined was his wife's lover and had then killed her a short time later.

The next morning, when his father told him that Lorelei had left, Harry took him at his word. Freddy then set out to poison his son's mind against his mother.

But really, Harry concluded his suicide note, it was him that had killed his mother by not reporting what he and Jack had seen on the day the aviator was murdered. That was the real reason why – all these years after his father's death – that he'd kept quiet about what Freddy had done. How could he ever explain to his family that he was a coward who had caused his own mother's death?

There was no way now to undue the things he'd done except to tell the world what had happened and then to stop himself, with his own hand.

Harry Nelson knelt at the edge of the road, in front of the fruit stand, and put the end of the .308 barrel into his mouth.

40.

"Hi Grandpa, it's Hugh."

"Hi Sunny Jim, what are you up to?" Robert sounded lucid today.

"I'm just waiting for Heather to get home. Her friend was involved in some bad business last night and Heather wanted to see how she was holding up."

"Bad business? What sort?"

"It's a long story. It was at a bar where Heather and Penny were."

"Some sorta fight?"

"Yeah. Something like that. When she gets home we're going up to the old farm again."

"The old farm?"

"Your parents' old place."

"My parents' place? The house at the end of the road?"

"What? Ah…" Hugh paused. He had no idea what house Robert was talking about. "We're going to the farm in PEI where you lived when you were a kid. Do you remember living there?"

Pause. "Yeah. Good soil."

"We're going to see Ellen Comer. I might drop in on Harry Nelson too while I'm up there. You remember him?"

"Yeah. We used to chum together. Him, me, Eddie, and Jack."

"You remember Jack too then, eh?"

"Yeah. Nice guy. He found a body once."

Hugh was shocked that, for the first time ever, his grandfather was speaking about the events of 1943. "Him, and Harry too," he replied.

"Right. A deserter from the air station who broke into our house looking for civilian clothes. He climbed through a back window. It was my and Eddie's bedroom but we were fishing in the creek. My mother heard him and pretended to be talking to us so he wouldn't know she was alone, and then she got out of the house."

"And they never found out who shot the guy."

"No. Jack told me once that he and Harry saw who did it,

214

but I don't know whether they really did or not. He wouldn't tell me who it was."

Shortly after Hugh hung up the phone, Heather arrived home. She'd gone to Penny's to see how her friend was doing and to ask her how her interview with the police had gone.

"Everything okay?" Hugh asked.

"Fine."

"Did the cops listen to Penny's recording?"

"Yes, but we should get going. I'll bring you up to date in the car."

Soon, the couple were in the Fiat driving north, to Ellen's.

"I may have been wrong about something I told you last night," Heather said as they drove through Charlottetown. "I thought that Hazel would be made to return the money that Alex put in the safety deposit box because it's the proceeds from crime: blackmail or illegal drugs. It's a substantial amount apparently."

"And you now think that she can keep it?"

"No, not if she's honest. Since the police only know about the blackmail money Alex was getting they might assume that everything he got was either spent or deposited in his store's account. They won't be asking where Alex's drug money was. There's no mention, on the recording Penny made in Hopkins office, about the safety deposit box or Alex being in the drug business. It only confirms that Hopkins burned down Alex's store to make it look like Alex was killed by drug dealers rather than him. Penny said the police never asked her about drugs and she didn't volunteer any information. She'll tell them soon about the company that sends illegal drugs to PEI, but anonymously. She also said that she called Hazel last night and told her what happened at the bar and what she'd told the police."

"So, it's up to Hazel to tell the police about the safety deposit box?"

"Yes."

"I think it might come out at the trial that Alex was involved in selling drugs," Hugh said.

"I agree. It might. And how much money Hopkins doled out in blackmail."

"And if they ask if there's a stash?"

"What Hazel will say then remains to be seen."

"And there's the handgun in her safety deposit box…"

"Which Hazel is apparently going to tell the police she found in the apartment."

"Is the insurance money for the store going to get seized?"

"Maybe, I guess. I don't know anything about the specifics of the policy. Penny told Hazel to get a good lawyer."

"So Hopkins is now in jail."

"Yes, Hopkins is now in jail. The police told Penny that he's been charged with first-degree murder in Alex and Clive's deaths. And I gather that there may be a lot of other charges for the men involved in Hopkins' little sex club with minors. And for Bethany Yeats, for contributing to Alex's death and for soliciting girls. God, I'm not looking forward to hearing about what went on at that bloody cottage."

Hugh brought Heather up to date on the conversation he'd had with his grandfather Robert.

"And you say he was lucid," Heather said, "and you believe him?"

"I do. What he says jibes with the conversation we had with Jack, where I thought he was trying to lead us to the killer. According to Robert, Jack saw who did it."

"And now Jack's dead."

"But if Jack saw who shot the aviator than Harry Nelson did too."

"Are you planning to talk to him about that?"

"I'd like to, but since the likeliest suspect is his father he may refuse to talk to me."

Panel from Heather Bruce's Siren video

It's counter intuitive but the male philanderer wants to go home. He imagines himself to be an Odysseus. He wants a home but one that allows him to roam (in many ways). This is not open-mindedness. It is personal privilege.

The male grouping – like the gang, military, or old boys network – is paramount, and owning a physical territory is critical, but so is controlling the culture within it. In spite of wanting to roam he wants to retain power at home. Sexual adventures are only acceptable for men.

During his journey, Nausikaa rejected Odysseus. Her name means, 'burner of ships'. Odysseus was defeated by her rejection. The seducer cannot accept this. He must overcome all resistance or he loses. It's the battle's objective.

Because the philanderer/sailor sees seduction as power, he must believe himself to be a seducer, as an indicator of his masculinity. Having many women on his hook is his due and reflects his power. Women are one of the spoils of war.

41

As she drove, Heather was wondering whether she should talk in her video about conservative traditionalists who blame women, the LGBTQ community, minorities, and the decline of Christianity for what they describe as an attack on 'the family' (and the methods they employ to silence members of those groups).

She felt that it wasn't really the family per se that they wanted to protect. Families weren't under threat – just the specific type where men rule, and where women and children are obedient, silent, and straight, and meeting traditional gender role expectations.

Best, she decided after some thought, to solely focus on siren myth since that is the exhibition's subject.

Craning his head to see, Hugh interrupted Heather's musing. "What's going on? That's Harry's place."

Heather slowed the Fiat to a crawl and crept past the entrance to the Nelson family farm. A police car and another emergency vehicle sat on the shoulder of the road. "I wonder if something happened to Harry," she said.

"Maybe he had a heart attack at his fruit stand," Hugh replied. "The death of Jack really took it out of him."

Hugh and Heather sat at Ellen's kitchen table in her trailer while Heidegger the dog slid around their knees, demanding attention.

Ellen was at the counter, pouring boiling water from the kettle into an old teapot, She then placed it on the table, where she'd already laid out milk and sugar. She next retrieved the plate of cookies that she'd readied, and set that on the table before sitting down.

Addressing Ellen, Hugh said, "On our way here, when we drove past the Nelson farm, there were a couple of emergency vehicles along the side of the road."

"I know," Ellen said, "my grand-daughter's a police officer. She and her son are staying at Leona's for now. When she was driving to work this morning, Laura found Harry's body by his fruit stand, laying on the side of the road."

"We wondered if it was something like that. Did he have a heart attack?"

"Suicide."

"Maybe he was depressed after Jack's death."

"Yes, he left a note. I don't know if I should be telling you this but it concerns you so you'll undoubtedly be getting a visit from the police."

"It concerns Hugh?" asked Heather.

"Both of you. Harry wrote that he couldn't live with himself. It seems it was him who killed Jack, that lovely man who wouldn't have hurt anyone, and apparently then took some shots at the two of you after following you."

"That was Harry?" said Hugh. "I'm amazed."

"So it's true then? He shot at you?"

"We had no idea who it was," Heather answered.

"Do you know why he did it?" Hugh asked.

"To hide the truth. It seems that, on that day in 1943 that the deserter from the air station was murdered, Jack and Harry were walking up by the creek to go fishing. They heard the gunshot and then saw Freddy Nelson with a shotgun, walking away from the body. They agreed to say nothing."

Hugh said, "When Jack's daughter phoned me to say that her father had been killed she said that he'd told her he was going to tell us something…"

"That's what riled up Harry. He killed Jack and then tried to kill the two of you, assuming that Jack had already told you what they saw."

"It's astonishing," Heather said. "When we saw him at Jack's funeral, it didn't look like he was capable of even driving somewhere little own following people and using a high-powered rifle."

"And yet he killed Jack…" Hugh's voice trailed off. "I don't understand why he wouldn't want anyone to know what his father had done. It was so many years ago."

"Family honour maybe," Heather replied, "the reason for a lot of silence."

"It seems," Ellen said, "that Harry felt Freddy also murdered his mother Lorelei and Harry blamed himself for it. If he'd told the world what he and Jack had seen then his father would have been arrested and Lorelei would still be alive. In his note, Harry accuses himself of being a coward for not saying anything the day of the murder."

"They were just kids," Heather said. "How tragic. You said that Harry felt his father had killed Lorelei. That sounds like he wasn't certain."

"I gather he didn't see Freddy do it, but realized later that he'd seen his father burying something the night after the aviator was killed. Harry figured it was just his shotgun and didn't connect it to Lorelei – even though it was the same day that she disappeared – because his father told him that Lorelei had left and he believed him."

"And no one else noticed that Lorelei had disappeared?"

"No one questioned it. I know I didn't. She had no life outside her house – her husband had made sure of that – so it was weeks before Freddy told anyone she was gone. He made out like she'd just left."

"Do you believe that Freddy killed Lorelei?"

"Oh yes, he was a mean, violent man. If he thought that she'd been carrying on with someone…yes, I can see him killing her in that circumstance." Ellen began to pour tea from the old teapot. "I've been chastising myself all morning about not following up more about poor Lorelei."

"How would you have followed up?" asked Heather.

"By trying to track her down. I knew she was planning to leave Freddy, so when she disappeared I put it down to that. I can't imagine anyone who knew Freddy thinking it odd that Lorelei would leave. I assumed she'd gone back to her family out west. But it wasn't like Lorelei to desert Harry. When we talked about her plan to leave she told me that, after she got some money together, she'd come back for him. When she didn't show up I imagined all sorts of things, but it never occurred to me that Freddy may have killed her."

"What sort of things did you imagine, if I might ask?"

"Well, the last time I spoke to her she said that she thought she might be pregnant. I wondered if she'd died in childbirth. She'd told me that she didn't want the baby and I also thought maybe she'd died having a back street abortion. She told me that getting an abortion was one of reasons why she planned to leave. I did try to connect with her. I sent her a letter. I didn't have an address so I sent it to the town where she said that she came from – to her, or in care of her family if she wasn't in town. I figured, since it was a small town where everyone knows everyone else, that it would be delivered or forwarded. But the letter came back to me with a stamp on the front saying that the recipient had moved and their forwarding address was unknown. I didn't know if it was Lorelei or her family that had moved. I'd indicated on the envelope that if she wasn't in town that the letter be given to her family, so when my letter came back, I assumed that they were either gone as well or had refused the letter. So I figured my only option was to wait to hear from Lorelei."

"I wonder if Lorelei told Freddy that she might be pregnant," mused Heather.

"I suspect she did, and since he murdered her, he may have thought the baby wasn't his. Lorelei told me that Freddy believed the stories the aviator was spreading about having an affair with a woman in the area and he'd decided it must be her."

"And was that possible?"

"Oh no," Ellen said immediately. "She wasn't having an affair with that man. She told me that he was chasing her, and saying that he was in love with her, but that she wanted nothing to do with him."

The framed photo from the buffet, the one of Louise and Ellen, sat on the table in front of Hugh. His request to borrow it, and make a copy, had been approved.

After Ellen went to the bathroom, Heather picked up the photo, smiling while doing so. She gave it a casual glance, at first, and was about to set it back down when she had the same thought that Hugh did when he'd first seen it. She was sure that she recognized the young woman in the photo.

Heather closely studied her face. She knew she'd seen it before but couldn't pinpoint where.

It was soon on the tip of her tongue. But it stayed there.

When Ellen arrived back from the bathroom, Heather said, "I was just looking at the picture of you with Hugh's great-grandmother."

Ellen smiled. "Louise was the sweetest person. She was a surrogate mother to me."

And suddenly Heather remembered. "That would have been nice for you, being here on your own, a long way from home."

There was something in the way that Heather had spoken that caused Ellen to look more closely at the woman sitting in front of her. In doing so she noticed how intently Heather was staring back at her.

"If you don't mind me asking, did you advise Lorelei on how to change her identity?" Heather asked.

Ellen didn't immediately reply, continuing to study Heather's face. "What exactly is it that you do?" she asked.

"I work with Hugh, teaching in the same school."

"Teaching what?"

"Art?"

"Ah, and…wait, I know who you are now. You're the woman doing the show on sirens they wrote about on the CBC News website."

"Well I'm one of them."

"And you don't, I think, see sirens as the cold-blooded killers of myth. You think that's only the way that men have portrayed them. You said that if the myths about sirens are re-written by women that sirens will be seen in a different light."

"Yes. I'm working on a video for the exhibition and re-writing the myth will be a part of it. I argue that myths support the status quo and that they come to be seen as encapsulations of truth – which only means that the world view of the powerful has succeeded in becoming accepted as reality."

As Hugh watched the interchange between the two women, and their intense focus, he became aware of being an outsider; that the real meaning of the exchange was hidden from him.

"So you'll write about sirens in a different way…" Ellen said thoughtfully, "from a woman's perspective, and in doing that you take away men's power to define women. Yes, I see."

To Hugh's dismay, Heather said to Ellen, "I'm wondering whether you would let me interview you for the show. Do a feature on you. A real mermaid as it were."

"It was a long time ago," Ellen said sadly. "A long time of hiding."

"But surely there's no need for secrets any more."

"I suppose not."

"And nothing to fear."

"No, apart from the loss of anonymity."

"So you knew that people called you 'mermaid' behind your back," Hugh said.

"Did they? No one ever said it to my face. One boy, Jimmy Sherman – he drowned in the pond near here – had been to the AGO in Toronto, recognized me, and was trying to blackmail me: sex for not outing me. It sounds like he'd already told some people."

"I don't know about that," Heather said. "Harry told Hugh the mermaid nickname was because you were a beautiful young thing who just showed up one day like you'd been plucked from the water by your husband."

"So maybe Jimmy was being honest that he hadn't said anything," Ellen said. "He wanted me to go to the pond, to meet him there in exchange for keeping quiet. I thought I had no choice but to go along if I wanted to stay hidden and safe from my father, and not rejected by my husband for my past. I was on my way to the pond…"

"But he drowned," said Hugh.

"Yes. Fortuitous for me I guess you could say, although I wouldn't have wished it on him. Apparently he was drunk. He had a bottle of whisky that they found in the water. They figured he dropped it in the water and when he went to retrieve it he got one of his feet jammed between two rocks on the bottom when he tried to push himself upwards. I'd already turned around when it happened so I didn't see anything. I'd decided to come back here and tell Larry the whole story but when he got home that day he told me about Jimmy. Someone had apparently seen Jimmy's clothes on the diving rock at the pond and a local diver recovered his body. His foot was still lodged on the bottom."

42.

"I'm lost," Hugh said. "You're saying you're a mermaid?" he said to Ellen, and to Heather, added, "And you're agreeing?"

Heather laughed. "You've been to the Art Gallery of Ontario. You've mentioned to me that you have."

"Y e s…" Hugh drew out the word, coaxing for more.

"And said that, just before you moved to PEI, you saw some paintings from the Maritimes at the gallery."

"I did."

"Well, one of them was probably a painting done around 1940…" Heather looked at Ellen for confirmation, who nodded back. "It's a painting of a mermaid."

"Oh… Yes, yes, one of them was. I bought a bunch of postcards in the gallery shop; reproductions of paintings by Maritimes' artists. The mermaid painting's one…"

"The nude model for it would have been, what, around sixteen?" Heather searched Ellen's face for confirmation.

"Exactly," Ellen said. "And not long after it went on display at the AGO as part of an exhibition of new Maritimes' artists. It's now on to permanent display."

Hugh looked at Ellen as if seeing her for the first time. "I knew I'd seen your face somewhere before – several times. It was the painting. I thought it may have been from a picture in one of Louise's photo albums but I went through them, after meeting you, and you're not in any of them. It was the postcard. I regularly come across them…"

"I made a concerted effort to avoid having my picture taken after I got married."

"So no one would associate you with the painting."

"Yes. I'd left home to get away from my father. He heard that I'd posed nude for a painting and he beat me. I was all black and blue, and I ran out of the house to escape. He was yelling that I'd shamed him and he kept saying he was going to kill me. He often beat us but this was a different level."

"But surely your father wouldn't have actually killed you," Hugh said incredulously.

"The beatings would have been enough reason to leave,"

Heather said forcefully.

"Yes," Ellen agreed. "I wasn't sure how far he would go but I didn't want to stick around and find out. Or to ever see him again for that matter. My mother was afraid to stand up to him so I had nobody on my side. I had no brothers, and my sisters sided with my father. People knowing that I'd been a nude model would equate it with being a woman devoid of any morals and they would have treated me as such…but anyway, I ran to Bathurst, took the name of a girl who'd drowned, got a job, and met Larry. We corresponded at first and then I went to meet him in Summerside."

Hugh recalled Ellen's comment on an earlier visit, that if a man and woman do something that is commonly deemed to be immoral that it is only the woman who gets judged for it. "And you got married in Summerside," he said.

"Yes. I didn't marry Larry for protection. I fell in love with him in spite of the age difference. If any one of us was using the other it was him using me. He'd lost his wife and may have simply wanted a woman at home to look after his young child. Which was something I could consent to… It may not have been my first choice of things to do with my life, but I loved him and I wanted a home, and that meant conforming to the expectations of the time of what a nice girl was."

"You thought that if Larry found out about your past you would lose him," Heather said.

"Yes, and I felt that I had to hide. So, you see, it wasn't just hiding from my father. It was hiding from society's judgment. Young women were trapped in these kind of dilemmas. They had to be silent about their pasts."

"The mermaid must give up her ability to speak if she wants a home with the prince…" Heather said, thoughtfully.

"Just so."

No one spoke for a brief time, but the silence was broken when Heather looked at Ellen and said, "Did you ever think of the possibility that Lorelei might have been abused?"

"I was sure of it. I confronted her about it. She denied it at first but I recognized what was happening in her life from the bruises, and she told me the truth. Freddy had heard a rumour about the aviator sleeping with a woman in the area and figured it was Lorelei because she admitted having known the man in Summerside. Then one day Freddy spotted the guy near his property. Of course, Freddy was the jealous type and felt that women were always trying to put one over on men, so he refused to believe that the aviator was really a stalker. Plus he was possessive. He called Lorelei a slut and a tramp, and beat her up. I suspect that Freddy told her to stay away from me because he figured out that she confided in me and I would see the bruises. I told Lorelei she had to go to the police, but she refused, so I convinced her that if she left, that Harry would be okay in the short term, and once she was settled somewhere I would help her get him. I talked to her about how to change her identity, and I gave her some money. The rest of the story is what I told you; that I guessed she'd suddenly fled and that something must have happened to her out west."

When the time came for Heather and Hugh to leave, Heather said to Ellen, "So, about the interview I mentioned. Would you consider letting me interview you and tell your story, as part of my group's siren exhibition?"

"An interview with a real life mermaid?" Ellen smiled.

"Yes. But only if you think that you or your world won't be harmed by outing yourself."

"I suppose certain secrets should have a lifespan… something Harry just taught me. So sure, you can tell my story; or make a myth of it if you want."

"When can I come to visit and interview you?"

"How about next Sunday?"

On the drive home, Hugh chastised himself about things he'd missed. He'd been right that Jack was leading them to who the killer was, but not about who he was leading them to. Likely, Harry had been in touch with Jack. How else would Jack have known about Edward's death?

And, Hugh thought, Harry's reason for dissuading him from talking to Ellen about the murdered aviator was now clear. Harry must have suspected that Jack had told his good friend Ellen about what he'd seen. Ellen had even told Hugh that Jack confided in her after finding the body.

Panel from Heather Bruce's Siren video

It is always the case in wartime that the sailor-soldier-airman must confront the fact that he cannot know anyone. The essential nature of everyone is hidden, so to protect home means to mistrust women...all women. And since they are unknowable, to see them as possible predators. Their supposed weapon being seduction.

To survive, men must make themselves deaf to women's voices.

That there is an essential antagonistic relationship between men and women is posited in Siren myth.

Panel from Heather Bruce's Siren video

The Siren, Witch, and Nymph are allegorical representations of women in *The Odyssey*. According to the tale, it is females who turn men into pigs, enslave them as husbands, and destroy their ability to have a home.

But if these creatures are viewed not as types of women but as allegorical representations of latent qualities in all women, then any man who absorbs these beliefs, to any extent, will see all women as needing to be be outsmarted and silenced if he is to have a home.

As well, all women will be perceived as a threat to a man's nomadism, freedom, and unity with other men.

All women will be seen as distractions that weaken the army, team, or gang, so they must either be tricked, silenced by some means, ignored, or seen as nobodies.

43. The next Sunday

"I wish we'd asked Ellen where she came from and what her real name is," Hugh said to Heather, who was driving them north. "Are you planning to ask her when we see her?"

"I've been thinking about it. They seem like natural questions but they're also private ones. I thought that I'd ask her if she was willing to talk about such things and, if not, to let it go. It's not as if the specifics matter. I've decided to tell her story in the form of a myth so it should be as universal as possible."

Shortly after 2:00 p.m., Heather pulled her car into the driveway of Ellen's farm and parked beside her trailer.

Hugh had come along on the trip, to return the photo he'd borrowed, and he was the one who knocked on the trailer door.

There was no answer. Not from Ellen and not from Heidegger, although a dog in the nearby farmhouse could be heard barking, aroused by the presence of Heather's car.

"What do you think?" said Hugh, turning to Heather. "Is she out for her walk."

"No. She knew we'd be here at 2:00…but her car's gone, so she must be as well."

"Sounds like she changed her mind about the interview."

"That would be my guess…too bad." As they turned to leave, Heather said, "Is that Heidegger barking?"

"I think it is, maybe. The other times I've been here there was no barking from the house, only from the trailer."

As Hugh and Heather walked towards the Fiat a man exited from the front door of the house and headed in their direction. "Hi," he said when he neared them. "You must he Heather and Hugh."

"We are," Heather said, alarm rising in her voice at the possibility that something had happened to Ellen. "We were expecting to meet Ellen here."

"Yes. She said so… I'm Anthony by the way, her daughter Leona's husband."

"Do you know where Ellen is?"

"She's not here. She told Leona that she wanted to

reconnect with her past, off the island, and didn't know how long she'd be away."

"Off the island?" Heather asked. "Is that Moncton?

"Moncton? I don't know. Leona says she has no idea where her mother is from. She says that Ellen always joked and told her that she was a mermaid but not to tell anyone. Leona figured her past must have been awful and she didn't want to talk about it, so she didn't press Ellen for details."

"Did Ellen say when she'll be back?" Hugh asked.

"No. I mean, she said that she will be back but not when. That's why I'm out here talking to you and not Leona. She's really upset. Leona's worried that her mother has gone to a place where she may be in danger."

Anthony, directing his words to Heather, said, "Ellen said that when you arrived, to tell you that you still have her permission to tell her story in any version you choose."

"I borrowed this from Ellen," Hugh said, and handed the framed photo he'd been holding to Anthony. Hugh managed a smile. "The woman in the picture with Ellen is my great-grandmother."

Heather drove the Fiat out of the driveway and turned onto the road, heading in the direction of Summerside.

"Did we do the wrong thing in talking to Ellen about herself?" she said. "Maybe she still wanted privacy."

"She could have said 'no' when you asked to interview her, but she didn't. It sounds like she maybe felt some curiosity about people or places in her past, based on what Anthony said."

"Yes… I wonder where she went."

"I don't know if we'll ever know."

"Do you know where the nearest beach is?" Heather asked after a long silence. "I have a sudden urge to be by the sea; to stand and look out over it, and imagine…"

"You want there to be myth in the world don't you?" Hugh said.

"Yes, I certainly do."

Panel from Heather Bruce's Siren video

Culture should not be seen as something that is owned by one group or another – where it is ruled over as an act of power. Culture is a living thing that needs to constantly evolve by drawing from new and varied sources.

Old myths allowed the voices of the powerful to rise above the white noise of equal voices. But myths can also be revised to counter this inequality and express other views.

Creating new versions of old myths, as well as writing new myths that reflect opposite assumptions to those of the past, and of power, can undermine fixed attitudes and beliefs.

We can plant a flag and declare this island to be a Sirens' Island; Sirens being women of a community who use their voices for many purposes, including mutual protection, and security. And who should be left alone if they so desire.

Here is a myth about the woman depicted in this painting: a Mermaid. She is sixteen. We'll call her Eleanor.

Text and Image Credits

I decided against reading any academic analysis of *The Odyssey*. I wanted this book to be an interplay between Heather's text, and the story: each shaping the other. The characters, groups, and society, therefore, are entirely fictional. Any resemblance to specific actual persons, groups, society, or opinions in academic essays, is unintended and coincidental.

I stuck to historical detail about sirens and mermaids that appears on multiple blogs and other online sources, so does not require citation.

'Mermaid' swimming in the pool of the Sip 'n' Dip lounge, O'Haire Motor Inn, Great Falls, Montana.

<u>Text</u>

Page 115.
Jean Baudrillard. *Seduction*. Trans by Brian Singer. Montreal: New World Perspectives (CultureTexts Series), 1990. (pages 7 and 8)

Page 144.
Taken from a saved clipping of an interview of Marshall McLuhan by Linda Sandler, which appeared in Chatelaine Magazine (uncertain of date or issue). Quotes are on page 81 of the issue. Tape of the interview is given as 1974-07-05 in:
https://search-bcarchives.royalbcmuseum.bc.ca/sociology-canada

Coney Island Mermaid Parade

No. 10 Bombing and Gunnery School, RCAF,
Mount Pleasant, P.E.I. 1944.

Images

Cover
Engin Akyurt. Public Domain. Cropped.
https://unsplash.com/photos/8fjB_w8G7nU

Frontispiece
Engin Akyurt. Public Domain.
https://unsplash.com/photos/MtX2d4n9Ny4

Page 25.
 John William Waterhouse. *Ulysses and the Sirens*. National Gallery of Victoria. Public Domain.
https://commons.wikimedia.org/wiki/File:John_William_Waterhouse_-_Ulysses_and_the_Sirens_(1891).jpg

Page 35.
W. Hethe Robinson. From *Stories from the Odyssey Told to the Children* by Jeanie Lang. Public Domain.
https://commons.wikimedia.org/wiki/File:In_the_Meadow_the_siren_sat_on_the_bones_of_the_men.gif

Page 42.
Christopher Campbell. Public Domain.
https://unsplash.com/photos/1QYtLPzPXb0

Page 47.
Gustav Wertheimer. *The Kiss of the Siren*. Indianapolis Museum of Art. Public Domain.
https://commons.wikimedia.org/wiki/File:Gustav_Wertheimer_-_The_Kiss_of_the_Siren_-_76.27_-_Indianapolis_Museum_of_Art.jpg

Page 51.
Henrietta Rae. *The Sirens*. Bought from the St. Larry Exhibition in 1904 by Mrs. J. R. Cardeza of Philadelphia. Public Domain.
https://commons.wikimedia.org/wiki/File:The_Sirens_by_Henrietta_Rae_(1903).jpg

Page 61.
Manuel Meurisse. Public Domain.
https://unsplash.com/photos/S7YmTR65fHA

Page 74.
Dmitry Zelinskiy. Public Domain.
https://unsplash.com/photos/gOErbMaVUk0

Page 83.
William Etty. *The Sirens and Ulysses*. Art UK. Public Domain.
https://en.wikipedia.org/wiki/The_Sirens_and_Ulysses#/media/
File:The_Sirens_and_Ulysses_by_William_Etty,_1837.jpg

Page 108.
Unknown photographer. State Library of Queensland, Australia. Public
Domain.
https://commons.wikimedia.org/wiki/
File:Young_women_enjoying_a_day_at_the_beach_at_Southport,_1940_
(3841385190).jpg

Unknown photographer. State Library of Queensland, Australia. Public
Domain.
https://commons.wikimedia.org/wiki/
File:Young_woman_wearing_a_swimsuit_at_Southport,_1940_(3840594
401).jpg

Page 115.
Stow Kelly. Public Domain.
https://unsplash.com/photos/2Ahs0MhQgRo

Page 129.
Vasily Vereshchagin. Detail from: Beating the fiances of Penelope
returning Ulysses. Original tile: Избиение женихов Пенелопы
возвратившимся Улиссом. Public Domain.
https://www.wikiart.org/en/vasily-vereshchagin/beating-the-fiances-of-
penelope-returning-ulysses-1862

Page 130.
Janosch Lino. Public Domain.
https://unsplash.com/photos/dftkVVKj4NM

Page 135.
Theodor de Bry. Depiction of Richard Whitbourne's encounter with a
mermaid in St. John's harbour. Public Domain.
https://commons.wikimedia.org/wiki/
File:Two_mermaids,_men_on_island,_ships_and_boats_LCCN20027161
05.jpg

Page 143.
Toni Oprea. Public Domain.
https://unsplash.com/photos/oDJ7UQXnCxE

Page 154.
Ange Loron. Public Domain.
https://unsplash.com/photos/8__e9QHVYOA

Page 160.
Stormseeker. Public Domain.
https://unsplash.com/photos/rX12B5uX7QM

Page 172.
Anonymous. Public Domain.
https://commons.wikimedia.org/wiki/
File:TheLadiessWorldMarch1896page18.gif

Page 195.
Engin Akyurt. Public Domain.
https://unsplash.com/photos/OUHAVSh3oIM

Page 217.
Johann Heinrich Wilhelm Tischbein. *Odysseus and Nausikaa.*
Großherzogliches Schloss Eutin. Public Domain.
https://commons.wikimedia.org/wiki/
File:Nausikaa_und_Odysseus_(Tischbein).jpg

Page 227.
Unknown (Whitear). National Archives UK. Public Domain.
https://commons.wikimedia.org/wiki/File:INF3-271_Anti-
rumour_and_careless_talk_You_forget_-_but_she_remembers.jpg

Page 228.
Jacob Jordaens. *Odysseus Threatens Circe.* Kunstmuseum Basel. Public
Domain.
https://commons.wikimedia.org/wiki/File:Jacob_Jordaens_-
_Odysseus_threatens_Circe.jpg

Page 231.
Elisabeth Jerichau-Baumann. Public Domain.
https://commons.wikimedia.org/wiki/File:Elisabeth_Jerichau_Baumann_-
_Havfrue_1863.jpg

Page 233.
V. Smoothe. "Mermaids" swimming in the pool of the Sip 'n' Dip lounge,
O'Haire Motor Inn, Great Falls, Montana. The original of this image is in
full colour and has been changed to black and white. CC BY 2.0 DEED.
Attribution 2.0 Generic (license link:
https://creativecommons.org/licenses/by/2.0/deed.en)

https://commons.wikimedia.org/wiki/File:Sip_n_Dip_mermaid1.jpg

Page 234.
Hypnotica Studios Infinite. Coney Island Mermaid Parade 2013. The
original of this image is in full colour and has been changed to black and
white. CC BY 2.0 DEED. Attribution 2.0 Generic (license link:
https://creativecommons.org/licenses/by/2.0/deed.en)
https://commons.wikimedia.org/wiki/
File:Coney_Island_Mermaid_Parade_2013_by_Hypnotica_Studios_78.jp
g

Canada. Department of National Defence. Library and Archives Canada,
e005176210. Two aircrew examining a target drogue at No. 10 Bombing
and Gunnery School, RCAF, Mount Pleasant, P.E.I., 1944. CC BY 2.0
DEED. Attribution 2.0 Generic (license link:
https://creativecommons.org/licenses/by/2.0/deed.en)
https://commons.wikimedia.org/wiki/File:Airmen
%2BTargetDrogueRCAFMountPleasantPEI1944.jpg

Page 238.
Enys Tregarthen. Taken from North Cornwall fairies and legends, first
published in UK 1906. Public Domain.
https://commons.wikimedia.org/wiki/File:Tristam_Bird_and_Mermaid.jp
g

*Illustration of Tristam Bird and the
Mermaid of Padstow, before he shot her.*

Page 239.
John William Waterhouse. *Ulysses and the Sirens*. Public Domain. https://
www.wikiart.org/en/herbert-james-draper/herbert-james-draper-the-sea-
maiden

John William Waterhouse. *The Sea Maiden*. Public Domain.
https://www.wikiart.org/en/herbert-james-draper/herbert-james-draper-
the-sea-maiden

Ulysses and the Sirens

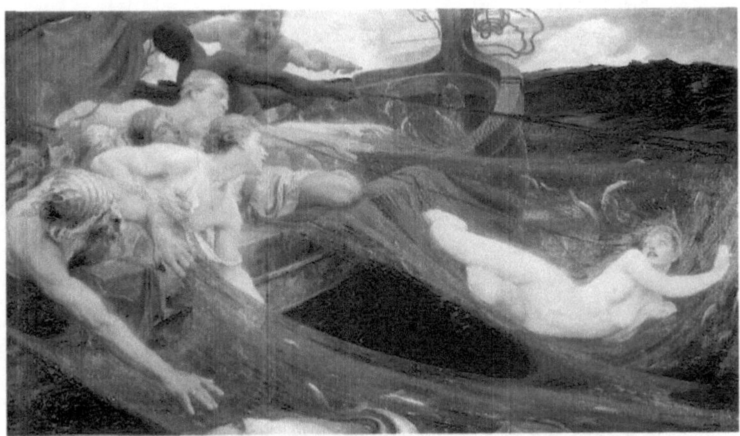

The Sea Maiden